# Rescue

ALSO BY ANITA SHREVE

**A Change in Altitude**
**Testimony**
**Body Surfing**
**A Wedding in December**
**Light on Snow**
**All He Ever Wanted**
**Sea Glass**
**The Last Time They Met**
**Fortune's Rocks**
**The Pilot's Wife**
**The Weight of Water**
**Resistance**
**Where or When**
**Strange Fits of Passion**
**Eden Close**

# Rescue

A NOVEL

## Anita Shreve

**Doubleday Large Print
Home Library Edition**

LITTLE, BROWN AND COMPANY

NEW YORK BOSTON LONDON

The characters and events in this book are fictitious.
Any similarity to real persons, living or dead, is
coincidental and not intended by the author.

HC ISBN 978-1-61129-024-0

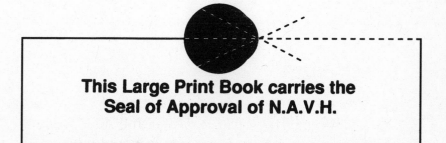

**for Jennifer Rudolph Walsh
with love and tremendous gratitude**

# Rescue

Webster jogs down the narrow stairs in stocking feet and says, "French toast," as he rounds the corner.

Rowan blushes over the pan, the one that has more scratches on it than Teflon.

Webster loves his daughter's face. Even when she was an infant, she had that extra, what, quarter inch above the eyebrows. As though someone took a pair of pliers, stretched her head a little. It makes her blue eyes open up. It makes her look a bit startled by life. Webster likes that. Rowan has the same widow's peak as Webster's, her hair brown, almost black. Rowan covers hers with bangs. Webster covers his, more pronounced, with a baseball cap. The widow's peak is a problem, always will be.

Webster, on automatic, opens the fridge for the juice.

"I already did that," Rowan says.

Webster turns and sees that the kitchen table is set with plates, silverware, napkins, and butter in the old butter dish instead of just a saucer, the juice in proper juice glasses. Rowan has on a pale blue sweater from J. Crew that he bought her for Christmas. Something is ending, and they want to mark it. Webster has been thinking this for months now.

The birthday has to be celebrated in the morning. Webster has the night shift.

Rowan slips the French toast onto the plates.

"You should have applied to culinary school," Webster says as he sits down and pulls the chair closer to the table.

Mistake. He sees the tiny wince at Rowan's mouth. It's there, and then it's gone.

Rowan has been rejected by three schools, one of them Middlebury, her top choice. Webster remembers his daughter waiting at the computer in the kitchen for five o'clock on March 15, the day and hour at which some of the schools sent out acceptances and rejections. Webster was messing around with the dishes, washing the same glass twice, pretending he wasn't there. He knew to the minute when five o'clock arrived. The minute came and went. More minutes came and went. Not a sound from Rowan. No joyous yelp, no happy shout. Maybe the schools were late with the results, Webster thought, though he knew that whenever you hoped for divine intervention, it never worked out.

That day, he gazed at her back. The girl was still, studying her hands, fiddling with a silver ring on her middle finger. Webster wanted to say something, to touch her, but he couldn't. It would embarrass her, make it worse. Better if Webster left Rowan her dignity. After twenty minutes in the same position, Rowan stood and left the kitchen. She went up to her room and didn't come down, even for supper. Webster was angry with the schools, and then sad. By morning, he had worked himself around to encouraging. He talked up the University of Vermont, which had been her safety school and to which she had been accepted in the fall. She didn't want to go there, though. She had hoped for a smaller college. What Webster minded most was the loss of the joyous yelp, that happy shout.

Rowan deserved it.

Webster deserved it.

"Delicious," Webster now says.

The bread is thick, drenched with egg and milk and perfectly toasted. Rowan loads her plate with syrup. Webster eats his toast plain, the way he's always done, though sometimes he covers the last piece with jelly. Webster doesn't recall buying the eggs, and he's pretty sure the syrup can had only crust at the bottom.

"I've got the four-to-midnight," Webster says. "Covering for Koenig. His daughter's getting married. Rehearsal dinner tonight."

Rowan nods. Maybe Webster has already told her. "I've got practice till six anyway," she says.

What to do about Rowan's supper? He's been asking himself that question for fifteen years. He lifts his head and notices a wrapped plate of extra French toast on the stove.

Done.

"Open your present now," Rowan says,

the first time either of them has acknowl-
edged the birthday, the father forty today.
Rowan, five nine and seventeen, stands
and glides into the dining room. She returns and sets the present to one side of
her father's plate. The box is wrapped in
gold paper with red Christmas trees. It's
almost June. "It's all I could find," she says.

Webster leans back and takes a sip of
coffee. He has the present in his lap. He
sees that Rowan has been generous with
the tape. With his Swiss Army knife, a
present from Sheila a hundred years ago,
Webster gets the package open and puts
the silver cube on the table. He begins to
fool with it. He discovers that if he lays it
on one side, it tells the time and date. If he
sets it on another, it shows the weather for
the next four days: two suns; a cloud with
rain coming out; and then a sun.

"It's hooked up to a weather channel
somewhere," Rowan explains as she moves
her chair closer to her father's. "It's better if
you keep it near a window. This side is an
alarm clock. I tried it. It's not too bad. The
sound, I mean."

Webster guesses the silver cube cost
Rowan at least three days' pay from her

job at the Giant Mart over the state line. She commutes from Vermont to New York and back again two afternoons a week and every Saturday if there isn't a game. Webster puts his hand on Rowan's back and lightly rubs it just below her long neck. "I can really use the outside temperature thing," he says. "And what does this side do?"

Rowan takes the silver cube from her father and demonstrates. "You rock it from side to side and then set it down. It tells your future inside the black square."

Webster remembers the black balls of his youth, the ones with sayings floating in who knew what liquid. Probably something toxic.

"Whose future?"

"Yours, I guess. It's yours now."

Rowan returns the cube, setting it on her father's lap. They wait. Abruptly, Webster flips the cube over, but not before he's seen the ghost of his future struggling to the surface. *Prepare for a surprise.* He refuses to own the prediction.

"Why did you do that?" Rowan asks.

"Surprises, in my business, are nearly always bad."

"You're too cynical," she says.

"I'm not cynical. Just careful."

"Too careful for your own good," she adds as she glances at the clock. "I have to go."

She slips from her chair and kisses his cheek. He watches her graceful movements, performed a thousand times. She holds up her hair, twists it, and lets it fall over her right shoulder. He's never seen this particular gesture from his daughter, and it hits him in the gut.

"Thanks for the breakfast and the present," he says.

"Sure."

Webster swivels back to his French toast.

He registers an odd silence in the hallway, not the rattle of the knob, the usual friction of the warped door in its frame. After a few seconds, Webster turns his head around.

His daughter is still in the back hallway, gazing out the window of the door.

"What's up?" he asks.

"Nothing."

"Rowan?"

**"Nothing."**

"Don't bite my head off."

Webster notices what might be the out-line of a hard pack of cigarettes in the pocket of her light jacket. He suspects his daughter is drinking. Is she smoking, too? Is she experimenting? Is this normal for a girl her age?

Webster can't remember the last time he's felt relaxed with Rowan. For a few moments earlier this morning, his heart lifted: Rowan remembered the birthday, Rowan cooked for him, she was excited about his present.

"Rowan."

*"What?"* Rowan asks, grabbing her backpack from a hook.

"I just . . . I just want you to be happy."

Rowan sighs and rolls her eyes.

Webster struggles for the high note of the birthday breakfast. "Love my present," he says again.

Webster can feel his daughter's impatience. Eager to be away.

He turns back to the table. He hears the tug and pull of the door, the necessary slam.

He walks to the window and looks out. As he watches his daughter get into her

car, an ache moves through his chest, sucking him empty.

Rowan is leaving him.

She's been leaving him for months.

# Eighteen years earlier

Webster got the call at 1:10 in the morning. "Unresponsive female half-ejected one-car ten-fifty." He made it from his parents' house in to Rescue in two and a half flat. He parked the secondhand cruiser near the building and climbed into the passenger seat of the Bullet as Burrows put his foot to the floor, turned down the lights and the siren, and swooped into the left lane. Webster had his uniform over his pajamas; his stethoscope around his neck; his gloves, trauma shears, flashlight, tourniquet, oxygen key, and window punch on his utility belt; his radio in its holster. In his head, he

ran through the protocol for a 10-50. Assess scene safety, including potential for
fire, explosion. Wires down, leaking gas
tank, turn-out gear and visor if extrication
indicated. Open the airway. Jaw thrust, if
necessary. Assess breathing and circulation. Stabilize spine. Check the pulse, get
a blood pressure check, and look for lacerations. Webster was twenty-one and a
rookie.

"Where?" he asked.

"Near the garden store where 42 takes
a bend."

Four minutes out. Max. Maybe less.

"Victim wrapped herself around a tree,"
Burrows said.

Burrows was a beefy guy with cropped
blond hair where he still had it. His uniform
shirt was missing two buttons, which he
tried to hide with a zippered vest. The guy
had a bad scar on his right cheek from a
melanoma he'd had removed a year ago.
He fingered it all the time.

Because he was a probie, Webster was
the packhorse. Burrows, his superior, carried only the med box and his own protec-
tive clothing. Webster dealt with the oxygen,

the trauma box, the c-collar, and the back-board.

"Fucking freezing," Burrows said.

"Whatever happened to the January thaw?"

In the distance, a cop with a Maglite directed nonexistent traffic. Burrows made a fast and expert U-turn, pulling to a stop on a flat piece of shoulder thirty feet from a Cadillac that had rolled and come to rest upside down.

"Just kissed the tree," said Nye, a weasel with a chip the size of Burlington on his shoulder. "And what I want to know is what's a fucking girl doing with a two-ton Cadillac?"

Not a girl, Burrows and Webster discovered. A woman, twenty-four, twenty-five. No seat belt. The Cadillac was at least a decade old with rust in the wheel wells.

"Unresponsive," Nye's younger partner, McGill, said as he moved to make way for Burrows and Webster. The medic and the EMT knelt to either side of the partially ejected patient. The shock of glossy brown hair in the artificial light registered with Webster, replaced immediately by acronyms: Airway. Breathing. Circulation. ABC. He maintained spine stabilization and took the vitals. Burrows handled the airway.

"A hundred twenty-two over seventy," Webster read out. "Pulse sixty-six." Even in the cold Vermont air, he could smell the alcohol. "ETOH," Webster reported. "Lips are blue."

"Respirations?"

"Eight."

"She's in trouble."

"She reeks."

Still, Webster knew, they couldn't assume.

A star pattern on the windshield had produced facial lacerations on her forehead. A crushed window had loosened a shower of sparkles. Webster gently brushed the glass from her eyes and mouth.

"Anyone know her name?" Burrows asked.

Webster watched the Weasel reach for the woman's purse, which had lodged under the car.

Nye opened a wallet. "Sheila Arsenault."

"Sheila!" Burrows said in a loud voice. "Sheila, wake up!"

Nothing.

Burrows administered a sternal rub to wake the dead.

The woman lifted her head in the direction of the pain. "Fuck," she said.

"Nice girl," Nye said.

"Responsive to painful stimuli only," Burrows stated for the record as he fastened the c-collar onto the woman's neck.

"Can we do a clothes drag onto the board?" Webster asked.

"Go around," Burrows said as he removed the rest of the glass from the woman's face and slapped on a non-rebreather mask. He made a slit with his trauma shears down the length of the denim sleeve of her jacket. He started a line in her arm.

From where Webster knelt on the other side of the car, he could see a piece of metal he couldn't identify, its sharp edge pushing into the woman's belly, making the front tails of a light blue shirt bloody. A sheared-off piece of the dashboard? Something that had come up from the floor? Through a slit in the metal, he saw Burrows working on the woman.

"Belly cut," he called out to Burrows. "Looks superficial. If Nye and McGill can bend this piece of metal a half inch toward you, you might be able to slide her out. I'll put a pressure bandage on her as soon as the metal is clear. You have yours ready when she comes through."

"Blood?"

"Yes, but not a lot. Wait for my count."

With his flashlight in his teeth, Webster pulled a pressure bandage from his pack. He reached forward to the metal barrier and wedged the bandage as best he could against it and thought that if the maneuver went wrong, he'd get a hand sliced open for his reward. He felt an obstruction at the place where the metal reached her skin. A set of keys and something furry. He unbuckled the woman's belt, eased the free end through a loop, and got the keys, the rabbit's foot, and the belt. He tossed them over his shoulder. He held the pressure bandage at the ready. He saw that the fastening of her jeans wouldn't get past the opening either. "I'm cutting her pants off," Webster said.

Nye, the cop, whistled.

With practiced moves, Webster slit the legs to the waist. He gently slid the pants down to her knees, removed her boots, and took the jeans off. He could see her white bikini underpants, her slim, pale legs. He put a warming blanket over her and tossed her clothes behind him.

"My count," he repeated. "One . . . two . . . three."

The cops pried up the metal a quarter inch. As they pulled from the shoulders, there was another spill of blood before Burrows could get his pressure bandage on. A spill but not a gush. A laceration but not deep. The slice looked clean. Another inch, she'd have split her intestines open. Webster folded the woman's feet flat to get her through.

The cops moved away as Webster brought the bundle of clothes around and joined Burrows. He and McGill had gotten her onto the backboard, strapped her on, and put a blanket over her. Burrows administered another sternal rub. Instead of an obscenity, they got only a weak moan.

"Move," Burrows said, and Webster heard the alarm.

They took the backboard to the rig and slid her onto the stretcher, Burrows climbing in with her. "Step on it," he said before Webster shut the door.

Webster pushed the Bullet to seventy, the most he dared on 42. Sometimes, he was able to take note of a rising sun on a hay-field or the reflection of the moon on the creek that flirted with the route, but that night his thoughts were at the back of his head, listening hard to Burrows, who was trying to get a response from the woman.

At Mercy, Burrows went with the patient to give a report to the ER. Webster wanted to follow the stretcher with the glossy brown hair falling over the metal edge, but his job was to clean up the Bullet and put all the gear away. Inside the ambulance, he found a dozen stained bandages, indi-cating more bleeding than Webster had previously reported. Burrows returned with the stretcher before Webster was done. Webster peeled off his gloves and stepped up to the driver's seat. Normally, as the rookie, Webster would have driven both ways, but, in the interest of time, Burrows had been at the wheel when Webster had pulled into Rescue earlier.

"Fine-looking woman," Burrows said as

they headed back to Rescue, a squad that serviced five towns besides Hartstone.

"Not a local."

"Blood alcohol point two-four."

"Jesus."

"Shame."

"Shit," Webster said.

"What?"

"I tossed the keys that were on her belt onto the grass."

"Find them on your own time."

"There was a rabbit's foot."

Burrows laughed. "Lucky girl."

After Webster had cleaned the equipment in the basins at Rescue, restocked the Bullet, and hosed off the outside of the rig, he got into his car and drove back to the scene. This time he noticed the quiet road, the .2 moon, the farmhouse just beyond the place where the Caddy had rolled. A tow truck was pulling onto the road. Nye put out a flare he'd lit behind the tow truck. "Why are you back?" the cop asked.

Never a *How's she doing?* with the Weasel.

"I tossed her keys onto the grass," Webster said.

"If it was her car keys, don't bother looking."

"No, it was something else."

"She oughta go to jail. She could have killed someone. Herself even."

"Then jail wouldn't do her much good, would it?" Webster said as he began to search the depressed grass where the car had come to rest. As Nye and his partner got into their blue and white Hartstone Police car, Webster thought he heard a faint snigger.

Webster had his flashlight for the search. He began to crawl around the frosty perimeter. Maybe the rabbit's foot did work, he thought. The woman didn't kill anyone. She didn't kill herself. She hadn't broken her neck. She hadn't severed an artery. She hadn't suffered a traumatic amputation.

The image of the shiny brown hair came and went. Webster wanted to find the rabbit's foot. He pictured himself returning it to the woman named Sheila. In his mind, she still had sparkles on her face.

An owl called out, and Webster could hear in the distance the whine and downshift of a semi. He turned off the flashlight, stayed on his knees, and turned his face away. After he felt the whoosh, he switched his light back on.

It took him twenty-five minutes to find the keys. With them, he stuffed the rabbit's foot and the coiled belt into his jacket pockets, got back into his cruiser, and let himself shiver until the heat came on. Fuck, it was cold.

Two hours later, Webster, showered and dressed, said hello to his father at the breakfast table. He lived with his parents, trying to save money for a piece of land he coveted. He was pretty sure he could convince the guy who owned it to sell it to him when the time came because Webster had helped to save the man's wife from dying of cardiac arrest a couple of months earlier. Normally, Webster didn't think like that. He and Burrows were a team, and it was usually his partner who shocked the patient and pushed the meds. But only Webster had known instantly where the farm was located, having driven past it a dozen, two dozen times, just to see the hillside with the view of the Green Mountains. He'd told Burrows over the radio where to go and had taken the cruiser. When Webster got to the farmhouse, the woman was barely responsive and sweating profusely. After she lost consciousness, he cleared her airway. He started CPR. He worked on her for over two minutes before Burrows arrived. They had her on a demand valve, an oral airway in place, and on the cardiac monitor inside the Bullet, pushed the meds seconds after that. With that kind of a call, a minute could make a difference.

Webster's father, Ernest, ran a hardware store in town and was up at six every morning. A man who believed in routine, he ate Raisin Bran and bananas for breakfast, four cookies with lunch every day, and had a nighttime ritual that seldom varied: two Rolling Rocks when he got home, the only time he and Webster's mother, Norah, kept to themselves; then dinner; then a half hour with the paper. Another half hour with the catalogs. One television show. Then bed at nine. Webster couldn't remember the last time he'd seen his father with a book, but the man knew everything there was to know about hardware and what to do with it. On the place mats at Keezer's Diner was an ad for his father's store: Webster's Hardware, depicted with a likeness of Webster's grandfather, a banner, and the tagline "Quotes Cheerfully Given."

Webster's mother taught fifth grade at Hartstone Elementary and, at sixty-one, was thinking of retiring soon. Webster had been a late baby, his parents unable to conceive until his mother was thirty-nine. Once a blond, but now gray, she had wide hazel eyes and a widow's peak she'd bequeathed to her son. Every night, she'd take an armful of papers out of her briefcase and sit down to grade them. She was the peacemaker in the family but could be stern when the occasion called for it. Webster had sometimes wondered what she was like with the more unruly students in her classes.

"Can I make you some eggs?" she asked as she stood by the counter.

"No, toast is OK," Webster said. "I have to get back to Rescue."

He didn't. He intended to return to the hospital.

"You were just there, weren't you?" she asked. "I heard you come in."

"Just some follow-up," Webster said. "I'll be back home soon."

"Well, I think you'd better," she said. "You need to get your sleep."

Webster was a part-time EMT, hoping to work his way into a full-time position, one that would require that he be at Rescue while in service. For now he got the calls at home, and his parents were used to the tones and to watching their son stand up from the dinner table without a word and take the stairs three at a time, or to hearing a car door close in the middle of the night.

Just before Webster's senior year in high school, when his father suffered his own mini-recession at the hardware store, Webster began to look at junior colleges he could commute to, convinced that by the time he graduated there would be money for the University of Vermont in Burlington. But when Webster graduated with a certificate in business—about as useful as an old Christmas card, he'd decided—he chose not to take over his father's hardware store, which had always been the family plan.

The idea of it filled him with dread. He wasn't for the open road like a lot of guys he knew, but he wanted to do something more exciting in life than stand behind a register six days a week. He remembered the evening he told his parents at the kitchen table, his father stoic and nodding, his mother stunned. They assumed he had something better in mind. He didn't, but he'd seen an ad that had triggered his curiosity.

"An EMT," he said.

"An EMT?" his father asked, incredulous. "You're kidding."

"How long have you wanted to do this?" His mother's voice was higher pitched than normal.

Webster lied. "A year or so."

"It doesn't pay very well," his father, ever the pragmatist, said.

"Eventually the pay's OK."

"You'll see horrible things, Peter." This from his mother, her eyes distant.

"Where do you train?" his father asked.

"I'm looking into that right now," Webster said, and with that his future seemed destined.

He took an EMT course at Rutland Hospital, went on observation tours, and passed the exams. His interest in emergency medicine grew steadily the more he learned about it, and it seemed to him that he had accidentally made the right choice for himself. He was twenty-one when he got certified.

For his graduation present, his parents gave him a sum of money that he used to buy a secondhand police cruiser, all the markings gone but still as fast as the day it had rolled out of the factory. Speed was everything for a medic, though in winter, when he had to put the studded tires on, he lost some of that.

Webster studied the woodwork around the window over the sink and guessed there probably wasn't a right angle in the entire house. He doubted the farm had ever been prosperous. When his parents had bought the place—Webster had been seven—the kitchen floor was linoleum, the walls made of lath and goat's hair, and the dining area was white with plaster dust. Up a flight of stairs was a sitting room with a blocked-up fireplace, a porch that had been finished off to make a sewing nook, and a decent-sized bedroom that his parents took over. In the attic were two small rooms that his cousins and aunts and uncles used when they visited.

Until Webster was twelve, he'd slept on a loft bed that his father had built in the sewing nook. When Webster turned thirteen and his body grew too long for the bed, his father knocked down the wall between the two attic rooms and made one big one. It had a sloped ceiling and a window at either end. The back window overlooked Webster's mother's vegetable garden, a large hydrangea bush, and a tall mimosa tree that produced puffy salmon-colored balls each August. Two Adirondack chairs were set underneath that tree, and it was there that his parents often sat in summer, trying not to pay too much attention to the vast tract of land they'd sold off to finance improvements in the hardware store.

Webster said good-bye to his parents and drove into the Vermont morning, the sun just rising, steam coming out the backs of the vehicles in front of him.

They couldn't have sent the woman home yet, Webster reasoned, not with that level of alcohol in her blood, three and a half times the legal limit. Webster wanted to see her face and hear her voice. He'd done an "after" call only once before, with a ten-year-old who'd nearly drowned in a marble quarry. Webster had needed to see the boy alive. Needed to feel the reward of what he'd done. Needed to hear the parents thank him. At the time, three months into the job, he'd had a two-week run of lousy calls that had caused him to want to quit before he'd barely begun. Two children burned to death in a trailer fire. A cardiac call they might have been able to do something about had they been summoned sooner. A three-car collision on the ice on 42, an entire family of French Canadians wiped out: mother at the scene, father in the Bullet, baby daughter at the hospital.

Webster parked and walked into the ER. The staff knew him, and they didn't. He cornered a nurse he thought he recognized.

"I brought a woman in last night," Webster said. "DUI, stomach laceration."

"They're giving her fluids. She's still got a Foley catheter. They're going to discontinue her IV in half an hour."

Webster checked his watch. "Half an hour? She could get the d.t.'s."

"Doesn't matter what I think. Towle's orders. Signs of old bruises on her body, by the way."

"I found something at the site that belongs to the woman," he said.

"I'll take it," the nurse offered.

Ordinarily, Webster would have left it at that. "I'd like to see her if you don't mind. Just to see how she's doing."

The nurse narrowed her eyes. "Visit away," she said. "Bed number eight."

Webster pulled the curtain aside. The woman's face was pale, with bruises ripening beneath her eyes. She had a mouth that might be French like her name. Her hair was still glossy. He moved closer to the bed. The alcohol was depressing her system. When they took the fluids away, she'd get a headache and the heaves.

Under the thin coverlet, the bandages made a runway across the woman's stomach. He noticed the narrow outline of her body, her nipples under the cloth. Her johnny was open at the neck, and Webster could see the place where Burrows had rubbed her sternum. Hell of a bruise, but you had to make it work. He remembered her long legs, the bikini underpants.

Webster said her name.

An eye fluttered.

He touched her arm and raised his voice a little. "Sheila?"

She opened her eyes. He watched as she tried to focus. She said nothing.

"My name is Peter Webster," he said. "I'm with Hartstone Rescue, and I worked on you last night." He paused. He hadn't meant to say it that way. "You had a close call. You nearly died."

"No, I didn't," she said, already defensive, the eyes sharpening up. In better shape than she looked.

He thought of walking out of the cubicle right then and there. Later, he would often wonder why he hadn't.

Webster let a week pass before he tried to find out Sheila's whereabouts. He assumed the wallet had been returned to her, but there might be a record of her address at the police station. Possibly at the hospital, too, though they were tight with information. That left Webster no choice but to call the station. He prayed it would be McGill at the other end of the line.

Webster wasn't surprised when he heard Nye's voice. The Weasel was everywhere: the left eye with its squint and the mouth in a permanent sneer—not necessarily the result of Nye's disposition, but because the man's right eyetooth stuck out a quarter inch. Webster wondered whether instead of developing a face that showed his character, Nye had grown into his face, viewing the sneer in the mirror every morning when he shaved.

Nye might not know that Webster had already visited the hospital. He decided to take a chance.

"The rabbit's foot?" Nye asked.

"Yup."

"What's the point?"

"She might need the keys."

"The car was totaled, her license was suspended for two months. Massachusetts license, by the way."

"Any local address?" Webster asked, and waited.

"You know I can't give out that kind of information."

"Jesus, Nye. I might have saved her life."

"That means exactly zero over here."

Fucking Nye was going to make him beg.

"I suppose as a probie, you're not familiar with proper procedure," Nye added.

Webster took a chance that guff would win out over pleading. "Cut the crap."

Nye made Webster wait so long, he was

sure the Weasel had hung up. Then he heard the tapping of a pencil point on a desk.

Nye gave Webster the address. "Don't do anything stupid, probie."

Webster knew where the house was. Just inside the northern town line stood a pale blue Cape with a front porch not fifteen feet from the edge of 42, the porch encased in jalousie windows. Webster pulled into what might have been a driveway in an unkempt yard. Before he opened the door of the old cruiser, he thought about what he'd say: he was just following up, wanted to know how she was. She would see right through that, might even call him on it. He remembered her defensiveness in the hospital. But Webster's curiosity outweighed his judgment, had been outweighing it all week. When he knocked on the door, it was Sheila who answered.

"Who are you?" she asked at once, both hands on the door, ready to slam it fast.

She had on a plaid shirt with the sleeves rolled to the elbows, a pair of jeans. Her hair was longer than he'd thought, curling at the ends, as glossy as he'd remembered.

He found it hard to take his eyes off her mouth. Did she really not remember his visit to the hospital?

"I'm Peter Webster. I was at the scene when you had your accident."

"Are you a cop?"

"No, I was one of the EMTs."

"OK," she said.

"I just wanted to follow up, see how you were doing."

She wasn't buying it. In her stocking feet, Webster put her at five nine, five ten.

"How do I know you're who you say you are? And, more important, why the fuck should you care how I am?"

Not as tough as she wanted him to believe. Something wary in her eyes. Webster took out his ID. She studied it and stepped to one side. "Come in," she said. "I'm freezing."

Coke cans, empty cigarette packs, a mess of Devil Dogs wrappers, and a Stouffer's box on the counter. A tin pail overflowing with trash and tissues. The rectangular table had a soiled green and white oilcloth tacked to the edges. A spoonful of purple jelly lay on the cloth inside a dozen coffee rings and toast crumbs and a smear

of what might be butter. Clots of illegal wir-
ing on the kitchen counter.

"This isn't exactly all mine. The mess, I
mean. The Devil Dogs are theirs," she said,
pointing to the ceiling.

"How long have you been here?" Webster asked, looking around.

"Couple of days."

He unzipped his jacket in the overheated
room. "Renting?"

"Not right now. I will be when I get a job."

"How'd you end up here?"

"A nurse."

Webster nodded.

"So you've seen me," she said. "I'm fine.
You can go now."

Webster didn't move.

"The old folks live upstairs," she said.
"They hardly ever come down except to
make a meal. *He* never comes down at
all." She crossed her arms over her chest.
"He's sick with something. I can hear him
coughing at night. I think I'm supposed to
do their dishes, but no one's ever said.
The old woman is the nurse's aunt. Why
the fuck am I telling you all this?"

He didn't answer, but the question didn't
stop her.

"The nurse came once and took the old lady out to do some shopping. The old lady's a mouse, hardly speaks at all. I think she's afraid of me, though I can't imagine why." She smiled as if she knew precisely why. "I have the 'front room' here," she added, putting her fingers in quotes, "and I can use the kitchen and the bathroom. I sit in the living room and watch TV. I steal their booze."

She raised her chin slightly, daring Webster to reprimand her.

"You drink too much," he said. "You were drinking too much the night you rolled your car."

"And that's your business how?"

"You might have injured someone else, and that *is* my business."

"What's next?" she asked. "The physical exam?"

She walked out of the kitchen and into the jalousie porch. Because it was frigid outside and overheated inside, the windows had steamed up, leaving a small ellipsis in the center of each pane.

"They keep the heat up to God-knows-what, and I can't touch it."

No curtains at the windows. A bed

pushed against the shingles of what had once been the outside of the house. The bed was neatly made. A few clothes hung from a portable rod on wheels. A suitcase had been tucked behind the portable closet. In the corner were a round wooden table and two chairs.

Sheila sat on the bed.

Webster pulled out a chair. "I wanted to see if you have any remaining injuries or difficulties from the accident."

"Are you a social worker?" she asked.

"No."

"OK. I don't have a driver's license anymore. I'm in this lousy shit hole. The nurse gave me a hundred bucks. I have to find a job. Other than that, I'm fine."

She reached over to a leather jacket at the end of the bed and removed a pack of cigarettes. "I'm here because the old lady needed someone in case of emergency." She took a drag on her cigarette. "Where do you live?" she asked.

"In Hartstone," he said, not mentioning his parents.

She gestured with her lit cigarette to her jacket. "The cops gave me the wallet back, but guess what? No license and no money."

"How much was in it?"

"Hundred and twenty."

Fucking Weasel.

"Did you ask for it back?"

She gazed at the frosty glass. "They said it was never there. Was I surprised? No."

"Do you mind if I ask you what you were doing in Vermont the night of your accident? The police said you had a Massachusetts license."

"Is this in your manual? Question number thirty-eight?"

"No."

"I live in Chelsea. Lived. Near Boston. I had a boyfriend who drank so much he started pissing the bed. I threw him out, told him to get lost. He came back. Stuck to me like a booger you can't get off your finger." She glanced quickly in Webster's direction to see how he was taking the booger. "Finally I couldn't stand it anymore. I packed a bag, got in the car, and drove. Didn't stop till I rolled the car."

"You could have called the police, got the guy arrested," Webster said.

"He was the police," she said with no emotion.

"Restraining order?"

"Really."

Webster noticed a half-empty bottle of Bacardi under the bed. The glass beside it still had liquor in it.

"Sometimes I walk to the hardware store down the road and buy bagels and coffee and cigarettes."

The hardware store. His dad's.

She didn't have rounded shoulders like most tall women he knew. She wore her hair tucked behind her ears. Her jeans were tight and slim and didn't come from L. L. Bean. He thought that when the bruises were gone her face would be pretty.

"I'm going to drive you to the Giant Mart just over the state line," he said, "so you can get some food. And then I'll drive you back."

"I think that's illegal. I'm not supposed to leave the state."

"You'll be fine with me."

"No," she said.

"You have to buy food," he argued. "And you need a paper so you can get a job. What did you do in Chelsea?"

"I waited tables."

"How old are you?"

"Twenty-four."

"Is that the truth?"

She nodded.

"I like your accent," he said.

"You mean the *Ahss-n-all?*" she asked, exaggerating the Boston pronunciation of her name.

He stood up. "You'll starve if you don't come with me."

"I'll get by," she said.

"Put your jacket on."

In the car, Sheila stared out the side window, as if they were a married couple, not speaking. She reached into her pocket and took out the cigarette pack. She glanced at him and put the pack away.

"You can smoke," he said.

"Wouldn't want to stink up your precious car. Where'd you get this anyway? It's a cop car, right?"

"Was. Got demobbed."

"What's that?"

"Stripped. After four years, the police buy new cruisers, and then they strip the old ones of any markings or gear and sell them. I needed a car that was fast. For my job. Hell of an engine."

"Rev it up," she said. "Go fast."

He held his speed.

She reached up, twisted her hair into a knot, and then let it fall over one shoulder. He drove another mile to the supermarket across the border.

"We're in New York now?" she asked.

Webster nodded.

"Liked it better in Vermont."

"Why?"

"Felt safer."

No one could attribute safety to an invisible line, but Webster had always thought there was a difference between Vermont and New York. In New York, the roads immediately deteriorated; the houses had less charm and looked to be in poorer condition; and villages gave way to street grids with stores on them. There was age in some of the New York border towns, but it was an unappealing redbrick age. When he crossed the state line, Webster always felt he was one step closer to a life he didn't want to live.

Still, the town had a supermarket, two gas stations, and a pharmacy. He turned into the lot of the Giant Mart and parked.

"So what's the deal?" she asked. "You

pick out the food and pay for it? You give me an allowance?"

"Let's just go in. I have stuff to get."

They headed for the door, but she wouldn't walk next to him, as if she didn't want any part of the awkward enterprise.

Webster grabbed a cart. "Find what you want and put it in. We'll sort it out later."

He bought more food than he actually needed so as to have the larger share when they reached the register. His parents would be surprised. He hardly ever grocery-shopped.

He put oranges, lettuce, white bread, lasagna noodles, and coffee into the cart, all the time trying to sense what aisle she was in. He added two pounds of hamburger meat and a plastic package of swordfish. The Giant Mart didn't sell booze, so she couldn't be doing that. He added detergent and napkins, having no idea whether these items were needed at home. He picked out an angel food cake and a pint of vanilla ice cream and found her in the canned goods aisle buying soups. She had saltines, peanut butter, and English muffins in her arms. She placed her items in the cart.

"How about some milk or juice?" he

asked. "A steak or hamburger meat? A to-mato?"

"You my daddy now?"

"You're older than me." He left the cart and returned with a chicken for roasting. "You know how to cook this?"

"What do you think?"

"I honestly don't know."

"I can do a bird."

He put the chicken into the cart. He went down another aisle and came back with a bag of potatoes, a plastic bag of string beans, and a carton of orange juice.

"OK, enough," she said.

"You don't want anything sweet? Cook-ies or something?"

"The old people have enough Devil Dogs in their cupboards to turn us all into diabetics. Besides, I don't like the stuff."

Sheila didn't join him at the checkout counter. She was standing by the auto-matic doors when he went through with the cart.

"Thanks," she said. And then immedi-ately ruined it. "Am I going to have to put out for you?"

Webster stopped the cart. "Your view of human nature is warped."

"And you have such a happy view of human nature?" she asked.

"I usually see people in distress. They're pretty happy if they live."

"Lucky you."

They returned in silence to the blue Cape. When Webster parked the cruiser, he got out and handed Sheila her bag of groceries.

"You wanna come in?" she asked. Almost shy, but not quite.

"No," he said.

Though he did.

He handed her a ten-dollar bill. "I didn't buy you cigarettes. I figured I'd let you walk for them."

She snatched the ten and headed for the house. He liked the way she walked—taking her time, as if she weren't freezing in her leather jacket. She opened the door and went in without so much as a glance in his direction.

She was sexy and beautiful, and Webster wondered if he could smooth out the rough edges. Though maybe it was the rough edges that he liked.

* * *

Webster didn't want to go home yet, even with the melting ice cream in the trunk. Instead, he drove up a steep dirt road to the ridge where he hoped one day to buy a piece of land and build a house. Fast-moving clouds made slashes of bright light on the hills below. In the distance, the Green Mountains had turned purple. Someday he would build a house with a large window pointed at those mountains. When he wasn't at work, he'd sit behind that window and look out. The earth and the mountains were fluid, changing every second.

In that house, Webster thought, he would feel free.

For the first time since he'd been driving to the spot, Webster pictured a woman in the house with him. Not Sheila necessarily, but someone.

He drove by her place every night for a week, each time slowing to see if he could spot her through the windows of the glassed-in porch. Once he saw a moving shape and thought about pulling over, but he knew he wasn't ready yet. Besides, he often had his uniform on, which might spook her.

On Saturday, he stopped. He expected lights to blaze. He guessed that neither she nor the old people had many visitors. The house remained dark apart from a dim light upstairs and a flickering blue from a television downstairs. He walked to the back door and knocked.

The overhead went on, and she opened the door. She wore a navy sweater over a pair of jeans. Her socks were bright red, and her hair was wet. The bruises on her face had all but faded.

"I came by to do the dishes," he said.

She flipped on the kitchen light and gestured with her arm. "Be my guest," she said.

Webster walked into a kitchen that if not spotless was at least tidied. No clutter on the counter, no overflowing trash.

"Guess I'm too late," he said, relieved that he didn't have to make his way to the bottom of the neglected sink.

"Couldn't stand it," she said.

She pulled a pack of cigarettes from the pocket of her leather jacket, which lay over the back of a kitchen chair. Webster noted her brown leather boots standing upright near the oven.

"You married?" she asked.

"No," he said.

She took a long drag on the cigarette, as if she hadn't had one in days. Maybe she was trying to cut down. She backed up to the counter and leaned against it, crossing her arms.

"You desperate for company?" she asked.

"Maybe." He liked the way her navy sweater fell over her hips. "Got a job yet?"

"No, but I have an interview tomorrow."

Webster stood by the door. She hadn't invited him to sit down. "Who with?"

"A place called Keener's."

"Keezer's," he said. "They're going to love you over there."

"You think so?"

"I know so."

"Want to take me to the interview to-morrow?" she asked.

"Keezer's?"

"Yeah."

Webster pictured showing up at the diner in his instantly recognizable cruiser and waiting for her. The rumor would be all over town before she was back out the door.

"What time?" he asked.

"Any time in the afternoon."

"I get off at two forty-five," he said, lying. Three o'clock was the least busy hour of the day at the diner. After lunch and before the four o'clock beers and shots on the way home.

"Cool."

"Just so you know, Keezer's a son of a bitch," Webster warned. "He'll have you up against the wall for a feel before the week is out."

She smiled. "Looking forward to it," she said.

"You going to invite me to sit down?"

"No," she said, dropping her cigarette into the sink and picking up her jacket. "I'm broke. I need a hot meal."

By the time Sheila had walked to the cruiser, gone back to lock the door, and returned, the tips of her wet hair had frozen. She played with the frost and broke the ends. "Christ, it's cold. I hope your car doesn't break down."

"You need a better jacket."

"You want to buy it for me?"

He did. That was the problem. He made a U and pulled out onto 42.

"Where are we going?" she asked.

"A place that serves good chili."

Webster drove north, past the town line, and then past the one after that. For a while, they didn't talk in the car. She spent the time looking out the window at the lights in the houses. "They still have their Christmas trees up," she mused.

"They'll be lit until the needles fall off. The wreaths will be up until Easter."

"How come?"

"Long winter in Vermont."

"Think we've gone far enough?" she asked after a time, a note of sarcasm in her voice.

"It's the best place around." A lie, and she knew it. "We can turn back if you want," he offered.

"What?" she asked, as if she hadn't heard him.

The parking lot was full. Webster let Sheila off at the door. He watched as she left the car and straightened her shoulders.

Webster searched for a spot, his frustration growing every second. He didn't want to leave her alone. By the time he got inside, some guy would be hitting on her. He parked at the edge of an adjacent cornfield. Illegal, but so what? A farmer was going to come out and slash his tires? He jogged back to the restaurant.

At first, he couldn't spot her as he glanced from room to room.

"She's in a booth," the guy behind the bar said. Webster gave a quick nod and headed for the red leatherette. The tables were highly varnished and slick to the touch, as if they weren't entirely clean. The whole place smelled of cooked onions and cigarette smoke. Sheila had her jacket off. She was sitting sideways, a beer in front of her.

She's comfortable here, he thought.

Three beers apiece and two half-empty chili bowls. Sheila was a delicate eater, and Webster had lost his appetite. Her skin was flushed, and the heat inside the restaurant had curled her hair at the ends. It softened her face.

"It's not that I'm trying to settle here or anything—fuck, no—it just seems like a good place to lie low for a while."

She said it as if she were used to lying low. As if she were an outlaw.

"You know you're in the police records," Webster said. "Your boyfriend being a cop, he can easily find you."

She shrugged, but he could feel the

vibration of the tip of her boot against the center pole of the table. Her eyes slid off his face.

"What did he do to you?" Webster asked.

"What do you think?"

The ER nurse had said evidence of old bruises. Webster felt anger toward a cop he'd never met.

"So what about you?" she asked. "You been here all your life? In Hartstone, I mean?"

"Sort of."

"Ever lived in a city?"

"Rutland. Didn't live there exactly, but I did my training there."

"That's a city?"

"Maybe."

"How can you stand it?" she asked, turning and stretching out again in the booth. Dinner over. She blew the smoke away from him. It didn't much matter. Webster could hardly see the pool tables against the back wall for all the fog.

"Stand what?"

"The . . . I don't know . . . the *nothing.*"

"People lead full, rich lives all over the planet," he said with a half smile.

"A philosopher now."

He liked watching her in profile, especially as she smoked. She had long fingers, a sophisticated drag, a lovely purse to her mouth as she exhaled. He hated smoking, but he knew the look was the reason girls took up the habit.

"And you would know this how?" she asked.

"I read," he said.

He was surprised when she let that go.

"You have family?" he asked.

"I've got a sister in Manhattan."

"You could have gone there."

"First place he'd look. Besides, she lives in a one-bedroom with her boyfriend and a baby on the way."

"You like her?"

"My sister? What's it to you?" She was facing him now, restless, but blew the smoke sideways this time. A mouth poised to play the flute.

"Just want to know if you like anyone."

"I like her," she said. "We're different, and she doesn't approve of me, but I like her."

"Older or younger?"

"Older."

Webster nodded, took another sip of

beer. He'd been glancing around from time to time to see if he recognized anyone. His being there—fraternizing with a patient he'd recently worked on—was questionable at best, unethical at worst.

"What about you, Mr. EMT? You have any sisters or brothers hanging around?"

"No."

"Only child," she said, mulling it over. "And where's your house?"

"I'm . . . ah . . . I'm living with my parents," he said. "I'm saving up for a piece of land I want to buy."

"Your parents. Wow."

"You want to go?" he asked, looking around for a waiter to give him a check. He thought he'd had enough.

"No," she said. "I want to shoot some pool."

"You any good?"

"I'm great."

"Next you'll be telling me you're a hustler."

"You give me seventy-five, I can double it."

He didn't believe her. If he gave her seventy-five with those sharks, she'd go home empty-handed.

"Those guys back there?" he said, pointing his finger. "They're good. They'll take your money in five minutes."

"Watch me," she said.

He gave her the seventy-five.

She chalked the end of the cue as if she were coloring it. She sidled up to a skinny guy with a blond mullet and asked if she could get into a game. Webster could tell that she'd already blown Mullet's concentration, but he wasn't the guy with the clout. Mullet looked to a large man with a black zippered vest over a blue and gray flannel shirt. The man's head was shaved, as if he'd just gotten out of the military.

"Luker, she OK?"

Luker took a long look at Sheila and nodded at Mullet. Webster could see that they both liked the way her jeans fit. A good-looking woman could always get a game. Sheila pretended to be more drunk than she was in a way that made Webster nervous. He could see that Mullet and Luker each thought he was going home with her. Two other men in their early twenties were at the table, too, but

Luker was the boss. "Lower the pot to twenty-five," he said. "Five bucks a piece. Race to three."

Sheila held the cue like a novice. It was clear she was watching Mullet and imitating his every move, as if she were new to the game. Webster was surprised they didn't throw her out then and there.

"Any house rules I should know about?" she asked in a voice Webster hadn't heard before.

"Yeah, Sweetheart, it's nine-ball."

The Mullet guffawed as if Luker had made a terrific joke. Sheila was all concentration as the balls were racked. "I go first?" she asked.

"The table's all yours," Mullet said.

Sheila bent, took her time, made her shot, and knocked the cue ball off the table. She put a hand over her mouth.

"Scratched it," Mullet said as he put the cue ball exactly where he wanted.

By the time the table was Sheila's again, the game was hers for the taking. One of the other players hadn't been able to sink the eight, but the setup made for easy shots. Sheila sank the eight but jawed the nine. If she were hustling, Webster thought, she was good.

"Nice one, Sweetheart," Luker said. "Beginner's bad luck."

Sheila lost the first race and begged to be allowed to continue. "Look, I almost got it in," she said, raising her left shoulder and then lowering the right in a sinuous move. She put a five on the table. "Let me win it back," she begged.

She laughed with Mullet, but it was Luker she had her eye on. If Webster hadn't known her better—and it occurred to him that he didn't know her at all—he would have sworn she was after him.

"Race to three," Luker said. "Ten bucks."

"Dickhead's shooting air balls," Mullet complained, pointing to one of the other players. "He hasn't got a dime left."

"That true?" Luker asked.

The man shrugged, put his cue in the wall rack, and walked away.

"The pot is forty. We'll spot Sweetheart the eight ball," Luker announced.

On her first shot, Sheila hung the eight and relinquished her turn. On her second, she caromed the nine off the eight and sank the eight, jumping up into the air and clapping her hands. On her third, she ran the table to seven and appeared to be unable to sink the eight.

*Careful,* Webster thought, a good ten feet behind her.

"You making lemonade, Sugar?" Luker asked, pretending indifference.

Sheila turned to Mullet. "What's he talking about?"

He shrugged. "He wants to know if you're hustling him."

Sheila gave a good laugh. "Oh, boy," she said.

But Luker had had enough. "Get lost, Sweetheart. This game's gonna get too rich for you." He turned to the other three players. "Pot is three hundred. Seventy-five apiece. Race to seven."

She put the ten she owed on the table and began to chalk her tip again, wiping the residue of yellow onto the thighs of her jeans, a move not lost on either Mullet or Luker. Still in the stance she began with (she was brilliant at this), she peeled the other bills from her jeans and laid down Webster's additional sixty, which made him take a deep breath.

"Honey, it's seventy-five," Mullet said, looking nervous now. "Go buy yourself a coupla beers."

Behind Sheila, the man with the best view of her ass reached forward and put fifteen on top of her sixty.

Luker stood to his full height and took his time cracking his back. "Not spotting you no eight ball," he said as he examined Sheila hard. When it was her turn, she bent forward and made a terrible shot that ratted in the nine. The man standing behind her whistled.

"Pure luck, Baby," Luker said. Mullet had gone silent.

Sheila lit a cigarette. Webster wondered if he should get her out. He didn't like the looks of Luker. On Sheila's second try, she ran the table up to eight and didn't sink the nine. The man behind her groaned. He didn't get it.

On her third try, she made a move a dancer might, bending to the table. The ash of her cigarette was nearly an inch long, the center of attention. A girl with frizzy blond hair who'd been hanging near Luker knocked on the back of his black vest. She let her arms slide around him, claiming him. Her hands almost met in the middle.

The ash was mesmerizing. Even Webster was certain she couldn't make a shot without leaving it on the table, an offense Luker would use to throw her out. Sheila ran the first six, caromed the seven off the eight, sinking the seven, and then sank the eight and nine. No one said a word. It seemed the whole back half of the restaurant was silent and waiting.

As she rose from the table, she elegantly caught the ash in the palm of her hand. As she bent to put the cigarette out in an ashtray, she mouthed the word *car* to Webster.

He took his jacket from a hook, went for the door, and heard her laugh at the back of the room. A sexy laugh he didn't like. He was worried for her. No man wanted to be hustled in front of a girlfriend hanging off his vest.

Webster braced for the cold. He'd be bracing until May, a good two weeks after the warmer weather had finally come. He brought his watch cap down over his ears and raised his collar. He jogged between rows of cars to his own, wanting to be exactly where he was supposed to be.

When he parked by the front door, the engine running, he took his hat off and tried to flatten his hair. He turned on the defroster to melt the ice from the windshield. He checked the gas gauge: he had maybe fifteen miles' worth left. He turned the engine off. After ten minutes of waiting, Webster grew worried. He thought of going back in, but if she had a good hustle going, he'd ruin it. After twenty minutes, he was picturing a back-alley rape, even though there wasn't a true back alley for fifty miles.

She was laughing as she opened the door of the restaurant. She lost the laugh as soon as it was closed.

She got into the car.

"Go," she said.

They were almost to the Hartstone town line before she spoke. "Smashed the rack and ran the table. Twice. The guy beside me was holding the pot and couldn't give me the money fast enough."

"That big guy looked like he wanted to kill you."

"Don't think so," she said, counting out Webster's seventy-five. "I'm pretty sure he wanted to fuck me."

"I wanted to get you the hell out of there," Webster said.

"You have rescue fantasies."

"Believe me, the last thing I fantasize about is rescue."

"That's why you do it, though. Your job."

"You're full of it," he said.

"You ever drive into New York at night?"

"No," he said, knowing she wanted to find another pool table.

"You're lying."

"Don't even think about it."

He had no authority over her. On the other hand, she didn't have a car.

It wasn't until they were a mile from her place that she asked to see the land.

Webster was taken aback. "It's dark out," he said.

"There's a moon."

He peered up through the windshield. Point nine. He stopped the cruiser and made a U on 42.

"You liked it," she said.

"Liked what?"

"Watching me hustle."

"How long have you been playing pool?"

"Since I could stand on a chair."

"You're very good."

"I'm better than you think," she said.

Webster wondered if he could beat her.

"Can I ride with you sometime?" she asked. "In the ambulance?"

"No."

"Why not?"

"It's against the law."

"I'll bet it wouldn't be the first time you've broken the law."

"It's not happening," he said.

As he drove up the hill toward what he thought of as his piece of land, the gas-hungry cruiser sucked the needle down to empty. Webster hoped it would pop up again when they reached the summit of the ridge. If not, he could always coast to Sheila's with a push or two.

Nearly every light in every house was out. No need for a light in the kitchen or living room to convince a potential burglar that someone was home. Everyone was home, everybody was asleep, and Webster knew all the doors were unlocked.

Though he routinely locked the cruiser because the novelty of the vehicle and the
equipment inside attracted teens, his parents had never locked either their cars or
the doors of their house. Most police calls
involved vehicular accidents or domestic
disturbances fueled by alcohol, with the
occasional after-hours attempted break-in
at a store or warehouse. McGill and Nye
had plenty of time, on their shifts, to play
poker.

When Sheila and Webster reached the
ridge and the best vantage point, he stopped
the car.

"This is it?" she asked.

"This is it."

She rolled down the steamed window to
get a better look. The cold bit their necks.
The moon and the frost lit the shape of the
land and the dark mass of mountains in
the distance. He seldom drove to the spot
at night, preferring the color and clarity of
the day; but he could see that from a cabin,
the panorama outside a picture window
would be worth staying awake for.

"You're going to build a house here?"
she asked.

"Maybe. Someday."

"Kind of isolated."

"That's the point."

She walked out onto the frozen grass and wrapped her leather jacket around her. Webster opened the trunk and took out his uniform jacket, which he had folded next to his personal emergency kit. He shook it out and walked to where she stood. He'd left his hat in the car, and his ears burned. He set the long jacket over her shoulders, and she slid her arms through the sleeves. They hid her hands. She hugged the jacket close, like a bathrobe.

"Where's the snow?"

"We had some in December. We'll get socked any minute now."

"You cold?" she asked.

"Not very."

"You just like being here."

"I do."

"I've never seen anything like it," she said from deep inside the jacket.

He was happy on the frozen grass, his toes going numb, his collar up to protect the back of his neck. It seemed that already the land was delivering on a promise.

"How long before you've saved enough?" she asked.

"I'm going to speak to the guy who owns it and tell him my plans. I won't have enough for a down payment for a few years, but I want him to say he won't sell it until then. For all I know, he might have promised it to a nephew."

All Webster could see were Sheila's eyes over the yellow and black collar.

"You know, Webster. This is the first time I've gotten a real vibe off you."

"What do you mean?"

"You're exactly where you're supposed to be, aren't you?"

"Maybe."

Surprising himself, Webster made the first move. He opened the high collar of the jacket and kissed her. Her lips were frozen into a half smile, but he didn't want to stop.

He felt the moment when she kicked in. As he took her to the ground, she began fumbling with his belt. He saw in his mind her slim legs and the white bikini underpants, though in fact he couldn't see anything except her face. He prayed that when she got him free, his dick wouldn't shrivel from the frigid air.

She kept him warm and hard.

"You on the pill?" he whispered.

He felt her nod graze his cheek.

It was a contest of wills to see who could hold out the longest. Mostly against the cold. He thought the icy ground must be painful for her, even through the jacket, which just about covered her butt. He never felt her breasts, felt hardly any skin at all. He wanted the act to mean something on this piece of land he coveted, but all he could feel was the contest of it.

When they were done, he pulled up her jeans for her, then did his own. In a minute, they would stand and run for the car. She leaned back and looked at him.

"Honest to God, Mr. Webster, that was the coldest fuck of my entire life."

Attention, Hartstone Rescue. We need a crew on Hawk Ridge. Female, fifteen, reporting injuries from domestic assault."

Webster reached for the radio. "You got any more on that?"

"Caller hung up. Attempts to call back, negative."

"ETA on the PD?"

"They're on another call."

Burrows and Webster arrived at a converted barn in the only tony part of Hartstone. There they discovered a slim woman in her forties standing by the door and a sullen fifteen-year-old girl in jeans and a black T-shirt, sitting on the sofa.

"You get over here and apologize to these men," the mother barked to the girl. "You tell them what you did."

The girl was silent, which seemed to infuriate the mother even more. The mother, dressed in a suit as if she were on her way to work, stomped her foot. She walked to the sofa and physically tried to get the girl to stand up by pulling at her arm.

"That won't be necessary," Burrows interjected as he wedged his body between the two females and broke the armlock. "You go stand over there next to my partner," he said to the mother.

When the mother was gone, Burrows stared down at the girl.

"What?" the girl finally said.

"You hurt?" he asked.

She had short cropped blond hair, a cheek piercing, and heavy purple eye makeup. She rolled her eyes with disdain, but shook her head no.

"Well, if she won't tell you, then I will," the mother, by Webster's side, blurted. "She called nine-one-one and said that my fiancé, her future stepfather, had beaten and raped her. My *God!* Does she look beaten up to you? When she saw the ambulance pull in, she confessed to what she'd done. I'm beside myself."

"Is there any truth to these allegations?" Webster asked the mother.

"Hell, no. She's out of her mind. My fiancé, Vince, hasn't been here since last night at supper, during which my daughter was so insulting and rude that Vince had to leave."

Burrows said nothing to the mother, but again addressed the girl. "Did this man harm you in any way at all?"

"In any way? Yeah, doc. He's ruined my life."

"I'm not a doctor."

"Whatever."

"Did he touch you or hit you with something?"

"He might as well have."

"Miss, I have to do a brief exam to determine if there are any injuries."

"Thought you weren't a doctor."

"I'm a medic."

"Poor you."

Burrows got down on his haunches and tried to take her wrist to check her pulse.

"Don't you fucking touch me!" she snarled, her face contorted into one of the uglier expressions in the teenage repertoire.

Webster joined Burrows, and they stood aside for a moment. Webster noted the open floor plan, the loft with the balcony, the kitchen with an outsized refrigerator. "What do you think?" he asked.

"I can't examine her without her permission."

"Obviously she called nine-one-one to piss her mother off," Webster said.

Burrows turned. "Ma'am, what's your name?"

"Natalie Krueger."

"And your daughter's name?"

"Charity."

Webster resisted the impulse to raise an eyebrow. What mother in her right mind would call her daughter Charity in this day and age?

"Actually," said the girl on the sofa, "it's Pure Scum, which is what her *boyfriend* called me last night."

"Ms. Krueger, where is Vince now?"

"He's in Massachusetts, where he lives," she said with smug satisfaction. "In Williamstown."

"When did he leave?"

"I already told you. Last night. I'm sorry you had to get dragged into this. I'd have stopped it had I known sooner."

Burrows tried to explain. "We can't do anything right now unless your daughter gives her consent."

"Which will be never," Pure Scum said from the sofa.

"The police will arrive soon," Burrows said to the girl. "You should be prepared for that. They're going to have a lot more questions than we do."

"Shit."

"What the hell did you think was going to happen?" the mother cried.

Burrows leaned into Webster. "We could call the cops off. Kids do stupid stuff to drive their parents crazy all the time."

"She's accused a guy of assault and rape."

"What's your gut tell you?" Burrows asked.

"Hoax. To drive the mother out of her mind."

"Yeah, me too."

"I gotta call it in," Burrows said. He took his radio off his belt. He called Dispatch. "Scene appears to be safe," he reported.

"Any weapons involved?"

"No. Can you give me a better ETA for the PD?"

"They're just finishing up now. Should be another fifteen to eighteen minutes."

"We going to wait until the cops get here?" Webster asked Burrows when he was off the radio.

"I guess," he said. And then he shrugged. "We'll wait in the rig till they come."

Had Burrows and Webster not been twenty minutes into overtime, Webster later thought, they might have shown better judgment.

Webster walked over to the sullen teenager on the couch. She lay back against the pillows with her legs wide open, as if she were either the most relaxed person in western Vermont, or the most seductive. "It's a serious offense to lie to a nine-one-one operator," he said. "Don't do it again."

As he walked away, Webster was sure he heard a mincing echo. *Don't do it again.*

He wanted to turn around and give her a harsh lecture. He didn't.

They climbed up into the rig. Webster drove to the end of the long driveway and they waited fifteen minutes before they saw the cops approaching. Nye rolled down his window. "What's up?"

"A hoax," Webster, in the driver's seat, said. "A girl trying to piss off her mother."

"Just what we need."

McGill groaned.

"It's up to you," said Webster. "Maybe the girl needs a talking-to, I don't know, but she's breaking her mother's balls."

Nye rolled his eyes.

Webster and Burrows took off for Rescue. They weren't a mile from the house when Dispatch signaled again. "Report of serious injuries at your previous scene."

"It's a hoax," Burrows radioed in. "A daughter trying to drive her mother nuts. Prank call."

"I don't think so," the dispatcher calmly disagreed. "Cop called it in. There's someone screaming in the background."

Webster reversed the rig and pushed it hard. He sprinted when they got to the house, thinking if this were still a hoax,

Burrows would have the girl arrested. He pushed through the front door. There was no sign of the girl, but the mother was screaming. There were burns and blisters down the right side of her face and along her throat. Her scalp showed where her hair had burned.

"Fuck," Webster said softly.

Nye was trying to get the woman to lie on the sofa.

"We'll take care of that," Burrows said. "You find the girl? She's probably upstairs."

"McGill's got her. Also found an empty bottle of toilet bowl cleaner on the floor." Nye pointed to where the bottle had rolled.

Burrows took over the airway. The vapor from the acid could burn the woman's throat. He intubated and then started an IV for the pain. He tried to calm the woman.

"Hydrochloric acid," Burrows said to Webster. "We have to flush it out. Get me a large pitcher of cool water. Jesus, it's in her eye. It's full thickness on the cheek."

Burrows cut her clothing off and removed all of her jewelry. There might still be acid on her clothing. He covered her with a blanket.

He gave the woman fentanyl for the pain.

When Webster returned with the pitcher, Burrows began the flushing, making sure he wasn't causing any acid to spill onto healthy tissue.

"You guys were just here, right?" Nye asked.

"Yes," Webster said, "but everything was fine."

Nye stared.

"Everything seemed fine," Webster amended. "No injuries."

"Why did you leave?"

Burrows spoke. "It looked like a hoax. The girl saying the mother's boyfriend had raped and beaten her. The girl struck me as lying about the injuries."

"Did you examine her?"

"No. She wouldn't let me touch her."

"You take the mother to Mercy. We'll deal with the daughter. I'd say you and the probie here just stepped in a big one."

It was worse than either Burrows or Webster had predicted. Evidence of sexual assault was collected from the daughter at the hospital. At least two crimes had been committed: a fifteen-year-old girl had been raped; the same girl had thrown acid at her mother. The mother had serious burns, including to her cornea.

"I'm gonna get my ass hauled," Burrows said to Webster on the way back from the scene.

"I was with you every step of the way," Webster said.

"Noble, but it doesn't fly. I was the crew chief. I was in charge."

"I'll back you up."

"You'll stay out of it. You hear me, probie? You followed my orders. That's it. Me, I'll keep my job. You? You'll be outta Rescue before you finish washing down the Bullet. They question you, you say you followed orders. Is that understood?"

Webster nodded.

"What was that?" Burrows asked again, this time in a loud voice.

"I got it," Webster said.

"All we had to do was fucking stay put," Burrows muttered, shaking his head.

Webster had had patients die on him, and that was hard enough. But to have harmed a patient by not remaining at the scene was brutal.

They drove past the town hall, a brick ranch turned into the seat of government. The library had two stories and a stone facade, but it, too, looked fake, as though it might once have been a feed and grain store. Webster had never been a scholar, but he read at night for pleasure.

The rig passed by Keezer's Diner, nearly full now at 11:30, every vehicle outside a pickup truck with tools and blue tarps in the back. He wondered if Sheila was working. Mother's Country Kitchen had gone out of business, but the Quilt Shop was still hanging in there. Webster was familiar with every shop and service in town. Sometimes he liked to cross the border into New York and drive to a place he'd never been before. Explore a town in which he knew no one.

They passed the Maple Leaf Gift Shop, Armand's Pizzeria, and Roberts Funeral Home. On a lane behind the funeral home was the American Legion Hall, the place where just four years ago his class had held its senior prom. Webster took the next left into Fire Rescue. He parked the Bullet in its spot: facing out, ready to go again. Burrows headed for the building.

Webster walked to the front of the Bullet and stared out into the morning. The snow was still on the trees from the night before, and the sun turned it all into crystals. He had a hankering to go skiing. He wondered if Sheila skied and thought not. He'd looked up Chelsea on a map, and it was a long way from anything with a chairlift.

He moved just outside the garage door opening. He would go to see her as soon as he got out of work.

He longed to get Sheila out of that porch room with the creepy landlords who ate Devil Dogs. He couldn't imagine what they looked like, and he hoped he'd never have to meet them. But get her out where? He couldn't bring her to his parents' house. Out of the question. She didn't have anything but the earnings from her hustle and maybe a week's paycheck. He'd like to get on a plane with her and go someplace warm. It would take him months to earn enough money for two plane tickets, without dipping into his savings. Where would they go? Florida? Mexico? The two of them on the beach, he in bathing trunks, she in a bikini, a pair of piña coladas between them.

"Webster!"

Webster turned to the door of the squad room.

"What the hell are you doing, probie?" Burrows asked. "Making snowmen?"

"No, sir," Webster said.

"You're still on duty, in case you hadn't noticed."

Webster pulled back the curtain. He knew what town he and Sheila were in, but he'd seen it only at night when they'd driven to the B and B, both of them a little drunk, she more than a little. The streets had been dead at eleven, but now the town had action: pedestrians pitched forward against a sharp wind, pickup trucks traveling in both directions, a glare already on the crust of the snow. The B and B was Sheila's idea. On recent successive Saturdays, they'd gone on day trips, stopping at a bar and a cheap place to eat on each excursion they made farther and farther away from Hartstone. But this time she'd wanted to make a weekend of it. Webster sometimes felt as if he were a rubber band, liable to snap back to Rescue at the first tones from his radio. He'd have to learn to ignore that summons. He was off duty.

He stood in his boxers. The room was overheated, and they had no control over the temperature. When they'd arrived the previous night, the heat had been welcome. Almost three months in Vermont, and still Sheila hadn't bought a winter jacket or hat or proper boots. *Spring'll be here any minute,* she'd say whenever Webster brought up the subject, as if she'd never have to experience winter again. Never another winter in Vermont anyway.

Two weeks after that night under the .9 moon, Webster had been promoted to full-time and stayed at Rescue during his shifts. He'd been given the graveyard tour: midnight till eight. Sheila worked days at Geezer's, as she'd come to call it, which made him wonder why someone else hadn't thought up the nickname earlier. When his tour was over, he'd hang around Rescue for twenty minutes to talk to the new team, and then he'd go over to the diner for breakfast. She looked demeaned in the shiny gray uniform with the white apron. She usually told him he looked like hell, and he told her she looked nice. Sometimes she'd manage to brush her hand against his. Once she'd bent down and wrapped an arm around him, pretending to be reading an article in a newspaper Webster had spread on the counter. For Webster, breakfast in the diner was a necessity, but he ached when he left. He thought of Sheila as a drug that had hooked him after only one hit.

Sometimes Sheila asked him questions about his night. He'd tell her everything about each case, getting rid of the images and smells. She never made wisecracks about his work. Maybe the memory of her own accident was too fresh. He wondered what she did at night.

Four days into the third week, he'd ridden into Rescue with Burrows. They'd had a bad night, and the images weren't pretty. Webster unloaded the back of the Bullet and hefted as much equipment as he could into Rescue and onto the counter in the squad room. So intent was he on getting the equipment into the basins without dropping something that he missed her over by the coffee machine. He noted an odd silence in the room and looked up to see Sheila with Callahan, a new recruit who'd arrived for the next tour.

For a moment, Webster felt paralyzed. What the hell was Sheila doing there? She had on her leather jacket, a black turtleneck, a different pair of jeans. Her hair was pinned up. A jolt traveled from his groin to his chest and back again. Burrows put a hand on his shoulder. "Relax, Webster," he said. "It's not as if anyone can keep a secret in this town."

Webster joined Sheila at the coffee machine, and Callahan slid away. A manufactured banter behind him broke the silence.

"What are you doing here?" he asked.

"I came to buy you a drink."

"It's eight o'clock in the morning. There isn't a bar open in the entire state of Vermont."

She leaned against the counter and cocked her head. "How about Albany?" she asked, teasing him. "That's a city, isn't it?"

"I'm not driving to Albany."

She put a finger to her cheek, mock thinking. "The bar at my place is open," she said, as if it had just occurred to her.

"At this hour?"

"Yup."

"Don't you have to work?"

"I'm at the dentist's," she said with a smile. "That's what Geezer thinks, anyway."

"I have to clean the equipment, pack it away. Talk to the next crew. Give me twenty minutes."

Webster worked steadily, aware of the glances of the other medics. If one of them was going to report him for fraternization, then so be it. He should be mad at Sheila for so casually jeopardizing his job.

After he left Rescue, he got into his car, Sheila already in the passenger seat.

Once inside the house with the jalousie porch, he took a quick glance around the kitchen, then grabbed her by the soft sleeve of her jacket, turned her around, and kissed her. She broke away and laughed at him. She guided him onto the porch. He didn't care about being close to the road. Let the whole world watch.

She sat on the daybed and took off her clothes in a perfunctory way, as if she were alone. Another woman might have made a tease of it. For the first time, Webster saw her breasts, her pubic hair, the scar across her belly.

"You're fucking gorgeous," he said. Then he nodded in the direction of the scar. "Won't that hurt?"

"I doubt I'll notice it," she said. "Though if you stand there with your jacket on much longer, I might get bored and fall asleep."

The Sheila who'd had a no-nonsense way of removing her clothes slipped into a woman who was at least as pent up as Webster. It might be weeks before they could learn to take it slow.

Webster watched Sheila sleep in the over-heated room of the B and B, the sheet pulled up over her breasts, a slender arm exposed and relaxed. The glossy brown hair on the pillow had always been a talisman for him. Around her, the flowered wallpaper and the antique reproductions faded out to nothing. In recent weeks, she'd become a tourist.

"You have wanderlust," he'd once said to her in the car.

"What's that mean? I like to fuck and walk at the same time?"

Webster slipped back into the bed, unwilling to be away from her. He knew how her skin felt everywhere—the down of her arms, the hard muscle of her inner thigh, the sweet curve of her hip. If she woke with a hangover, she hid it well, apart from a terrible thirst.

He stroked her arm from the shoulder to the wrist. He wanted to wake her. He liked to see her eyes flutter open, the moment of pleasure when she saw him. Sometimes, she smiled. He had the water glass ready. She would prop herself up on an arm and drink it down, and eventually, after they'd had sex, he'd get her another and a couple of Excedrin.

That morning, however, she woke as if reluctant to enter the world. Webster enjoyed the anticipation. But then she bolted up in bed, putting her fingers to her nostrils.

"What's that awful smell?" she asked.

Webster sniffed the air. "Coffee? I used the coffeemaker on the bureau. It's terrible, but I didn't want to walk out naked in search of a coffee shop." He ran his fingers from the base of her spine to the nape of her neck.

"Webster," she said, bowing her head.

He didn't like the way she'd said his name. He waited. "What's wrong?" he asked.

"Fuck."

She can't do this anymore, and she's going to say it. He shut his eyes. He couldn't stop her.

"You want it straight out?" she asked.

"Always."

"I'm pregnant."

The word stunned him. Pregnancy had never crossed his mind.

"You sure?" he asked.

She brushed the hair off her face and turned to look at him. "Very."

"How far along?"

"Ten weeks."

"Have you seen a doctor?"

"Yes."

A dialogue repeated, he imagined, thousands of times between thousands of couples. Only this time it was unique, as if he were the first man ever knocked out by a single word.

Under the .9 moon, he'd asked her if

she was on the pill, and she'd nodded.
Then later, she said she preferred a diaphragm. Had she really nodded? Had he
been mistaken?

Fucking biology. It didn't give a shit what
Mother Nature was doing on the outside.

He almost said, "How can you be sure
it's mine?" but stopped himself just in time.
**Don't go there.**

"I don't know what happened," she said.
"I was on the pill, and then I started getting
these bleeds and I switched to a diaphragm.
They're both supposed to work."

He studied the quilt. A blur of colors
slowly came into focus. He noted red flowers on an ivory background, whole squares
of blue, knots of thread in the corners of the
patches. For a moment, he imagined Sheila
happy, the happiness infectious. Then he
pictured her wanting an abortion, and sup-
porting her decision. Finally, he saw her as
frightened, at least as confused as he was.

"I'll be such a good mother," she said,
and Webster was surprised a second time.
She turned and stared at him, as if she
knew she might have pushed him too far,
as if he might still be in shock.

"How will you know what to do?"

She kissed him. "We'll figure it out together, Webster."

She was not going to ask him how he felt about the pregnancy.

Again, Webster imagined Sheila happy. He tried to see past the sheet to the flat of her belly. His child was lodged somewhere just below the runway scar.

All he had to do was let go, let it happen.

If he asked another question, she'd see his uncertainty, and once the baby came, she'd never forget that waffling and would always wonder. Webster would regret that. He loved Sheila, of that he was certain. The idea of not being with her hurt. Besides, he was just as responsible for the seed inside her as she was. More so. He was the guy, for Christ's sake. He was an EMT! Why hadn't he just used a condom?

He stroked her hair where it fell against her back. He liked the way the two sides curled toward each other. He imagined other women paying big bucks over the years to achieve what Sheila came by naturally.

A baby. Settling down. Maybe a place of their own. And he'd be with her every step of the way. As much as he could. He thought about the long nights he'd be gone, and for just a second, he had an image of Sheila with a baby sleeping in her lap, a glass of Bacardi under the sofa. He made the image vanish as quickly as it had come.

He thought about how much she'd had to drink the night before and felt a little sick. Why had Sheila done it? She'd known. A last hurrah?

He told himself to flatline his anger.

This was risk. Risk of the most dangerous and wonderful kind. To bet your life on something as tiny as a sprout.

"I'm in," he said.

Webster, in a clean shirt and a pair of khakis, fresh from his day's nap after a Friday-night call, found his father, two Rolling Rocks in hand, in the kitchen.

"OK if I join you?" Webster asked. Occasionally, during the last year, Webster had been invited to have a drink during his parents' hour together. Sometimes he would. Sometimes not.

"Sure," his father said, clearly happy to have his son spend time with the old man. He nudged the fridge open with his elbow.

"I'll get that," Webster said.

His own beer in hand, Webster followed his father into the living room. If his father had looked happy, his mother was delighted. Webster winced. If either of them detected a summit, they didn't let on.

A cheese ball, studded with chopped walnuts, had been placed on a dinner plate, surrounded by saltines. "We hardly ever see you," his mother said, patting her hair. She plumped the cushions next to her with something like giddiness. "You must be working all the hours of the day."

His mother drank beer in a wineglass. Webster sat next to her and fingered the condensation on his Kelly green bottle.

"In another few weeks," said his mother, "we'll be sitting on the porch this time of night. I really have to clear out all that winter dirt."

"How's the job going?" his father asked. "You save anyone I know?"

His father knew almost everyone in Hartstone.

"Asa Bennet had a fall yesterday," Webster said, forgoing the "Mr." as he wouldn't have just two months earlier. Crazy how a single word could signal a change in a father-son relationship. "Broke his hip."

"What will the poor man do?" his mother asked. "He's how old now?"

"Eighty-four."

"And Alice passed away, oh, at least two years now."

Three, Webster knew from the patient report. "I don't know what he'll do after he recovers," Webster said. "I see them only as far as the hospital. Sometimes I know what happens after that, but most of the time I don't."

"What a job you have!" she exclaimed, not for the first time. Webster was never sure if she meant, "What a horrible job you have," or "You have such a wonderful chance to help people." As far as being an EMT went, both were true.

Webster cleared his throat. "I've been seeing someone," he announced.

His mother coughed on her beer. Webster patted her back. "That's nice," she said when she could speak, her voice scratchy.

"Who is she?" His father sat in the upholstered wing chair, always known, since Webster was a boy, as "Dad's chair."

"Her name is Sheila Arsenault. She's from Boston but is in the process of settling in Vermont."

"I used to know some Arsenaults," his mother mused, "but they were from Quebec."

"How long have you been seeing her?" his father asked.

"About four months," Webster replied, exaggerating a bit.

"What does she do?" his mother asked.

"Right now, she's working as a waitress, but she's looking for a better job."

"Where does she work?" his mother continued.

Webster wished he could name a better place. "Keezer's. But that's just temporary. For now."

"I see," his mother said, more curious than concerned. "Tell me what she looks like."

"She's tall and slim. Beautiful brown hair. Blue eyes. Pretty."

"And where did you meet?" his father asked.

"I met her in the diner," Webster lied, knowing that the truth would steer their thoughts in an unfortunate direction.

Webster knew that his father had picked up on something. He was staring at Webster, as if searching for a tell. When had

Webster ever told his parents he was seeing someone?

"You should bring her to dinner," his mother offered, probably already thinking about a menu.

"Thanks. I will. But there's one other thing." Webster bent forward and held the nearly full Rolling Rock between his knees. "Sheila's pregnant."

Both parents froze, their arms in midair. In other circumstances, it would have been comical.

Webster had to remind himself to breathe. The house sounded the way it did when he was alone in it. Silent except for the clock and the fridge and the heating system.

His mother lowered her drink. His father finished off his and set the bottle down hard.

"It's mine," Webster said, short-stopping the inevitable.

His father rolled his head back in disbelief. "How can you be sure?"

His father asking the question the son had stopped himself from asking the girlfriend.

"I'm sure," Webster said.

"Peter," his mother moaned. "You're only twenty-one!"

"Almost twenty-two," Webster said.

"How far along is she?" his father, persistent, asked. His mother looked as though she might cry.

"Three months," Webster said.

It was simple math.

His father looked away. Webster thought his dad would get up from the wing chair and leave the room and then the house and maybe not come back for a couple of hours.

"You're only twenty-one," his mother repeated, seemingly unable to move beyond that thought.

His father wasn't leaving, though. "Is she going . . ." He seemed unable to finish the sentence. Webster did it for him.

"To keep it? Yes."

"Do you love her?" his mother asked.

Finally, an easy question. "I do," he said. "Very much." But even as he said it, and as sure as he was that he did, he wondered if he really knew what love, in these circumstances, meant.

His father left the room and returned with three more Rolling Rocks. Medicinal, not celebratory.

"You going to marry this girl?" his father asked, his voice gruff. Man to man.

"She has a name," Webster said.

"But we don't know her!" his mother wailed before his father could tell him not to be fresh.

"How the hell . . . ?" His father pressed his lips together hard and gave a short shake of the head.

"I think we'll probably get married," Webster said.

"You think?" his father asked.

"We're taking it slow," he said.

"I should say not!" his mother protested. "Slow? I should say not!"

"You're an EMT, for Christ's sakes," his father said, referring, Webster guessed, to the failed contraception.

Webster set his jaw. He'd expected the conversation to take an ugly turn, but it was still hard to live through it.

"This whole thing has been rolling along, and we don't even know her?" his mother asked. "This isn't what we envisioned for you."

Webster was silent. He didn't want this initial talk to end in more acrimony than it had to. In five minutes—no, less, maybe three—his mother had gone from delighted to curious to shocked to angry and now was quickly moving to disappointed. His father remained disgusted.

"You know we love you," his mother said. "We want only the best for you."

Webster wished he'd told his father first.

"I'm a grown man, Mom. I know how to save people's lives. I'm working hard. I sometimes volunteer for twenty-four-hour shifts."

"You've never even seen the world!" his father said, gesturing with his arm to take in all the places his son might never see.

"Did you?" Webster asked.

His father narrowed his eyes.

"Look," Webster said. "I'm going to start studying to be a paramedic, the next step after EMT. Once I'm a medic, I'm pretty sure I can make enough money to support us."

His father drank the rest of his Rolling Rock in one go. Webster waited for the belch.

"What's she like?" Webster's mother asked.

Webster thought. "She's strong. Strong-willed. She's funny. Very pretty. I said that." He paused. "She likes to travel to other

parts of Vermont to see them, so we sometimes take long drives."

"Wanderlust," his father said, with all that
that implied. Webster remembered Sheila's
quick retort in the cruiser.

"She's got a Boston accent. I think you'll
like her." Though he didn't think so. Not one
tiny bit. "Obviously, we'll have to get our
own place. A small apartment. I was thinking of renting something in town. Closer to
Rescue."

"Can you afford that?" his father asked.

"Just."

"Well," said his mother, sitting up straight
and smoothing her legs as if she had an
apron on. "When would you like us to have
her over for dinner?"

Ever the peacekeeping, let's-move-on
mother. For which Webster was grateful.

"I'm theoretically home next weekend,"
he said. "We could do it Saturday night."

"Settled," his mother said, and she might
as well have had a gavel.


"Did you do it? How did it go?"

Sheila had her arms crossed over her
chest.

Webster moved into the kitchen and

looked around. He was hungry. A meal at home hadn't been possible. "Peachy," he said.

Sheila closed the door. "Well, it's done."

"I'm hungry," Webster said. "Have you got anything here I could eat?" He snuck a look at her stomach. How could she not be showing yet? Or was there stress on the belt? Yes, he thought maybe there was.

"Go sit in there," she said, gesturing to the jalousie porch.

Webster, though he'd slept from nine to four thirty, felt exhausted. Bone-weary, mind-weary. He could hear Sheila moving around in the kitchen. He could have used three more beers in quick succession, but he wouldn't get them at Sheila's. He hoped he wouldn't, anyway.

He supposed the announcement had gone as well as it could have. His father hadn't stomped out. His mother hadn't actually wept. There would be yet another chapter to the new saga. He laid his head against the back of the wall and dozed until Sheila came in with a tray. She set the food down.

"You think you can make it to the table?" she asked.

He smiled. "Spaghetti and meatballs," he said. "Perfect."

After he was seated, he glanced up and saw Sheila for the first time that evening. Did he imagine that her face was fuller? "How are you?" he asked, a question he should have asked the minute he'd walked in the door.

"OK," she said. "Still can't stand the smell of coffee, which is a real problem at work. When I get outside and breathe in the air, it's like a happy drug."

"No morning sickness?" he asked.

"Not morning. Sometimes in the afternoon I get a headache and I feel nauseous. But I hate throwing up so much, I'm willing my body not to do it."

"You look beautiful," Webster said.

"Jesus, you really were hungry."

He slowed down. "You have any bread?"

"Sure."

"With butter?"

"It was that bad."

"It was that bad."

They sat at the edge of her bed, Webster not sure if they would make love or not.

"We're invited to dinner next Saturday," he said.

"Won't that be a disaster?"

"It has to happen," Webster said. "There's no avoiding it."

"Can't we just have a secret baby and stay in a secret place?" She had her fingers in his hair. He hoped that she was kidding.

"And another thing," Webster said. "We have to start looking for a place to live."

"Our own apartment?" she asked, drawing back so that she could see his face.

"Of course."

"We don't have to live with your parents, and we don't have to live here?"

"Sheila, did you really think we could possibly do that?"

She ruffled his hair and drew her hand away. "I didn't know what your finances were. Mine aren't too great."

"Combined, I think we can just make it. It has to be small, and it has to be something close to town."

"Close to town? Where there are shops and people, and I could walk to work?" she asked, wide-eyed. The couple from whom Sheila rented the jalousie porch had given her the use of their ancient Buick, insisting they never drove it. Sheila was planning on buying it when she'd saved enough money. She had needed a car to get back and forth to work, and Webster guessed the old folks were more than happy to aid their tenant in that endeavor. Sheila didn't make as much fun of them as she used to. "This living in the sticks is driving me nuts."

The northern border of Hartstone could hardly be called the sticks. Unless you thought the entire state of Vermont the sticks.

She wrapped her arms around his neck. "This is so cool."

Webster smiled. "Yeah, I suppose it is." The idea of their future being cool hadn't really occurred to him.

He undid her belt buckle and smoothed her belly. "You're showing," he said.

"I am not."

"Go look at yourself in the mirror."

"I don't have a mirror," she reminded him, and he thought about the small circle high over the bathroom sink.

"Well, I think we'll have to go somewhere that has a full-length mirror."

Webster thought. It had to be a place that

was still open. A bar? A full-length mirror in the ladies' room? A bad idea. And then he had it. "The Giant Mart," he said. "They're bound to have a ladies' room with a big mirror that goes down to the sinks. If you wear your boots, you'd be high enough to see."

"This is so weird," she said and kissed him on the cheek.

"After we find a place, and I think we should start tomorrow, even though it's a Sunday, the first piece of furniture we're going to put in there is a full-length mirror."

She cocked her head and gave a little shake.

"So you can see how beautiful you are. And will be when you're eight months pregnant."

"I'll be fat."

"You'll be gorgeous."

She frowned, and it occurred to Webster that he'd never known Sheila to be even slightly vain.

She'd undone his shirtsleeve and was rolling it up his arm. "What kind of a place will we be able to get?" she asked.

He looked down at his arm. "I've done a little hunting," he said. "When I was thinking about getting out of my parents' house.

Not that I don't love them and appreciate the meals. I do. But it's past time. I've seen a few places. A one-bedroom at best."

Sheila stroked the inside of his arm. "We have to have someplace to put the baby," she said.

"Well, two bedrooms if we get extra lucky." The only two-bedroom Webster had seen during his short quest had smelled of dead animal. Tomorrow he'd walk over to Carroll & Carroll and see if there was anything new in the window. And he'd buy the Sunday paper, look at the ads. The problem was that the apartment had to be in Hartstone. Rescue had a bunk room and a living room with a TV for use during tours. All the furniture was from grateful patients. The kitchen had three spoons. Webster didn't understand why the medics didn't just go out and buy a dozen spoons. He'd thought of doing it himself, but couldn't presume until he'd earned a little more seniority.

The search for an apartment might be hard.

"OK," he said. "Let's go."

Sheila, drawing her fingers away from his arm, seemed confused.

"The Giant Mart," he said.

They took the first apartment they could afford: a one-bedroom the size of Webster's parents' living room situated over an ice-cream shop. That the apartment had a washer and dryer sealed the deal. If they'd been willing to look further, they might have been able to find a better place, but this one was available, and Webster was impatient. Now that the decision had been made, he wanted to make it a reality as soon as possible. They could move in any time, the owner of the ice-cream shop had said.

They transferred Sheila's belongings

the following Saturday morning. Webster wouldn't start moving in until the next day, after they'd had the dinner with his parents. He didn't want to appear too eager, even though he'd move no matter what they said.

Once Webster had paid the security deposit and the first month's rent, he and Sheila walked into their new home together. The kitchenette allowed only one person inside it at a time, but the round table Webster would bring from home could seat three in a pinch. The appliances looked tired, but they worked, which was all Webster cared about. They studied the small living room, noting water damage on the ceiling. They didn't much like the blue wall-to-wall either. Someday they'd own their own place, Sheila said, and Webster wondered if that would ever be true.

They walked into a single bedroom with a slanted ceiling and one window. They debated where to put the bed, a short debate, there being only one section of wall without a door or a window. They drove to the Giant Mart to buy a broom, a wastebasket, kitchen and bath supplies, and enough food to get by for a couple of days.

When the parental dinner was behind them, Webster would go to his father's hardware store and purchase a full-length mirror for Sheila. The only place he could put it would be inside the only closet in the apartment, the one in the bedroom. The owner had put hooks, in lieu of a coat closet, by the front door.

Sheila had asked the nurse if she could borrow the mattress from the porch for two nights until Webster moved his own bed in the next day. The nurse had been annoyed at the abrupt notice but had said yes to the mattress. Webster hauled it up the outside stairs. "Let me sweep first," Sheila said.

Together they settled the mattress on the floor of the bedroom. After it was in place, Webster asked where the sheets were.

"I don't have any," Sheila said.

"You didn't bring them?"

"They weren't mine."

"But . . ." Webster shook his head. "A towel?"

"Nope."

"We'll just have to be careful, then," Webster said.

"Careful with what?" Sheila asked.

"We have to christen the place," he said with a grin.

"Your father's going to recognize me," Sheila said from the passenger seat of the cruiser.

The hardware store.

"You didn't go wild in there, did you?" Webster asked.

"No, I just bought a lot of cigarettes."

"Well, I wouldn't light up during dinner."

"Jesus, Webster, give me some credit."

He was inclined to give her a lot of credit. When she'd emerged from the bedroom, she was wearing a loose light gray dress. Not a maternity dress, but one that could become one. She had put her hair up, which showed off her long white neck and the pearls at her ears. She had on stockings and a pair of white flat shoes. He whistled and made her turn around and told her she looked beautiful, which she did, though he hardly recognized her, and that threw him a little. It was as if she had on a costume for a theater production.

"I'm not sure this is a good idea," she said in the cruiser.

"I can't tell them no at this point. Besides, you're pregnant with their first grand-child. We have to do this."

"Doesn't it seem like everything is hap-pening too fast?"

It did. The pregnancy had put the normal timetable into overdrive. Then he wondered if there would have been a normal time-table at all. If Sheila hadn't gotten pregnant, what would they be doing now? Taking drives? Still visiting B and Bs? All of that seemed another lifetime ago.

He'd barely absorbed the news of the pregnancy himself. Now he had to help his parents comprehend what their son had done.

*Pregnant.* Hell of a word.

Webster and Sheila arrived at his par-ents' house at exactly 6:30. "Stay in the car," Webster said. "I'm coming around to get you."

"You've got to be kidding."

When he opened her door, and she stepped out, Webster was proud of the way she looked. "I don't want to sound like an asshole," he said quietly, "but you might want to get rid of the gum. My mother hates girls who chew gum."

"You are an asshole," Sheila said as she wrapped the gum in a tissue from her purse. "How long is this dinner going to last, anyway?"

Webster sighed. "Can you hang in there for two hours?"

"And I'm not a girl," she said.

Webster's mother, who'd had her hair done for the occasion, declared straightaway that she was happy to meet Sheila. Sheila said, "Me, too," while his mother's eyes slipped to Sheila's waist, not really visible beneath the gray dress.

Webster's father was cool. "I know you," he said, not a trace of a smile on his face. "Toasted bagel, butter instead of cream cheese, a carton of Virginia Slims, coffee black. You used to stand outside the store, juggling the bagel, the coffee, the cigarette, and the carton. I wondered how you could do that."

"Held the carton between my knees," she said, leaving the unfortunate image hanging in the air.

"Haven't seen you much lately, though," Webster's father said.

Webster could only imagine how Sheila

had looked in his father's store. Bored? Sullen? Impatient?

"I have a job now," Sheila said, maybe as embarrassed as Webster was to have had that initial portrait laid bare.

"Well, you have other things on your mind, don't you, dear?" Webster's mother said, deftly slaying the elephant. Webster was grateful. "Come right through," she added. "We're having drinks and some appetizers on the porch."

Webster sat next to Sheila, who had her hands in her lap. When asked what she wanted, she said lemonade, a large pitcher of which stood next to a bottle of wine. Webster followed suit, which caused his mother to copy them as well. Only Webster's father had the wine.

"I understand you're from Boston," his father boomed from his chair as if Sheila might be deaf. He had on a white shirt and tie and had groomed his hair with something that made it shine.

"Chelsea, actually," Sheila said.

"And what's that like?"

"It's a small city near Boston. Most people only ever see it from the Mystic River Bridge."

Webster's mother was seemingly mes-merized by Sheila's waistline, visible now that Sheila was seated.

Webster endured a long silence, unable to think of a single thing to say. Nervous, he ate all the nuts in the bowl.

"How did you end up in Vermont?" Web-ster's father asked, even though he'd been told the answer.

Sheila looked at Webster. She didn't know her lines and was desperate for a prompt.

"Car trouble," Webster answered. "I al-ready told you that."

"And how did the two of you meet?"

"Dad, stop grilling her," Webster said, willing to risk a confrontation. His father wasn't buying Sheila as the sweet new-comer to Vermont. He knew better. He'd seen the woman in the parking lot.

Webster's mother didn't care how the two had met. She wanted to talk about the baby to come. "You're taking care of your-self?" she asked Sheila. "I had such a hard time bringing that one"—she pointed at Webster—"into the world."

"Mom."

"Well, I didn't mean to suggest that you

would," she said to Sheila. "Every birth, as I'm sure you know, is different."

"I hope I'll be a good mother," Sheila said.

"Oh, you will, dear, you will," Webster's mother said, patting Sheila's knee, the first time the two had touched.

Sheila blinked. Webster's father stared at Sheila's face. Webster's mother stared at Sheila's waist. Webster was horrified. They had just under two hours still to go.

At dinner, Webster and Sheila talked about the apartment they'd found over the ice-cream shop, causing Webster's mother to reminisce about the years when "Petey" had always liked his chocolate cones with jimmies on them.

Webster shut his eyes.

Sheila complimented the meal, which seemed to be a soupy concoction of chicken, mushrooms, sour cream, and bread crumbs, with sprigs of parsley around the border of the casserole dish. Webster guessed that Sheila would have a hard time getting it down. When she did, he thought her heroic.

His father brought the bottle of red wine

to the table, poured a glass, and offered it to Sheila, who hesitated and then took it, surprising Webster. He then felt compelled to mention that some doctors thought that an occasional glass of red wine was beneficial to the mother and not harmful to the baby. He also wanted to tell his father to fuck off, but that wasn't anywhere in the script.

Webster checked his watch so often it became a tic. Sheila asked him if he had a shift that night, perhaps hoping that he would say he did.

She drank the glass of wine quickly and used the words *shacking up* to describe her move with Webster into the apartment above the ice-cream shop. Webster's father seemed pleased and even went so far as to smile. Was his initial distrust waning, or was he merely proving himself right in his character assessment? By the time Webster's mother served up a Boston cream pie, Sheila was on her second glass of wine, and his father was laughing. Sheila was flirting with the man, which made Webster as nervous as hell. Or was she merely opening up, being charming, trying to save the occasion?

Webster's mother had a pleasant smile on her face and could be pulled from her happy daze only when spoken to. She roused herself to ask for coffee requests.

Webster knew the coffee would make Sheila feel sick. He didn't ask for any, but his father did. Sheila devoured the pie and told Webster's mother that she would love to learn how to make it.

"Surely, you've had it before, being from Boston."

"I've had what passes for Boston cream pie," Sheila said, "but nothing that compares to this one."

When the coffee arrived, Sheila put the backs of her fingers to her nose and immediately went pale. She glanced at Webster across the table.

Webster pushed his chair back. "I think I'll take Sheila for a little stroll around the house. She's never seen the yard before."

"I'd like to help with the dishes," Sheila said in a weak voice.

"Nonsense," Webster's mother insisted. "You two go enjoy yourselves."

Webster held Sheila's hand as they walked into the backyard. Her heels dipped into the soft sod. Out of sight of the parents, she whispered, "You ate every last nut and piece of cheese!"

"I was so afraid you were going to give an answer other than car trouble. I just had to stop the questions."

"I wish I'd worn a pillow for your mother."

"She couldn't take her eyes off your stomach."

"What do you think they're saying about us?" Sheila asked, glancing up at the kitchen window.

Webster didn't want to know. His father would be saying that he didn't trust the girl as far as he could throw her. His mother would be defending Sheila, saying, "Don't be silly. She's lovely." His father would shake his head and use it as an excuse to leave his wife to do the dishes alone.

"You really want to know how to make Boston cream pie?" Webster asked.

"God, no," Sheila said. "I've had enough Boston cream pie to sink the city of Chelsea."

The next afternoon, Webster's father arrived with a set of tools just as Webster was moving in his few possessions. He'd let Webster get the mattress from his old bedroom by himself, but he helped his son haul it up the back stairs to the new apartment. "Small," he said to Webster when he saw the place.

Webster's mother had found an old love seat in the basement that was in decent condition, even if the slipcovers were flowered print. She had curtains to match, which seemed a bit much to Webster, but which solved the problem of the open windows. His father fixed a leaky faucet, spackled and painted over large holes in the wall, and checked the electrical outlets, putting new covers over them. Webster's mother had brought bedding, declaring that Webster's old sheets and blanket weren't fit to bring into a new home. She and Sheila made the bed together, and when Webster caught a glimpse of them in the bedroom, his brain filled with white noise.

Too fast, too fast.

He couldn't imagine what Sheila was thinking. Would she feel that they'd been invaded? Would she be glad that she'd been welcomed?

Sheila and his mother opened cartons— mismatched dishes, glasses, a toaster, all unearthed from the Webster basement—while Webster and his father each had a beer. Webster thought his parents' kindness a sign of acceptance. Maybe his mother had won the previous night's argument after all.

When his parents left, Webster and Sheila stood at the counter, looking at the stack of Tupperware his mother had brought, all filled with parts of a meal and a coffee cake for breakfast. They shook their heads, bewildered. Two weeks ago, they'd had each other and nothing else. Their time together had been a secret. Webster was afraid that something precious was in jeopardy now. Their relationship was public, subject to scrutiny. He longed to be back in that moment in the B and B, stroking Sheila's arm before she woke up.

"What did you say when they left?" Webster asked.

"I said 'thank you.' What did you think I'd say?"

"I don't know."

"Your father glances at me when he thinks I'm not looking. As if I might be going to steal something."

"He came to help."

"Yes, he did."

Webster put his arm around the woman he'd slept with, who was his girlfriend, who would be the mother of his child, who might, one day, be his wife.

"Can we crack these open?" Sheila asked, pointing to the food in the Tupperware. "I'm starved."

Attention, Hartstone Rescue. We need a crew on Deertrack Road, number forty-five, suspected stroke, male, seventy-two, wife present at scene, blurred speech, apparent paralysis of left side."

"Let's go," Burrows said.

In the rig, Burrows got on the radio. "Car sixty responding. Can you say when symptoms first occurred?"

"Approximately fifteen minutes prior to our call. Can I have your ETA?"

"Six minutes," Burrows said and signed off. "It'll be twenty minutes down when we get there. You know where you're going?"

Webster was pretty sure he knew where Deertrack was. He'd once had a girlfriend who'd lived out that way. He nodded.

"You know the guy?" Burrows asked.

"No, do you?"

"Not really."

At the destination, Webster made a U and backed expertly up the driveway of number 45. Each carrying their usual equipment, the EMT and the medic opened the front door and walked in. The house was old, built around the 1920s, with a lot of dark molding and small rooms stuffed with furniture.

They found the man still slumped in his recliner, the wife trying to hold him up.

"I know who you are," she said, recognizing Burrows. "You're that nice medic who helped my daughter's son with his asthma."

Burrows was a lot of things, but *nice* was a stretch.

Burrows checked the airway and applied the high-flow oxygen. Webster whipped out his pad and pen. "I'm going to have to ask you some questions," he said to the woman.

While Webster took a history, Burrows dealt with the patient.

"Sir, can you tell me your name?" Burrows asked.

The patient answered, but his speech was garbled. Burrows asked the man to lift each leg. He could lift only the right one. Webster wrote that down along with the garbled speech. Burrows then asked the man to smile. The left side of the smile drooped.

Diagnosis confirmed. Injury to right side of the brain.

"I'm going for the stretcher," Burrows said to Webster.

"Ma'am," asked Webster, "can you help your husband sit upright? You can put your hand here on this left shoulder. I need to examine him."

The man said something else in garbled speech.

"What's he saying?" the wife asked, beginning to panic.

"I don't know, ma'am, but it's a good sign that he's trying to talk."

When Burrows returned, Webster reported: "BP two sixty-two over one twenty-eight. Pulse ninety-two. Respirations twenty-four. We need a line in. Sir, can you squeeze my fingers?" he asked the patient.

Webster felt something, but he wasn't sure he was getting a good response. He needed to know the level of the man's cognition. Had the stroke affected only motor skills or had the entirety of the right side of his brain been compromised?

Webster got in the man's face. "If you can hear me, sir, please blink."

He watched as the man blinked once. OK, then.

"We were fine," the wife said. "And then he just slumped over."

"Ma'am, you can ride up front. There's no time to change. Just put some shoes and a coat on."

Webster and Burrows slid the man into the rig. They helped the wife, in her bathrobe and coat, up into a seat. Webster slammed the back door, got into the driver's seat. The wife was already crying.

Webster drove as fast as he could. Minutes counted with stroke victims.

Burrows and the wife went with the patient into the ER, Burrows grabbing Webster's written notes to take with him. While the medic was gone, Webster wrote down all the items that would have to be restocked in the rig. He cleaned up the back,

stuffing the medical waste into the appro-
priate container. He stood by the passenger side, waiting for Burrows. The sun was
up strong already. But it couldn't do much
against the late April chill.

A doctor Webster recognized waved as
he passed by. Off duty? Going for coffee?

Webster could have used a cup.

Where the hell was Burrows?

Seventy-two and a stroke. Not uncom-
mon. The couple had probably lived in that
house for years, their routines established.
Alone now since the kids had moved out.
The wife had seemed caring. They had
each other. Maybe they bickered; maybe
they didn't. He'd looked for pictures of
grandchildren but hadn't seen any.

Burrows finally climbed into the rig.

"Where were you?" Webster asked as
he checked his watch. Nearly thirty-five
minutes.

"The guy stroked out again. And then a
third time with the wife watching."

"How is he?"

"Bad shape. Real bad. Cognitively, he's
got nothing. I wanted to stay with him. I
knew if you got a call, you'd come get me."

"Poor bastard," Webster said. "One

minute he's reading the *Hartstone Herald* and having his Nescafé, and the next he's a veg."

"Seen it plenty of times before," Burrows said.

"You think it gets easier?"

Burrows sat back. "Yeah, I do. But every once in a while, it hits you. That could be me, I think. That could be Karen."

"I think like that sometimes."

"You?" Burrows hooted. "You ain't seen nothing yet."

"What are the odds the guy will make it?"

"Zero," Burrows said.

Webster parked his cruiser in front of the ice-cream shop. He thought of bringing a treat up to Sheila but then decided to ask her first. These days, she was finicky about food. He stood and stretched his back. He'd stayed in service later into Saturday morning than he had imagined he would, Rescue having been shorthanded for four hours. He'd eaten peanut-butter cookies Burrows's wife had made and had studied his course work for medic certification. Anatomy fascinated him. But all he wanted now was a bed with Sheila in it. His face and vision felt grainy. Sheila should be home. She almost always had weekends off.

With his uniform jacket on, Webster climbed the long outdoor stairs to the apartment. He opened the door and stood still. He felt a surge of adrenaline, as if he'd barked his shin on the edge of a coffee table. A cop sat at the table, Sheila across from him. Webster thought, DUI.

Webster shut the door behind him. Not a DUI. The cop was too casual, leaning back in his chair, his legs crossed, ankle on knee. It took Webster another two seconds to register the insignia on the uniform. Chelsea. Massachusetts.

"You didn't tell me he was an empt," the beefy man at the table said, grinning. "Quite a comedown, Squirrel. From a cop to an empt?"

**Squirrel.**

The cop had the same accent as Sheila did. He was built, 220, outsized shoulders. He did something else besides ride around in a cruiser all day. Football league? Weight lifting? "What's going on?" Webster asked, hands moving into fists.

"This is the man I told you about," Sheila mumbled, her face pale, her posture in the chair saying it all. She'd narrowed her shoulders together, as if she were trying to hide her breasts, her entire body. When Webster saw that she was trembling, rage flooded him.

But you couldn't manhandle a cop who outweighed you by forty pounds, who had a gun in his holster.

"Hey, I got a name, Squirrel."

"This is Brian Doyle," Sheila said, not looking at Webster. Webster wanted to add, *The guy who pissed the bed.*

The cop didn't get up, didn't offer his hand.

Webster stared at the man, waiting for an explanation from somebody. The cop's chin had so many acne scars, it looked chewed. The eyes were pale green, washed out.

"An empt," the guy said again, as if he'd made a terrific joke. Nodding all the time. Establishing rank. He examined Webster head to toe. "Quite a surprise to find my sweet little Squirrel shacked up preggers with an empt in Vermont."

Why didn't Sheila say something?

"Get out," Webster said.

"Whaaa? I drive all the way from Chelsea, and you want me to leave without a proper meal?"

"There's a diner down the road," Webster said.

Engaging him.

Mistake.

"Squirrel and me have things we need to talk about."

"Not in this house," Webster said.

"This a house? Fuck, you coulda fooled me." The cop took a sip of coffee, as if he were Webster's best friend.

"What things?" Webster asked.

Second mistake.

"Hey, man, the bitch ran out on me," the cop said, as if appealing to a fraternal bond.

Sheila looked up at Webster. She put her hand on the table. "He says I owe him money," she said.

"Do you?" Webster asked.

She shrugged.

"How much?"

"Eight hundred."

"Eight hundred fifty," the cop corrected. He slid his hand across the table and covered Sheila's. She flinched.

"Take your fucking hand off her," Webster said, quivering with fury.

The guy was thirty, maybe thirty-three. Maybe he weighed 225.

"Simmer down, probie."

Was the gun in the holster the reason the guy had driven through three states in his uniform? It would have taken him four hours to get to Hartstone.

All Webster could hear was Burrows's voice in his ear, warning him months ago: *Never approach a guy with a gun. Even if he's hurt. He's hurt, too bad for him. Nine times out of ten, you approach, he'll shoot you.*

"She's a squirrely little hustler," the cop said, looking in Sheila's direction and then back at Webster. "She hustling you?"

"I'll say it one more time," Webster said, enunciating each word. "Get. The. Fuck. Out."

"Or what?" the cop asked. "You'll call the cops?" The guy grinned.

Webster pictured Nye and McGill arriving at the apartment. Looking from Webster to the cop and back again.

"What did she tell you?" the cop asked. "She tell you everything?"

Sheila twisted out of her chair, walked to the stove, kept her back to the two men.

"Like how she used to be standing at the top of the stairs in her nothing at all when I got off my shift? All pink and rosy from her bath? Me with the bottle of Maker's Mark in my hand? She tell you I saved her from a life on the streets?" The cop turned to look at Sheila's back. "You'd think she'd be more grateful. An apartment? A car to tool around in? I guess she likes guys who save her."

"Sheila," Webster said. "Get your jacket. We're leaving."

"No, you're not," the cop said. "I got business here."

Webster was silent.

The cop hitched himself forward in his chair, the seat barely containing his thighs. "Well, empt, I'll tell you what. I'm hungry. So I'm going to go to that diner you mentioned and have a big meal. And when I've finished with my coffee, I want Sheila to be sitting on a stool next to me with the money in large bills inside an envelope."

The cop stood.

"Don't go to the diner," Webster said, hating that he had to speak at all. But he couldn't have the guy at Geezer's. "Go to the pub at the inn."

The cop grinned again. "You're a stand-up guy, you know that? But you're an idiot. Don't waste your time on that fucking whore."

Never had Webster wanted to throw a punch more than he did at that moment. With every muscle screaming, he moved to one side.

The cop put on his cap, completing the uniform more than a hat ought to.

"You wouldn't last ten minutes in Chelsea," the cop said.

Sheila turned to Webster the moment the door was closed. "I'm sorry," she said, pressing her eyes with her fingers, as if she wanted to blot out the image of the cop.

"Why did you let him in?"

"I didn't. I heard footsteps on the stairs. I opened the door, thinking it was you, and then he was inside."

Webster's legs shook. He put his coat over a chair and sat down. "How'd he find you?" Webster asked.

"Is that a serious question?"

"I fucking wanted to cream the guy."

"I was terrified you were going to do something."

"Come over here," he said. He patted the chair beside him. Not the one the cop's ass had filled. "He's one dangerous son of a bitch."

"Unless I pay him, he won't go away," she said in a small voice.

"What are you going to pay him with?" Webster asked.

"I'll think of something."

"How much have you got saved?"

"Two hundred? I was saving to buy the Buick."

"Why do you owe him eight fifty?"

"He staked me."

"To what?"

"Pool."

"What happened?"

"I had some nights I shouldn't have been playing."

Webster let out a forceful breath. "You actually *lived* with this guy?" he asked.

Sheila abruptly got up from the chair.

"Fuck." Webster stood. "I'll get the money and take it to him."

Sheila walked into the bedroom, lifted

the mattress, and gave Webster her two hundred. "It should be me that goes."

"Yeah, well, it isn't going to be."

"Wait, let's think."

Webster waited. "There's nothing to think about," he said. "I either give him the money or I call the cops. If I call the cops, which is ludicrous, he's only going to come back another day, and he isn't going to be as congenial."

Sheila was silent.

Webster would never be able to rid himself of the image of Sheila, rosy and pink, waiting at the top of the stairs.

Webster drove to the bank and made a withdrawal. He ignored the questioning eyes of Steph, the teller, who would wonder what he was buying. From the bank, Webster walked to the pub, knowing with every step that he shouldn't be giving money to an extortionist. But if he didn't give the guy the money? Webster didn't want to think about it.

He entered the gloom of the pub. The cop was finishing a piece of lemon meringue pie. From the back, the man looked even bigger than he had in the apartment. Webster put the envelope on the stool beside him.

The man turned. "I said Sheila, dickhead."

"You want this or not?" Webster asked in a steady voice.

The cop stuck his jaw out and thought for a second. Then he gave a cold laugh.

"Don't ever come back here," Webster warned.

"Or *what?*"

"I'll kill you," Webster promised.

He turned before he could see the smirk on the cop from Chelsea's face.

When he entered the kitchen, Sheila was sitting at the table. It appeared she hadn't moved since Webster had left. All the color had gone from her face.

"What happened?" she asked.

Webster whirled and punched the wall. He made a sound of frustration mixed with pain. He couldn't feel the full extent of the hurt yet, but he knew he would.

He could hear Sheila getting up, putting ice into a dishcloth.

Webster turned. "There's so much I don't know about you," he said.

Sheila, with the bundle in her hand, was silent.

"I think you need to tell me everything," Webster said.

When Sheila finished talking, it was nearly dusk outside the window. She had held the ice to Webster's hand. She had smoked two of her three allotted cigarettes, but she hadn't poured herself a drink. She had paced and sat down and paced again. She had put more ice on Webster's hand. She had stood and walked through the tiny living area. Webster had listened to every word.

By the time she was done, she'd told him about the father who drank, who'd spent her seventh birthday in a city jail and shortly after had left the house. She described the mother who worked as a seamstress and behind the register at J. J. Newberry's, who tried her best but was never home. Who died too young of colon cancer when Sheila was thirteen. She told Webster about how she and her older sister, Nancy, had been taken in by their aunt and uncle, who lived three streets over. The aunt wanted them, the uncle didn't. He punished them with a belt. Nancy got the worst of it. She was a good student, but Sheila wasn't. She didn't care, she said.

When she finished with that story, she told Webster about what it was like to be a waitress in Chelsea, a city rife with gangs and drugs and crime. About how the streets were dangerous, especially at night when she got off work late. About how she was constantly approached and threatened or approached and hit on. About the cop who came into the Italian restaurant where she worked and walked her to her car one night, and how after that no one ever hassled her again. And about how the cop had set her up in a cheap apartment that had rats, but a place that finally got her away from the aunt and uncle. About how she'd foolishly traded one nightmare for another. She left out the parts that had led to the bruises Webster had seen, but by the time the sun was beginning to set, Webster wanted to smash in the man's face and break all his teeth.

"He's married," Sheila said. "He has kids. When he called me a whore, he meant it."

She never wept. She never indicated she felt sorry for herself.

She held Webster's hand between her own and gently massaged it. She told him about the night she knew the cop was coming over, and she'd heard from a girlfriend that he'd been drinking since noon. She put a few things into a bag, got into the Cadillac, and drove. When she reached the New Hampshire border, she stopped and peed and ate and had a couple of drinks. An hour later, she stopped and peed and had a few more drinks. The alcohol helped with the fear. She was terrified the whole drive that he was right behind her.

"You were headed to New York," Webster said.

"I was going to go as far as I could go."

"And you ended up on my stretch of road."

"That's one way to put it."

For a long time, Webster sat with her story while Sheila made dinner. He hated her history, but he didn't hate her. He decided to think of her past as "the time before

Vermont," and the tree against which her Cadillac had come to rest as the dividing line between "then and now." He decided he could live with that.

They ate, and she washed the dishes. After all the talk, she was silent, as if she had no more words. When she was through with the dishes, he took her to the couch and held her and waited for all the poisonous spores to leave the apartment.

Sheila entered the apartment announcing she needed a shower straightaway. She shed her uniform as she walked, as if she couldn't get it off fast enough. After the shower, in reverse, she collected the bits and threw them in the washing machine before she presented herself to Webster—wet hair and clean skin.

She glowed. Though she was doctor-phobic right from the get-go, he made sure she kept her monthly appointments and took her hefty vitamins.

"Why were you so eager to get your clothes off?" he asked when they sat down to a London broil he had just grilled. "My amazing charm?"

"Geezer rubbed my belly. Usually I don't care. My body's not my own anymore, and that's fine. But it made my skin crawl when he did it."

Webster had bought candles and a tablecloth. Sheila seemed not to notice.

"Well, you can rest now." He took a bite of steak.

For a minute, she looked around the room as if searching for something. Then she was silent. She picked up her fork but didn't touch the meat or the baked potato or green beans.

"I thought maybe I'd paint the bedroom tomorrow," Webster said.

Sheila lifted her glass of water and drank it straight down. She set the glass on the tablecloth. He reached for her hand and startled her.

"There's something I want to ask you," Webster said, and grinned.

Sheila was wary. Not smiling.

"Will you marry me?" he asked.

Sheila paused, fork in midair. She put her fork down.

"What?" she asked.

Webster was silent.

"This is kind of a surprise," she said.

"Sheila."

"Do we have to do this now?"

Webster let her hand go. "Do what now?" he asked.

"Talk. Make plans."

"We make plans all the time," he said.

"We don't make concrete plans."

"Yeah, we do. We're having a baby. That's a pretty concrete plan."

She pressed her lips together.

"What the hell, Sheila?" he said, sitting back. "This isn't your average plan. I'm proposing to you."

Sheila rubbed her eyes with the heels of her hands. "It's so good the way it is," she said wearily. "Let's not mess it up."

Sheila's skin was pink from the hot water, and her hair was flowing damp and straight behind her ears. She wore no makeup, as she did when she went out, and he felt, when he saw her naked face, that he was seeing the real Sheila.

"I'm not asking you just because you're pregnant," he explained.

"I know."

"Then what is it?"

"Why formalize everything?" she asked, lighting a cigarette.

He stared at her.

"See?" she said. "You want me to put this out."

"I do."

"Why?"

"Sheila, you know why."

"That's just it! I don't want all these fucking rules. You're smothering me."

**She wants a drink.**

Knowing that, Webster couldn't argue further. There was no persuading Sheila that she didn't want a drink or that the reason she was picking a fight was her need for the booze. As much as he wanted to remind her that it was dangerous to drink with a sprout the size of his pinky growing inside her, she wouldn't listen to him. All he could do was distract her, the way he dealt with alcoholics on tours.

"I take it back," he said. "I don't want to marry you."

She glanced up. "Make up your mind."

"I did want to, but now I don't."

"You teasing with me?"

"Do I look like I'm teasing with you?"

She stubbed out her cigarette, picked up

her fork, and ate a bite of the green beans. Behind her head, an empty bottle of Dawn rested on a sill under a window. The dirty pots from the meal listed in the sink.

"I've got a tour," he said, checking his watch.

"What? It's Friday night."

"A probie called in sick."

"You mean there's someone greener than you?"

Webster pushed his chair back. He felt something drain from his chest as he did so.

"You're lying," she said.

He was but said nothing.

"It's because I don't want to talk about getting married, isn't it?" she asked, sipping her water.

The sight of the candles made Webster sad. Why play house?

He went into the bedroom to change. He had nowhere to go, but he put on his uniform anyway. He grabbed his radio and his utility belt.

When he emerged from the bedroom, she was blocking the front door. In her hand, she held a Tupperware container in which she'd put the rest of his dinner.

He stood ten feet from her.

"You need a fork and knife?" she asked.

"They've got forks and knives at Rescue."

"Will you marry me?" she asked.

"No."

"Please?"

"What about all the rules?" he asked. "And the smothering?"

"Fuck the rules," she said. "We'll make our own rules."

"Such as?"

"We could get married on that piece of land of yours with just a few dogs for witnesses."

"The land's not mine."

"Details," she said, though he could see in the way she turned her gaze aside that she was just this minute registering the results of an equation Webster had solved weeks ago. Webster + Sheila + Baby = No Land. The land by itself was meaningless without Sheila and the baby. And he would need whatever was left of his savings to help support the three of them when the baby came. He would take twenty-four-hour shifts if he had to.

He watched her glance from the corner of the room to the floor to his face. "You can't do this," she said. "You've been saving for that land all these years."

He didn't remind her that she had let him pay the cop. "Hey, no rules, remember? I can do whatever I want."

"This isn't funny, Webster. This is serious."

"Asking you to marry me was serious."

She stared at him, then gave a half smile. "So where's the ring?" she asked.

He pulled the blue jeweler's box from his pants pocket. He hadn't wanted her to find it while he was gone. She took it from him and opened it. It was a small diamond set flat in a gold band.

"Jesus Christ, Webster," she said. "I was kidding."

They were married by the minister at the Congregational church where Webster had been confirmed just before he gave up on religion. The soul was an entity he felt ambivalent about.

Webster's parents came to the ceremony, along with Burrows and his wife, Karen. Two of Webster's cousins drove down from the Northeast Kingdom. No one from Sheila's side showed up, and it felt to

Webster, for a moment during the service, that his soon-to-be wife was standing on air, as if she might tumble into oblivion for lack of roots. Sheila's sister, the only relative who might have made the trip, was near her ninth month of pregnancy and couldn't travel. Sheila didn't seem to mind. "I wish it was just me and you," she'd said the night before.

She wore a high-waisted black dress, which surprised Webster, who hadn't been consulted and who'd assumed white. After the ceremony, when he complimented her on the dress—it was fluid and elegant and made her skin light up—she explained that she'd wanted to buy a dress she might be able to wear again.

"To your next wedding?" he asked.

She cuffed him with her bouquet, one his mother had picked out.

After the ceremony, the eight celebrants walked in the July sunshine to a wedding luncheon in a private room at the Bear Hollow Inn. Webster's cousins, Joshua and Dickie, both of them farmers, had keen senses of humor, which Webster remembered from his childhood when they'd lived closer. The jokes got Burrows going, and once Burrows had had a few, there was no stopping him. Webster sat back and stroked Sheila's arm. He liked seeing his mother laugh to the point of near hysterics. Even Sheila joined in the conversation when she could, though for minutes at a time she was eerily quiet.

"You OK?" he asked.

When she turned to him, he thought he saw tears forming at the corners of her eyes. He put his elbow on the table to shield them from the rest of the group. He'd never seen Sheila cry. His face was inches from hers. The tears frightened him.

"What is it?" he asked, taking her hand.

"Nothing. I'm fine."

Webster thought it might be the loneliness of having no family at the service and was about to say that he was her family now. He and the bump.

"This is stupid," she said. "I never do this. I'm just so happy." She bent her head to his chest, as if embarrassed by emotion. He wrapped her in his arms. "I never thought this would happen to me," she said. "Not like this. I don't deserve you, Webster."

"Are you shitting me?" he whispered into her ear. Sweet nothings from the bridegroom to the bride. "I'm the one who can't believe his luck. You roll your car precisely on my stretch of road, and I just happen to be in service? What are the odds that the love of my life would do that?"

He felt her laugh.

He pulled a clean handkerchief from his pocket and handed it to her. If he glanced up, his father, who'd insisted Webster carry one in his suit pocket, would be smiling. Webster held Sheila until she'd fixed herself up. "I really do love your dress," he said, a compliment that allowed him to pat the deliciously round contour of her lap.

"Do I have mascara all over me?" she asked.

He pulled away and scanned her face. "Right eye, just below the outer edge."

She swept the mark away, gave the handkerchief back to Webster. She lifted the champagne glass she'd been avoiding. The gesture caught Webster's mother's eye.

"Oh, honey, I've been waiting this whole time for you to do that." She and Sheila clinked glasses.

That night Webster and Sheila lay in bed on the first of their three nights of honeymoon. They had chosen to forgo a trip. Webster was happy enough to be in their bedroom cocoon with the prospect of two more days off. On Monday, they would shop for a car seat and a crib with the money his parents had given them as a wedding present. Tomorrow he and Sheila would decide in advance where to put the crib—which tiny part of their already tiny apartment they could carve out as a nursery. But that night they had no worries and no plans. Webster's mother, like the church lady she was, had arranged for the inn to make up two dinners and to save the rest of the cake, all of which she handed to Sheila when the lunch was over. "A woman doesn't cook on her wedding night, no matter where she spends it," his mother said. Sheila hugged her for the first time.

Webster gave his mother an A+ for trying. She seemed to be their biggest fan. Then again, Sheila had something his mother wanted: a grandchild to hold.

Webster put his hands on the bump and thought: *This, right now, this is my family.*

Sheila drifted in and out of sleep while Webster held her.

They're contractions," Sheila said when Webster opened the door at eight thirty in the morning. He'd had an easy night. Not too many calls, and nothing serious. "Not too bad." She was just into her ninth month. She sat at the kitchen table, a glass of water in front of her, her robe stretched as far as it would go around her belly. She could barely tie the sash. Being pregnant was sometimes funny.

"Braxton Hicks?" he asked.

"Maybe."

They'd gone to the classes, even though Webster already knew the drill. He kept it to himself, not wanting to stand between Sheila and the information she needed to know. He'd delivered an infant his first month as a probie. Burrows said the second-timers always waited too long. Webster knew about the blood vessels and aorta that twisted into an umbilical cord, the suctioning and the precious seconds waiting for the baby to pink up, the pointed heads the nurses always covered with caps shortly after the birth. The nurses said that the caps kept the babies warm. Webster thought it was because their pointed heads were ugly. He'd never seen a beautiful baby spring right out from the chute. Usually it wasn't until the infants were a month old, when the mothers came in to Rescue to thank the medics, that he could attach the word *cute.*

He set his radio and belt on the table. He watched as Sheila caved inward and closed her eyes.

He waited until she came back.

"That's not Braxton," he said.

"No, probably not."

"Your water break?"

She nodded.

"When?"

"Around two a.m."

"Why didn't you call me?"

Sheila shrugged.

Webster assessed her. He checked his watch and waited for another contraction. It came at four minutes, and this time she made hard fists to ward off the pain. He squatted in front of her.

"Do you remember about the breathing?" he asked.

"Of course I remember it. I just can't do it."

"You did fine in class," he reminded her.

"Does this look like class?"

"Try to breathe while you're having the contractions even if it isn't the way they taught you. Can you get dressed?"

"Probably."

"We're going in."

"To the hospital?"

"You bet," he said, standing.

"Am I going to be one of those idiots they talked about in class? The woman who goes in too soon and then has to go home?"

"No," Webster said. "Your water broke. You have to go in."

She struggled to stand, and he helped

her. "I hate it that you know more about this than I do," she said.

"Why?" he asked. "If this baby comes in the car, it's me you're going to want with you."

They dressed together in the bedroom, Webster unwilling to go into Mercy in his uniform. Sheila wasn't his patient. She was his wife, and he was about to become a father. Still, he knew all the things that could go wrong: the breech, the stillbirth, the cord around the neck. He asked if he could feel her abdomen so that he could locate the baby's head. "Don't touch me," she snapped when he moved toward her.

He took his utility belt, which had a pair of shears on it. He brought an armload of blankets. He carried her suitcase.

She leaned against the wall, breathless. "You really think it's coming now?"

"No," he said.

He helped her down the long flight of outside stairs. Stairs that were treacherous in winter, easy in September. The sun was up strong, and the leaves were translucent with color. Twenty-two years in Vermont, and it never got old.

Sheila had three hard ones in the car.

She pushed one arm against the dashboard, the other against the door. They were coming fast. He took the cruiser up to sixty, which was all he dared. He never knew when some lost asshole tourist might bolt onto the highway.

"Oh, God," she cried and looked at him. "I want to push."

"Don't," Webster said firmly. "Whatever you do, don't push. Breathe, Sheila. We're only half a minute out. Do the breathing. Are you listening to me? Don't push."

"I can't do the fucking breathing."

Webster wanted his wife on a sterile bed, her legs in stirrups, the attending listening to the fetal monitor.

He watched her cave in to another contraction. Before, as an EMT witnessing a birth, Webster had wanted to know what the pain was like. Now he was glad that he'd never know it.

Webster skidded into the loading dock, opened the door, and was inside the ER in one motion. He signaled to the first nurse who looked familiar.

"Mary, your name is Mary, right? My wife wants to push."

The nurse snagged a stretcher and ran

toward the cruiser. She yanked the door open. Sheila, white-faced, lay back against the seat. "OK, hon," Mary said. "Everything's going to be fine. Can you stand?"

Sheila's legs were wide apart. She shook her head no.

"We're going to get you out now."

Webster hooked his arms under Sheila's armpits, turned her sideways, and pulled. Mary, who was surprisingly strong considering her small stature, caught the feet. They hoisted Sheila onto the stretcher.

In the ER cubicle, Mary swung the flower-print curtain closed. She and Webster sheeted Sheila onto the bed. Sheila began to make mewling sounds during the contractions. Mary whipped off the maternity trousers and underpants, spread Sheila's legs, and put them into stirrups. Sheila still had on a purple batik maternity top with a peace sign in front.

"Crowning," Mary said.

Webster stopped himself from saying *Fuck.* He didn't want to panic his wife.

"Where's the attending?" he asked.

"ICU."

Webster swallowed another *fuck.*

"The baby's coming," Mary said. "You

stay up by your wife's head and hold her shoulders. You're here as her husband. She needs you more than I do."

Mary stepped outside the cubicle to hail a nurse named Julie.

Webster held Sheila by her shoulders and told her that he loved her, that everything was going to be fine. The baby was coming, and she could push all she wanted.

"Thank you, God," his wife whimpered.

Her face scrunched up, and a sweat broke. Within seconds, Sheila's hair was wet. She'd begun to grunt, and the sound spooked Webster. He'd heard it before, but not from Sheila. He tried to go into EMT mode and make himself calm, but when he felt the grit in Sheila's muscles and heard her cries, all his training left him. He was both excited and terrified, as if he'd never witnessed a birth before.

"Come on, Sheila," he said into her ear. "One more big push."

Sheila bore down with everything she had. Then she lost it, arms flailing. "Jesus, Jesus, Jesus," she cried, and Webster wondered if it was a sort of prayer.

"Sheila," Webster said in a firm voice. "Sheila, bear down. A quick one. You got it. You got it. It'll all be over in a second. Just do it one more time."

And then Sheila's body took over and carried her helplessly along.

Webster knew the moment the baby was out. He held his breath during the seconds of silence that followed.

He heard an infant's cry. He bowed his head, so grateful.

"OK, Daddy," Mary said. "You want to cut the cord? You got yourself a beautiful baby girl."

Webster snapped on a pair of gloves, and Mary gave Webster the sterile shears from a tray. He made a clean snip. While Julie dealt with the afterbirth, Mary sterilized the nub. She swaddled the baby and handed the infant to Webster. He nudged the swaddling aside so that he could see all of his daughter's face.

**His daughter.**

Her presence flooded him. He brought the infant to her mother, who had her eyes closed.

"Sheila," Webster said in a low voice. "I've got her. I've got our baby. She wants to nurse."

Sheila woke with a start and held out

her arms, which Webster saw were trembling. He helped prop her up. He laid the
baby on her chest, carefully folding Sheila's arms around their daughter. He knew
that Mary was watching.

"Oh my God, she's beautiful," Sheila said,
as if surprised, and Webster laughed. Sheila
looked like hell and so did the newborn. But
he couldn't hold that thought for long. He
was the daddy now. He hovered over both
of them.

The baby latched on to a nipple. Sheila
looked up at Webster. "Isn't this where we
met?" she asked.

Sheila picked out a Webster family name
that she liked: Rowan. Webster cobbled
together enough time off to last two weeks.
After he returned to his job, he was given
Tour 1. The chief called it a restructuring,
but Webster suspected he was giving him
a break. The day shift allowed him to be
home with Sheila and the baby by four
thirty in the afternoon.

Each day after work, Webster sprinted
up the stairs, nearly desperate to see his
little girl, who was rapidly approaching per-
fection. He found Sheila playing with the

baby on a pad on the floor, or dozing on the couch, nipples making wet circles on her shirt while Rowan slept in a crib. Though Webster couldn't feed his daughter, he changed her and put her to Sheila's breast as his wife gradually woke. Once the feeding was over, Sheila rose and started dinner while Webster gazed at the baby.

Rowan had hair just like Sheila's, which Webster thought the best genetic luck. The baby's eyes were blue, and her limbs were long, a characteristic from either parent. Webster's mother swore that Rowan looked just like Webster's grandmother, but when Sheila and Webster examined the picture of a dowdy woman Webster couldn't remember, neither could find any resemblance. Webster's parents were christened Nana and Gramps.

Webster's life upended itself. Sheila and he slept on different schedules, neither of them getting enough and neither of them minding. Webster convinced himself that Sheila and he had produced the most beautiful baby he'd ever seen. His mother took up her knitting needles, and it seemed that every time she came to the apartment, she had knit another item for Rowan: baby clothes and blankets when Rowan was a newborn; stuffed toys and sweaters and a beautiful green and blue coat for when she could sit up. Burrows and his wife gave Sheila and Webster a snazzy stroller that came apart and seemed to be able to do everything except cook dinner.

With Rowan in his arms, Webster rubbed noses with her and told her she was a pain in the ass. He walked her all over the apartment showing her the lights. He did and redid the same five-piece puzzle with her a hundred times while she smacked her mouth in surprise whenever she made it come out right. He imagined that Rowan, at nine months, must have found the backyard a vast and exciting territory. In the summer, Webster's mother brought over fresh vegetables that Sheila cooked, put in the blender, and then froze in ice cube trays. When she fed Rowan each lunch and dinner in her high chair, she defrosted a cube, warmed it up, and spooned it into Rowan's mouth, employing the same airplane trick Webster assumed every parent used.

Webster found himself using the word *love* all the time and indiscriminately. He felt he'd stumbled into a life that he was meant to live, though he couldn't have described it before he met Sheila.

Sheila, with her gradually slimming silhouette, seemed to experience life as her baby did, first living within a cocoon that stretched the sixteen feet from bed to couch to sink, then expanding into a car for drives to Nana's with the baby and then for errands at the supermarket, Rowan behind her in the car seat.

One late afternoon in August, Webster arrived home to find Sheila and Rowan asleep on the grass in the backyard. He hadn't wanted to wake them and so had pulled up a chair next to them and watched. A warm breeze blew over the three of them, keeping the mosquitoes away.

He wondered what had happened. Sheila and Rowan were sitting together and had just decided to have a nap? What a funny picture they made, the two females with the same shade of glossy brown hair, one tiny head tucked beneath another. Were they breathing in sync? Webster wished he had his camera with him, but he didn't dare move to get it. He could hear the bustle of customers out in front of the ice-cream shop. A perfect day for a cone.

The yard had privacy when the leaves were on the trees. The patch of land that Sheila and Rowan slept on had the most grass.

Rowan woke first, which then woke Sheila. Sheila brushed the grass off each of them. "Hi," she said dreamily. She stood with the baby in her arms, and Webster stood with them.

"I suppose I should get dinner going," Sheila said. Webster stopped her with a kiss.

"I've got a better idea. Let's just go around front and get ice-cream cones."

Sheila didn't protest as he thought she might. Usually she made sure that Rowan ate only healthful food. This time, however, she smiled.

"You have wonderful ideas, Mr. Webster, you know that?"

He picked up Rowan, who was still wiping the sleep out of her eye. "What do you say, ice cream for supper?"

She nodded her head and laid it against his shoulder.

Webster knew he was the happiest he had ever been.

It was SIDS, the infant dead for hours when Webster and Burrows got to the house, a small cottage at the edge of the creek that paralleled 42. It was built to be a summer place only, and at first Webster wondered if the mother was a tourist. The home had no insulation. The mother insisted to the 911 dispatcher that the baby was still breathing.

Blankets and stuffed animals littered the crib. No one knew for sure what caused the senseless and heartbreaking death. Webster felt only sadness and disgust.

He reached for the brachial pulse in the arm. He wondered at what point the mother had last looked at her baby and for how long she'd been avoiding reality. Burrows began CPR, even though both medics knew the child was dead. For the sake of the survivors, they had to do everything they could.

Webster glanced around the tiny living room, the crib next to the sofa. He always tried to get a picture of the life inside the house when they made a call. A one-bedroom, baby in the living room. The infant was maybe ten weeks old.

Burrows called in to Dispatch to tell them they needed a police officer and a coroner to meet them at the hospital. With SIDS, there had to be an autopsy.

"Ma'am, what's your name?" he asked.

"Susan."

"Susan, where is your husband?"

"He's at work."

"Where is that?"

"He's on a construction site near Rutland."

Her answers were quick and lucid. Her hair was dirty, and her teeth were a bad shade of yellow. Webster could smell the foul breath from six feet away. Despite the sunny day, it was gloomy by the sofa.

The woman pulled the sides of her pink cardigan closer together with her fists. "Why aren't you working on my baby?"

Webster squatted in front of the woman. "We are working on your baby. See that medic there?" Webster was sweating through his uniform shirt. "What's the baby's name?" he asked.

"Britney."

Webster wouldn't be the one to break the horrific news. That would happen in the hospital. It was working on a dead baby that screwed with your head.

"She's dead, isn't she?" the woman said.

"We're still working on her. We're doing everything we can."

"I know she's dead."

Grief hit the woman full force. Her face crumpled, and her body sagged to the sofa. She brought her hands to her mouth, beginning a series of *Nos*—wails tapering off to whimpers. Webster sat beside her and put a hand on her sleeve. She, not the baby, was his patient now.

Webster stood and quietly asked Burrows if meds were indicated for the mother, but he shook his head. "When the cops are done, we'll see how she is, maybe bring her in then."

"It's unbearable," Webster said.

"This your first SIDS?"

Webster nodded.

"It's the worst," Burrows, never a softie, said. "A whole life gone, and for no good reason. No matter how many times you've seen it, it makes you crazy."

"The mother's known for hours, hasn't she?"

"You blame her for not wanting to face reality?"

"No, not at all."

"You're shaking," Burrows said, suddenly examining his partner.

"I'm fine."

"Look, it didn't happen to you," Burrows said. "Rowan is fine. She will be fine. She's long past when you have to worry about that."

"I know," Webster said.

"You go outside and wait for the cops. I'll sit here with the mother."

"You sure?"

"Go," Burrows said. "That's an order."

Webster walked outside. He felt tears

popping into his eyes and stared up at the sky so that they could leak back into his head. He'd never live it down if Nye showed up and he was bawling. He thanked God out loud, wherever he was. With Rowan, there had been no SIDS, no respiratory distress, no abnormalities, no twisted cord, nothing. He could hear the cop car bumping along the dirt road. He had no excuse for why he was outside. He turned and walked back into the house. Things would happen fast now.

Webster shed his equipment as he walked, calling out, surprised not to see Sheila with Rowan in the living room. He called again and heard an answer from the bedroom. There, in the dark of a late October afternoon, Sheila sat on the bed nursing their fourteen-month-old daughter. Sheila had on a pair of jeans and a white button-down shirt that allowed Rowan easy access to Sheila's breast. Webster pounced on the bed, joining them. He laid a finger against Rowan's cheek.

"Don't get her going," Sheila said. "I'm trying to put her down. She hasn't slept all day."

Webster registered the snappish tone. Sheila's hair was stringy, and there were dark shadows below her eyes. If Rowan hadn't slept all day, neither had Sheila.

"As soon as she's done," Webster said, "put her down and then you can sleep. Or if she won't go down, I'll take her."

"You've been working two shifts."

"I'm in better shape than you are."

Sheila nodded.

Webster stood and undressed. He didn't want any part of his job to touch the baby. Taking off the uniform was a way of putting aside one life and taking up another.

He slipped on a pair of jeans and a black sweater, then went into the bathroom to wash his face and hands. Back in the bedroom, standing in front of the mirror at the dresser so that he could finger-comb his hair into place, he caught a cameo of Sheila and Rowan on the bed. On impulse, he turned and swooped in to give Sheila and the baby a kiss. His foot kicked a glass, and Sheila turned her head away.

He picked up the glass from the floor. It still had a residue of amber liquid in it. He smelled it. The whiskey shook him.

"Where is it?" he asked.

Sheila didn't answer. He could tell by the set of her jaw that she was angry. Hell, *he* was angry.

"I'll find it," he said, "so you might as well tell me."

"Be my guest," she said.

"What the fuck, Sheila? You're nursing. It's like giving Rowan a shot of Jack Daniel's straight."

"Don't exaggerate," she said.

Webster took Rowan from his wife. Sheila's arms hung empty. After a few seconds, she stood and slipped behind him. She slid her feet into her boots.

Rowan, ripped from the breast, started crying. She began to flail, revving up for a good one.

"Now look what you've done," Sheila said.

"What I've done?" Webster asked. "What I've done? How long has this been going on? Sheila, I need to know."

"I don't have to explain myself to you."

"Yeah, you do. It's my baby who's been sucking on whiskey."

"Your baby."

"Our baby."

"Oh good, I thought maybe I was the wet nurse."

"Sheila, stop this."

She walked out into the living room, and Webster followed. He watched as Sheila picked up her purse.

"Oh, Christ," he said. "Where are you going?"

"I don't know."

"Don't go."

"If I don't get out of here, I'll go nuts."

Webster placed himself between the door and Sheila, Rowan wailing.

"What the hell happened?" he asked. "Everything seemed fine when I left yesterday."

She faced him, her stare hard. "It's fucking eight degrees out, and it's not even November. I can't take the baby anywhere. She's been crying all day. This whole thing is a mess. Just a fucking mess. I feel like a trapped lunatic."

"Everybody feels like that when winter starts. Baby or no baby."

"But at least you're out. You're someplace."

"Maybe it's time to think about going back to work," Webster said.

"I don't want to go back to work. I just want to . . ."

Webster felt his blood go cold. "What, Sheila? What is it that you want to do?"

"Get in a car."

For a time, he couldn't speak.

"You were my best shot," Sheila said.

"Best shot at what?"

"Safety. You *exude* safety, Webster."

His head spun. Webster shifted the baby in his arms and patted her back to calm her.

"It happened once, OK? I had a drink. You happy now, Mr. EMT? It happened once, and it won't happen again. And you should take another look at your precious medical books. A mother has a small drink, you know how little gets to the baby? Practically nothing."

"Where's the bottle?"

"Rowan needs a change. And she needs to take a nap. And you're standing in my way."

She put her hands on him and pushed him to one side. Though he could have stopped her at any time, he stepped away from the door. He thought of telling her not to come back unless she was prepared to stay sober, but he knew the threat to be an empty one.

After Sheila left, Webster sat on the couch with Rowan. Had Sheila really picked him out as her best chance in life? The thought sickened him. Didn't she love him as he did her? Hadn't they fallen into their life together?

Or were Sheila's words merely tossed out in the heat of the moment? Would she come home and take them back?

When Rowan began to squirm and cry again, Webster fetched the pink diaper bag from the bedroom and selected what he needed. He laid his daughter on the pad on the coffee table to change her. She smiled as if he were tickling her. Though Rowan might have sensed the tension in the air, she'd never know what her mother and father had said to each other. Sheila's words were pebbles at the bottom of his stomach.

After he changed his daughter, he put her into her yellow pajamas. He sat for a moment in a kitchen chair, holding her, making faces and clucking.

Had Sheila deliberately gotten pregnant because he was her best shot? Who would do that? But then Webster thought about the confusion over the contraception the first time they'd been together. He shut his eyes. The night under the .9 moon had been a precious memory for him.

Sheila wanted to break the rules. OK, fine. But Webster could change the rules.

He struggled to get Rowan into her light blue snowsuit. Sheila had left the car seat at the foot of the stairs. Webster held Rowan's face close to his chest to protect her tender skin. He put the car seat in the cruiser. After he strapped her in, he walked around to the front seat, sat down, and put the key in.

He turned to look at his daughter, but all he could see was a pair of blueberry eyes in a snowsuit. Something fragile bounced around his chest. The edgy, restless Sheila had returned. The Sheila who drank.

Webster backed out onto 42 and drove to the Giant Mart. With Rowan strapped against his chest, he searched the aisles for baby formula. He could figure out how to make up bottles. In the morning, he would tell Sheila to stop nursing. He thought she might agree if only for the freedom it would give her.

When he returned to the apartment, he put Rowan to sleep and searched for liquor bottles. He found nothing. Either she'd taken it with her or she was more cagey than he'd thought. The word *squirrel* popped into his head, and he made an ugly sound.

Sheila returned during the night. Webster didn't ask her where she'd been.

In the morning, he made up four bottles of formula before he left for work.

The tones sounded, and the deadpan voice from Dispatch requested help. "Suspected cardiac, male, severe chest pain radiating through the jaw." Webster asked for the address. Burrows said, *Fuck*. He continued swearing the entire way as the Bullet took a beating over the frozen ruts. Burrows was unusually attached to his rig.

"Where is this place, anyway?" Webster asked.

"Hell if I know," Burrows said.

They reached a fishing cabin at the edge of a small frozen lake. Five trucks were parked outside. The enormous late-model vehicles looked ridiculous next to the tiny shack.

"Ice fishing," Webster said.

"You ever see the movie *Deliverance*?" Burrows asked.

"No."

"Never mind."

Webster noticed that Burrows knocked on the front door instead of barging in as he usually did. Maybe he thought there might be a shotgun on the other side. A man yelled, "Come in," and it didn't sound like an ambush. Not that any medic Webster knew had ever run into an ambush, but he'd read about them happening in the cities.

Inside, there were four men standing, one lying on the floor. Five men, five trucks. Nobody offered anyone a ride?

The floor was made of gray indoor-outdoor carpet tiles, badly stained. With what, Webster didn't want to know. The man down was crying and pressing his chest.

Webster and Burrows pushed their way through pizza boxes and beer cans.

When Webster knelt beside the patient, he was confused. The patient's skin looked too pink to be cardiac-related, but the man was panting hard. Webster went through the basic assessment. The patient wasn't sweating or short of breath, and he wasn't nauseated. His blood pressure was high.

"What's his name?" Webster asked.

"Sully," a man over by the sink said.

"Sully," Webster said. "Have you ever had this pain before?"

"Once," the fisherman cried out. "At my niece's wedding!" He spoke as if he were in agony. "They almost called the medics then."

"Sully, on a scale of one to ten, how high is your pain?"

"Eight," the man said. "Maybe nine! It's terrible!"

"Can you show me where it hurts?" Burrows asked.

The man put his fingers just under his ears and ran them to the middle of his chest.

"Chest pain radiating to jaw," Webster said.

"Call my wife!" the man yelled.

Webster stood and spoke to Burrows. "We got to take him in," Webster said.

"Nice ride."

"Long ride."

Webster sat Sully up and asked if he

could walk to the ambulance. Sully tried, and after several attempts was able to stand on his own. Webster heard the belch before they'd reached the front door. Sully said, as Webster had expected, "The pain is easing off a little. I'm feeling a little better. Let's wait a second."

"Let me check your vitals," Webster said, as protocol demanded, though both he and Burrows knew exactly what they were dealing with. "Sit down right here."

Webster cuffed the patient, then reached for a radial pulse. Before Webster could report, Sully stood again as if he'd had a tentative recovery from a near-death experience. After another minute, he had his arms in the air. "I'm saved!" he shouted.

The fisherman over by the sink sniggered. "Sully, I told you it was fucking heartburn."

The five men tried to thank the medics with offers of fresh fish. Burrows turned them down. One of the men pointed out to Webster the tiny shack in the middle of the frozen pond. Inside, Webster knew, would be a stove and some chairs and a hole through which the men dropped their lines.

He also knew this: most of a medic's calls were mundane.

"Rescue should send the asshole a bill for wear and tear on the rig," Burrows said as Webster drove.

"Why did you pass on the fish?" Webster asked.

"You like to clean them?"

"Not really."

"Neither do I, and Karen won't touch them. Don't imagine Sheila would either."

Webster couldn't picture Sheila cleaning a fish of any kind.

The ambulance bounced along the ruts. "Fuckers," said Burrows.

It took them twenty-one minutes to emerge onto a road that wasn't made of dirt. Thirty-six minutes from Rescue, twenty minutes at the scene, another thirty-six back. Nearly an hour and a half wasted. Burrows was in a mood.

"You look like shit, Webster, you know that?" Burrows said. "Baby not sleeping?"

"Baby's sleeping fine."

"Marriage good?"

"Fine," he said.

"It's my job to ask questions. You not performing at top notch, I gotta be paying attention. What's up?"

"I'm not performing at top notch?" Webster asked, concerned.

"No, you're fine. You look like you're on dialysis, though. So what's up at home?"

"Not sure," Webster said.

"Bingo. I knew it was the marriage."

"You're full of shit," Webster said. "I could have financial troubles, for all you know."

"But you don't. I'm right, aren't I?"

Webster sighed.

"Man, that woman had you pussy-whipped. You were so fucking nuts about her."

"I still am."

"She love you back?" Burrows took out a toothpick and began to clean his teeth.

"Yes," Webster said.

But *did* she?

"So what's the problem?" Burrows asked.

"I don't know," Webster said. "Look at this. A traffic jam in Hartstone?"

"You could use the siren."

"We're almost there."

A sudden siren might give the guy ahead of him a heart attack.

"Sheila's restless. Chafing at the bit."

"To do what?" Burrows asked.

"She won't say. She can't say."

"You sure it's not that postpartum shit?"

Webster could see the beginning of town, but he couldn't get to it. A large semi blocked his view. "Is there a parade today?"

"Dunno."

"It's not that. She's not depressed," Webster said.

Burrows turned and squinted at Webster as he drove. "So what is it?"

Webster had never discussed Sheila with anyone. It felt like a breach, going outside the marriage. But he knew Burrows wouldn't stop until he had what he wanted. And there might be some relief in talking about it.

"She's drinking," Webster said.

"Oh, sweet Jesus." Burrows briefly closed his eyes. "You drinking?"

"No."

"Well, that's all right."

"It's not all right."

"I'll bet it was romantic in the beginning,

right?" Burrows said. "The first bottle of wine . . . the second . . ."

"Yeah, maybe."

"Then you find you're drinking at every meal because it's just so fucking romantic, right? Candles, the pretty glasses, you get laid. It's cool, right?"

Webster was silent.

"Then one night you discover that one of you has a problem, and it's not you."

The jam broke up for no good reason that Webster could see. No parade. No accident. "How do you know all this?" he asked.

"Been there, done that. You need a marriage counselor?"

Webster shook his head, as much from surprise as from denial. "I think you can pretty much forget that. Not happening."

"Good, 'cause I don't know any!" Burrows cackled. "Just curious, though. Would Sheila go?"

"Would you?"

"Not on your fucking life."

Webster felt as though he lived inside an irregular heartbeat. For weeks, Sheila seemed normal, loving, and even, on occasion, sassy in the way Webster had once liked. Each time the three of them went sledding or shopping or to Webster's parents' for a Sunday lunch, and he watched the way Sheila read to Rowan, or took her for walks in the woods, or smiled when Rowan smiled, Webster had hope. For a moment, his heart seemed lighter, and he'd think, cautiously, *We'll be fine now*.

Even so, he continued to be vigilant. Inevitably, after a month or six weeks, he would see a sign that rattled him. The one sign made him look for others. Sometimes he felt that he was poisoning the marriage simply by looking for the tells, that somehow the search made them appear: a looser face, a slight slur of words, an unwillingness to kiss him. Sheila sometimes went out, but not with him. Webster searched for liquor bottles and found them. A cloud of distrust filled the apartment.

One night, Webster found a bottle of Bacardi behind Rowan's stuffed animals on a shelf. That Sheila had used Rowan's toys for a hiding place especially infuriated him.

"That's it," he said to Sheila as he went into the living room, brandishing his find.

Sheila turned her head away. Rowan looked up at her dad.

Webster thought his daughter had caught on to the tension between him and Sheila, and, now that she was starting to talk, might understand more than he wanted her to. He put the bottle behind him.

"We're going to get you to AA," Webster said to Sheila.

"The person has to want to go."

"Believe me, you're going to want to go."

"And how's that, exactly?" asked Sheila whose eyes never strayed from the TV.

Webster had an answer. It was something he'd been thinking about for weeks. "I'm taking Rowan, and we're going to my parents'."

Sheila turned off the TV. "What's that mean, exactly?" she asked.

"It means Rowan and I will be living at my parents' house, and you will not."

"Nana?" Rowan asked.

Webster smiled at his daughter. "We'll see," he said, and he thought the words *We'll see* the most used phrase in a parent's repertoire.

"You wouldn't dare," Sheila said.

"Try me."

Webster turned, went into the bedroom, found his suitcase at the back of the closet, and began packing his clothes and personal items. When he headed into Rowan's room with a large canvas bag, Sheila stood.

"All right," she said in a small voice.

"All right what?"

"I'll go. To AA."

Webster took the suitcase and the canvas bag back into the bedroom. "I'll find out where and when the nearest meeting is."

"I already know," Sheila said.

So Sheila had gone as far as to investigate AA? That was a start.

"Mommy sad?" asked Rowan, who always needed to know. As if asking whether she should be worried or not.

"No, Pumpkinhead," Webster said. "It's all good."

It wasn't all good. But it might get better.

He parked outside the church, as far away from a streetlight as he could. It was illogical, since Sheila would be walking into the basement meeting soon enough. He thought maybe he was protecting her identity—although preserving one's anonymity was almost impossible in Hartstone, or even the next town over. Behind them, Rowan was asleep in her car seat.

Sheila had smoked two cigarettes in the car. Ordinarily, Webster would have called her on that, too, with the baby in the backseat. Maybe he really was becoming a self-righteous prig, an epithet Sheila had once hurled at him. Lately, Webster had found himself wanting to go to a bar with his buddies at Rescue. Stay out all night, come home with a good one on. He couldn't. She'd never listen to him, then.

"You'll be OK," he said to her.

"I want to do this about as much as I want to have a root canal," she said.

"You ever have a root canal?"

"No."

She had on jeans and a white shirt. It was getting dark later and later, even though the early April nights could be frigid.

Webster checked his watch.

"I know, I know," Sheila said. "I have three minutes before I have to go. Actually, I could go in at any time."

"You'll just draw more attention to yourself."

"It's not going to work in just one night," she warned. "So don't get your hopes up."

She turned to look at him. "Are your hopes up?"

"I don't know whether I dare," he said.

He patted the middle of her back. He thought she flinched. It reminded him that they didn't touch as often as they used to.

But this touch seemed to have released something in Sheila. She sighed and bent her head. "I'm sorry, Webster," she said.

He wanted to hold her, but their positions were awkward, like those of teenagers trying to make out in a car. He wondered if Sheila would one day feel compelled to make amends. He didn't want amends. He wanted her to stop drinking.

"I love you," she said.

He undid his seat belt and pulled her close. "You do?" he asked.

She nodded, and he kissed the top of her head. "I love you, too."

She put her hand on his thigh. "It's not like a hypnotist, you know. I won't come out cured."

"I know that," he murmured, resting his chin on her head. "You just keep going to meetings," he said.

After a minute, she wiggled out of his hold and stepped out of the car. She hesitated a moment. He watched her walk, hands in pockets, shoulders straightened, toward the basement door.

When she came out, she was smiling. Webster's heart soared, even though he'd told himself not to expect too much. He watched her saunter to the cruiser, a streetlight illuminating part of her walk.

Drop-dead gorgeous.

When they went home, they put Rowan to sleep and made love the way they had in the old days. Webster couldn't believe his luck. If only he'd managed to get Sheila to AA sooner, they wouldn't have done so much damage to each other. Now life would be different. He was sure of it.

Before the week was out, Webster smelled alcohol on Sheila's breath. He was so angry, he could hardly speak.

"Just tell me one thing," he said before walking into the bedroom and willing himself to sleep, too tired and crushed to leave the apartment with Rowan or even threaten to. "That smile, when you came out of the meeting, that was a con, right?"

"I don't know," she said.

Webster made it clear that he wouldn't fight with Rowan in the room. Sheila agreed but sometimes forgot herself. In the worst of the bad episodes, Webster thought again about bailing. It sometimes seemed like Sheila was asking him to abandon her. Then he'd convince himself that Sheila was just going through a really bad patch in a young mother's life. Any minute now, she'd go on her own to AA, or she'd find a way to level out.

They had periods of calm. All would be forgiven during a night of great sex. Love of a certain kind would be rekindled. Webster and Sheila would inch closer and closer, each waiting for the other to give.

Sheila went to AA by herself and stuck with it for a month.

Webster knew that once he had been as happy as a man could be, but he couldn't feel that happiness anymore. Even when he and Sheila were good together, Webster couldn't get there. He closed his eyes and remembered the details, but it was as though a piece of him had floated beyond his reach.

Within this irregular heartbeat, Rowan grew.

Sometimes, riding in the Bullet to a scene, or chopping wood with his silent father, Webster wondered if all marriages had this pattern—some good periods, some bad periods. He thought they probably did. The doomed marriages would be the ones that got stuck in the bad periods, when neither husband nor wife knew how or cared to climb out.

During his training, an instructor had talked about "stressors." He'd meant them in the context of the job, the horrors the medics would inevitably see, the way they could, over time, make a medic indifferent to his patients. Webster had experienced some of those stressors, and though they sometimes rattled him, he had for the most part found a place to put them. Webster had no idea where to put the stressors of his marriage. They were making him indifferent to his wife.

His mother was on her hands and knees, patting the floor, playing a game with Rowan. Webster hadn't been paying attention. *Mister Rogers' Neighborhood,* a show that made Webster want to grit his teeth, was still on the television. He wasn't paying attention to that, either.

Sheila was at work.

Rowan's lips still had tracings of purple frosting. Webster let his mother feed Rowan anything she wanted. His mother had never had a girl she could spoil before. It tickled Webster.

His mother, breathless, got back up on

the sofa. Rowan seemed mesmerized by a show that reminded Webster of grass growing.

"You're Mr. Quiet today," his mother said, giving him a poke.

"Mom, cut it out. You sound like a character in that stupid show."

"Mr. Testy now," his mother said, her beatific expression unchanging.

Webster tried to smile but couldn't quite manage it.

"You want something to drink? Iced tea?"

"No," he said.

"What's wrong?" she asked, the expression on her face switching to one of concern. "You're worried about Sheila's drinking, aren't you?"

"How did you know?"

"It's pretty obvious. We have eyes."

"You and Dad have talked about it?"

"Only to each other."

Webster looked away, embarrassed.

"It's not your fault," his mother said.

"How do you know that?" Webster retorted. "Who's to say that something I'm doing or not doing isn't driving her crazy?"

"Has she said as much?" his mother asked. She turned to look at Rowan to make sure her granddaughter was still involved in the television show. "You both have this utterly precious child," she added.

"I know that."

"You look so dejected."

"I am. It's been a hell of a ride lately."

"Does Sheila love you?"

"I think so."

"Then she'll stop this nonsense," his mother said. "For you. For Rowan."

"It's not that easy."

Webster noted that his daughter was beginning to squirm as the program neared to a close.

"Get out more," his mother advised. "Get outside. Go for walks together. Instead of one of you with Rowan at a time, do things together."

He knew his mother meant well. But it was like offering a man a straw to stop a leak.

Rowan toddled to her grandmother and mashed her face, snot and all, into her knees. His mother didn't seem to mind. "Just remember this," she said, patting Rowan's head, "you can't regret anything that leads to your children."

*   *   *

The following Sunday, Webster heeded his mother's advice. The night before, he'd talked Sheila into taking Rowan to a park in the woods. It had picnic tables and benches and trails and even a place with playground equipment. All three of them would go. "I'll bring a picnic," he'd said. "Let's do breakfast."

In the morning, he packed up matches, bread, bacon, long skewers, paper plates, juice, paper towels, a skillet, a thermos of coffee, and a couple of mugs. "That looks interesting," Sheila said.

"You just wait."

Rowan seemed giddy at the notion of a family outing, and Webster wondered why they hadn't done more of this before. They'd gone shopping together, had been together when doing other errands, and they'd eaten at his parents' at least once every two weeks, but outings to the park were infrequent.

While Sheila ran around after Rowan, who had to try out every piece of equipment, Webster made his fire in one of several barbecue pits that dotted the beautiful acreage. As he worked, other families came into the area as well. Most of the kids had just dads with them. The mothers, Webster knew, were sleeping in or simply desperate to have time to themselves.

Webster set out the skillet on the grill above the fire. He cooked the bacon the way his father had taught him to—slowly and with a good scald. The scent made its way over to Sheila, who raised an eyebrow. He set out a paper plate padded with paper towels and left the bacon to drip. Next, he grilled the toast using the long skewers, browning each piece until it started to show dark spots, just as it should be. He poured the juice into paper cups, the coffee into the mugs. Then he put three slices of bacon between two slices of the toast. He made a sandwich for each of them. He thought the other fathers might be envious right about now. When he had everything ready on the picnic table, he called to his wife and daughter. "Come and get it."

He could tell by the pleasurable moans from both that he'd got it right.

"When you oversell something, I'm usually skeptical," Sheila said. "This is even better than I imagined."

"You have to do it outdoors, and you

have to use a wood fire. Otherwise it tastes completely different," Webster said. He watched his daughter open her mouth as wide as it could go to get a bite of sandwich.

"Wish I'd brought the camera," he said. "You do realize that this is an important milestone?"

"Her first bacon sandwich?" Sheila asked. "I think you need to get out more."

"My mother said that to me on Tuesday. I am out. We're all out."

Sheila drank her juice.

"Want another one?" Webster asked. "I've got plenty of bacon cooked already. Just take a second to toast the bread."

"I'll take another," Sheila said.

"Me, too," Rowan said, though she had just learned to open the sandwich and tear the bacon apart.

Sheila and Webster each had another sandwich. All three sat on the benches facing one another. Webster felt a tenuous flutter of happiness.

Sheila cleaned up while Webster took Rowan for a short walk along a trail. He didn't want her on the equipment until she'd settled her stomach. The walk turned out to be even shorter than he'd intended because Rowan, like a dog, felt compelled to look at and touch all the rocks and pine-cones along the way. When they turned back, he saw that Sheila was idling on a swing.

"Want a push?" he asked when he reached her.

"Sure," she said.

"I want a push," Rowan echoed, trying to sit on a swing next to her mother.

Webster pushed both Rowan and Sheila until Sheila was laughing and Rowan screaming in delight. He loved the sounds. Loved them. Finally, Sheila asked him to slow down. "I'm getting dizzy," she said.

Rowan and Sheila hopped off the swings, and the three sat on a bench along a path not far from the table where they'd had their picnic. Rowan slid off the bench and began exploring the natural treasures on the ground. Sheila was silent. Webster feared a curtain was slowly descending.

"Sheila," he said. When she turned to him, she had that half smile that he'd learned to distrust.

Webster could create moments, but he couldn't string enough of them together to make a life.

Webster laid his arms along the bench but didn't touch Sheila. He kept his eyes on Rowan. He could tell that Sheila was aching for a drink. He told Rowan not to put a pebble up her nose. She looked at him with lids lowered as if weighing the pros and cons. An older woman, sitting on a bench not far from them, leaned forward. It was the first time Webster had noticed her.

"These are the best years of your life," she said, smiling.

Webster nodded at the woman to acknowledge her pronouncement. Sheila bent her head as if examining the dirt.

"Really," she said to no one.

The backyard of the ice-cream shop wasn't much to look at, but Webster and Sheila had spent an hour hanging balloons from trees, decorating a picnic table with red cups and birthday hats and plates, and setting up games that two-year-olds could play. Overly excited, Rowan crisscrossed the yard. She already had grass stains on the yellow and white dress her mother had bought for the occasion. Sheila and Webster stood and surveyed the lawn.

"It looks like a birthday party," she said.

"Thank God it hasn't rained like they said it would."

"They always get it wrong."

"Rowan's fit to bust," Webster said, smiling at his little girl.

They'd had a long run of calm. Webster hadn't dared to hope that he and Sheila were on solid ground, but enough time had passed that he felt like celebrating their long good spell as much as his daughter's birthday. Sheila had made the birthday cake, a slightly listing chocolate cake with yellow frosting. Three candles, one of them for good luck.

They'd celebrated Rowan's first birthday party with family. This time Sheila wanted to invite four children Rowan knew from day care as well as their parents. Webster didn't know the parents; he'd seen them mostly in passing. Rowan's grandmother and grandfather would come to the party, too.

Sheila seemed happy. She poured Coke into one of the taller red cups meant for adults and asked Webster if he wanted some. He was about to say yes when the first of the parents arrived with their child, a boy named Jason. Rowan dragged Jason off to see the games her dad had set up. Sheila offered the parents a beverage and pointed out the chips and dips. Conversation was awkward, and there were a lot of jokes about living over an ice-cream shop. Webster had heard every one before, but he chuckled nevertheless.

Sheila laughed loud and long with the mothers. She knew them better than Webster did.

Webster lost himself in his job as master of ceremonies.

It wasn't until an hour had passed that he noticed that Sheila was never without her red cup. A ping of alarm went through him. She was nervous, he told himself, she needed a prop. When it was time for the cake, Rowan made a wish and puffed herself up. To Webster's astonishment, Sheila bent in and blew out all the candles herself. He was certain Rowan would cry, but instead she whapped her palm flat on the top of the cake, disturbing the icing that said "Happy Birthday Rowan." Only Webster saw the gesture as angry. Sheila chose to think it adorable and laughed. Webster glanced at the parents and noted their wary eyes.

While Webster oversaw the remaining games, Sheila leaned against the cement wall of the ice-cream shop, red cup in hand. By one thirty, she was slurring her words when she said good-bye to the parents. Webster noted how they drew their children close to them when Sheila approached. Webster was furious, embarrassed for himself and for Rowan. When the last of the guests had left, he told Sheila to go upstairs, that he would clean up and watch Rowan, too.

Sheila pulled herself up the stairs. Webster's mother took over the cleanup, while Webster stood next to his father under a red maple, both watching Rowan.

"Sheila's in a bad way," his father said, getting right to the point. "Something has to be done."

"I've tried everything I can think of," Webster said, "short of actually leaving her."

"You're going to have to do more. Maybe look into some of those programs."

"You mean a rehab program?"

"That's it."

"They're expensive, Dad."

Webster winced. His father would think that he was asking for money.

"We could help . . . ," his father began.

Webster put his palms up. "I'm sorry I

mentioned the cost. That's the last thing I want. Whatever we do, we do on our own."

His father put his hands in his pockets. Neither Webster nor his father had taken their eyes off Rowan, who seemed to have forgotten the incident with the cake. "I'll tell you this, son," his father said. "There's no better place your mother and I could ever put our money than to see you and your family have an easier time of it."

"Thanks for offering, but it's something I have to think about."

"You're a fucking lush," Webster said to Sheila in the bedroom while Rowan was watching television in the living room. He tried to keep his voice down, but there was too much anger behind it. "At your daughter's birthday? Are you shitting me? Did you see the way the children clung to their parents when you got close to them? My God, Sheila, can you imagine what they think?"

"I knew it," she said, looking smug. She took a pack of cigarettes from the bedside drawer and lit one. "You care more about what the neighbors think than about what's happening to me."

"I know what's happening to you. All I have to do is look at you."

She tucked her hair behind her ears and tipped her chin up, as if she didn't care. "What are you going to punish me with?" she asked. "No more birthdays? That's super. Then Rowan gets punished, too."

"She's already being punished," Webster argued.

"Was she embarrassed by her mommy today?"

"You bet she was. She knows when you're drinking. She pulls away from you. I shudder to think what's going on when I'm not here."

"You 'shudder to think.' Jesus, Webster, when did you turn into such an asshole?"

"I think you should go into a rehab program."

"Who made you king?" she asked, standing. "And not that AA shit again. The meetings make me sad. I have nothing in common with those people. Besides, you exaggerate my drinking, like you exaggerate everything. Does Rowan look hungry or unhappy or dirty to you? You think I don't love her as much as you do?"

"I think you love Rowan as much as I do. You just love drinking more."

"I don't."

"Sheila, stop. Just stop."

The defeat in his voice made her bow her head.

"Can't we just get through the night?" he asked.

"Sure," she said. "'One day at a time,' right?"

They had one good month followed by a bad month. Then they had three good weeks followed by a horrific week. During the bad weeks, Webster began repeating a single phrase over and over, like a tune he couldn't get out of his head: *My family needs to be rescued.* It galled him that he could prevent heart attacks, minimize injuries, and reverse overdoses when he couldn't suture the simple lacerations in his home life.

Just opening the door after work made Webster anxious. He might find Rowan, tired and sullen, on the sofa watching TV, with Sheila asleep in the bedroom. Webster had to fix it. Once he found Sheila cooking with a half-empty bottle of wine beside the stove. "One for the pot, one for the cook," she said, smiling, as if she'd forgotten all that had gone before.

"Where's Rowan?" he asked in a panic.

"I sent her outside. She's making a snowman."

Webster ran down the stairs. He had to fix it.

Webster made Sheila promise she would never drink and drive. Twice she forgot to pick Rowan up, and the owner of the day-care center had to call Webster at work, the message put through to his radio. *Go get your daughter.*

Webster searched the house, inside and out, again and again. One morning, he found a white plastic bag in the ice-cream shop's trash that contained several dozen airplane-sized bottles of vodka and whiskey. He closed his eyes. To have gotten all those bottles would have required Sheila to make any number of stops at different liquor stores so as not to draw attention to herself. He wondered if Rowan had been along on those trips.

Webster did everything he knew how to do, followed every procedure in the book,

but still he was afraid that his patient—
their marriage—would flatline.

One night in the week between Christmas
and New Year's Eve, Webster arrived home
from work and saw that Rowan was asleep
in the crib they'd tucked under an eave. A
Christmas tree took up all the remaining
space. They'd had a good Christmas together, Webster taking pleasure in watching his daughter's face when she woke to
the sight of presents. Webster's only difficulty had been finding a present for Sheila.
In the beginning, all he wanted to do was
give her presents. Now he felt worn out,
his imagination dulled. Anything romantic
or pretty felt false. He settled on a Crock-
Pot, which Sheila had asked for. The present depressed Webster.

They needed a bigger apartment, and
they couldn't wait much longer. At least
he didn't have to worry about waking his
daughter when he came in at night. Rowan
had turned out to be an excellent sleeper.

Sheila, from the bedroom, called his
name.

"Be right in," he said.

She came to the door of the bedroom.

She had on a pair of black thigh-high stockings with a matching lacy bra and panties. Her stomach was perfectly flat. How had she done that?

"Wow," he said. "To what do I owe this?"

"Come on in and see," she said in a coquettish voice.

He took off his clothes in front of the washer and dryer and had one of the fastest showers of his life. He dove into bed with his wife. No smell of cigarettes. No whiff of alcohol. Webster began to relax.

Sheila lay on top of him and stretched his arms wide. "I love you, Mr. Webster," she said, "and I want you to always remember that." She bent down for a kiss.

She released his hands, and he ran them up and down the back of her body, a wonderful sensation. She kissed him again and rose up while he admired the lacy purchases. He grabbed her and twisted her so that she was lying in the crook of his arm, and he was able to examine her face. Their eyes met, and he felt that each was saying a hundred words to the other, all the *sorrys* and *double sorrys,* but in a language unknown to either of them. He told her he loved her, and she kissed him hard, igniting the kind of competitive love-making they'd had in the old days. Webster felt anguish and lust in equal measure. Anguish for all that had been lost and lust for Sheila's body, which had never failed to excite him. He knew that each was trying to break the other, and that in this contest neither of them would win. He wanted Sheila. He wanted her forever. Most of all, he wanted everything to be different from how it was.

Sheila held herself back, though he could see that it was taking all of her will. When the moment came, they looked nowhere but at each other. When they fell back, they were laughing.

Webster, for a week and another week, lived his life.

The tones came in at one forty-five in the afternoon. Webster took the call. Burrows glanced up from his winning hand.

"Ten-fifty," Webster said. "Two vehicles. Route 222, north of town."

"Four minutes, twenty seconds," Burrows said without even needing to think about it. He bolted for the Bullet, Webster right behind him.

"Asleep at the wheel," Burrows said when they were under way. "Wanna take the bet?"

Webster thought. One forty-five in the afternoon. No traffic. No weather. Could be a drunk, but unlikely. Could be a cardiac, more unlikely.

"Too easy," Webster said as he set off all the bells and whistles. He stepped on the gas. "Could be a deer."

"I was about to win seven bucks off you," Burrows said. He smoothed the top of his crew cut.

"So you think."

"You had nothing," Burrows said.

"You actually have to play the hand to win," Webster reminded him.

Burrows gave him the finger. "We it?" he asked. "Or are we backup?"

"We're it for now. Their medics are at a fire."

"A guy speeding to the scene? Volunteer firefighter?"

"Could be," Webster said.

"Head on?" Burrows asked.

"Sounded like it."

"Oh, jeez."

They sped past the old jalousie porch. He took a sharp turn onto 222.

"How far up?" Burrows asked.

"Not sure."

Webster hated 222. All hills and winding curves, the route was dangerous. It was hard to go fast when you couldn't see more than fifty feet ahead of you.

He stood on the brakes when he spotted the flashing lights. A green and gold state police car, its doors open, blocked his view.

But not Burrows's. "Shit," the medic said, opening the door. He grabbed the med box and a backboard and ran.

It was then that Webster saw the Buick.

His chest ignited. He couldn't get out of the rig fast enough.

He ran to the car, saw Sheila in the front seat, Burrows already treating her. Webster opened the door to the backseat. Where was Rowan? Day care? He tried to think. Had Sheila left her off with his mother? What was Sheila doing on 222 anyway?

A state cop stood in front of him. "Unconscious woman in driver's seat of Buick," he reported. "Toddler thrown thirty feet. Other driver, male, swerved at the last minute. Pinned in truck. We're trying to get him out now."

"I need someone over here," a policewoman called, and Webster saw a bundle on the ground. He sprinted.

"Fastened into the car seat," the policewoman said, "but not belted into the car. The toddler went through an open window. She's alive."

Webster got on all fours, covering Rowan. Under the blanket, his daughter was still inside her car seat.

"Rowan, baby," Webster said.

The part of him that still worked as a medic noted the contusions, the facial lacerations, a possible broken wrist from the way it lay. He thought his daughter was in shock. He didn't like the glassy stare. Blood covered her face.

"I need help here!" Webster cried.

"Must have hit at an angle that protected her head," the female cop said. "Like a helmet."

"It's my daughter!" Webster yelled again.

The cop, who'd been squatting, stood and whistled. Another cop ran toward them.

"A second rig coming?" she asked.

"Less than a minute out," the male cop said.

"Where's the other medic?"

"Treating the victim in the Buick."

"Critical?"

"Doesn't look like it."

"Get him over here, then call for backup

and more backup. This medic right here is out of service."

Burrows pulled Webster up, his knees soaked from the wet mulch. "She's my patient now," Burrows said when he could see Webster's eyes. "You let me do the care. You can hold her hand."

Webster stepped back.

"Get the pediatric c-collar and splints," he told a second medic, who ran as fast as he could to the rig and back. Webster saw a third rig pull in.

He watched as Burrows put a splint on Rowan's arm. He heard his daughter wail, a beautiful sound, a beautiful sound. But the sight of his daughter on a shortboard made Webster want to vomit.

The *what-ifs* were punching the side of his head. What if the guy hadn't swerved? What if Sheila had hit a tree? What if Rowan, flying, had hit a tree?

Burrows put a hand on his shoulder. "Your daughter's going to be OK," he said. "Broken wrist. Broken leg. She landed on her right side. I've got a firefighter to drive the rig. Sit in back with me. Once again, I'm treating."

When Webster helped Burrows slide

Rowan onto the stretcher in the rig, he thought that the earth had tilted on its axis.

"Your wife," Burrows said when they were seated in the back.

"My wife."

"She's going to be OK."

"Alcohol?"

"Two-six."

Webster clenched his teeth and nodded. "She could have killed Rowan," he said.

"But she didn't. You want to know the injuries?"

Webster said nothing.

"Broken collarbone, lacerations on the forehead and chest. Multiple contusions. Maybe some damage to the spleen."

In other words, thought Webster, she would be fine.

"She was sobbing," Burrows said.

"Fuck her," Webster said.

At the hospital, after being examined in the ER, Rowan was transferred to a double room in the pediatric wing. Webster stayed with his daughter every minute. He gently gave her a sponge bath to wipe the blood away. He fed her from the trays the nurses provided. He watched the monitors. He read to her when she was awake. During the forty-three hours Webster was in Rowan's room, he slept for only six of them. He never went to visit Sheila.

On the morning of the third day, Webster's mother came to collect Rowan and Webster. They would stay at her place for a few days. His mother never said a word about Sheila.

Webster's mother had brought a newly purchased car seat and a blanket in which Webster wrapped his daughter. He sat in back and fastened them both in. Stuffed animals from the nurses filled the rest of the backseat, and Rowan giggled when Webster began to name them. Burrows followed in the cruiser. A probie would pick him up.

At the house, Webster gave Rowan to his mother. He knew there was a treat waiting for his daughter on the kitchen table. He waited on the porch.

"You're out of service for a week," Burrows said when he arrived.

"OK."

"They're going to release Sheila tomorrow morning. A cruiser will come to get her to take her to the station, where they'll charge her."

"The guy in the truck?"

"Fractured his hip and his knee. He might get out next week. But the knee is bad, and he'll need surgery and months of rehab. Not a volunteer firefighter, by the way."

"What are the charges?"

"Reckless endangerment, driving under the influence, vehicular assault, who knows."

"She'll do time?"

"For sure. Second accident. Now she's hurt a guy."

Webster looked away.

"The cops won't show up for her until ten o'clock," Burrows said carefully.

Webster nodded again.

"This is coming straight from Nye."

Webster was surprised. "Who knew?"

"Who knew?" Burrows said.

The next morning, Webster entered Sheila's room at eight o'clock. She was dressed in her old leather jacket. Burrows must have warned her. She looked grotesque, her lip split, forehead and cheeks bandaged.

Rowan had a broken leg and wrist, unlike Sheila, who could walk.

"You almost killed three people," he said. He stood ten feet from her, his fists in his pockets.

She bent her head. "I'm sorry," she said.

"You almost killed Rowan."

"I'm so sorry."

"I don't care about that."

"I'll go to rehab," she promised.

"You'll go to jail." He paused. "I'm supposed to take you to the police station now."

She looked up. "But you're not."

"No."

Voltage crossed the distance between Sheila and Webster. A current composed of anger and remorse and something else—the last flicker of attraction.

Webster pulled the cruiser around to the front of the hospital. Mary wheeled Sheila down. Nye, Burrows, and Mary making it happen. Webster would owe Nye forever.

In the cruiser, Webster asked Sheila what she had been doing on 222.

"I don't remember," she said.

His hands clenched and unclenched on

the wheel. He couldn't keep his jaw from jutting forward. He was furious with her for what she'd done, for making him do what he had to do now.

He stopped a mile short of his parents' house. He faced Sheila, but she didn't look up.

"I'm leaving the keys in the car," he said. "There's fifteen hundred dollars in the glove compartment. Keep driving until you're past New York. Then ditch the cruiser at a twenty-four-hour convenience stop. Find a bus and get on it and go as far as you can. Don't come back. You come back, you'll be arrested."

Sheila began to cry.

"And you'll go to jail."

He waited. He thought she might ask to see her daughter. He was prepared to refuse her. She never asked.

Webster stepped out of the cruiser onto the road. He shut the door, aware that he was shutting the door on a life. He walked forward, his shoulders hunched, as if waiting for a bullet.

He was a thousand feet away when he heard the cruiser start up. He listened as the engine moved toward him.

A wild hope flared, a skinny flame. He imagined Sheila stopping. He would tell her that he loved her. Something miraculous would happen, and the three of them could be a family again.

Sheila drew abreast of him, hesitated, and then drove on.

He watched the back bumper of the cruiser until he could no longer see it.

Webster collapsed onto the dead grass at the side of the road. He wept, and he didn't care who saw him.

**2009**

After Rowan leaves for school and Webster washes the birthday breakfast dishes,
he climbs the narrow staircase, the house
his own now since the death of his parents. Both had been under hospice care
in the front room, Webster with his fully
loaded belt, helpless in the face of the
cancers that ravaged each of them. Pros-
tate for his father; lung for his mother.
She'd never smoked a day in her life. Even
at the end, or especially at the end, watching his father take his last breaths, each
followed by seconds of nothing, Webster,
with his training, felt panic. It was all about

the morphine and the hospice nurses and sitting in the dim light then, his father in the hospital bed in the front room, his hand light and cool in Webster's. It was not Webster's first experience with death by any means, but it rocked him nevertheless. Traveled inside and screwed around with his innards and his brain so that by the time he brought ten-year-old Rowan in to say good-bye to her grandfather, Webster felt the fear and responsibility of fatherhood stopping up his chest. He was it. Nothing between him and the morphine drip at the end. Sheila already gone eight years.

Rowan is seventeen now.

Webster lies down on his daughter's bed.

Overhead, Rowan has painted a mural of all the New England ski areas she's visited. The mountains are rendered with intricate trails, a dry blue sky behind them, the distances among the mountains shortened by curving roads dotted with Jeep Cherokees and Subarus and Rowan's Toyota, all of them with ski racks on top. Sunday River, Stowe, Okemo, Loon, Killington, Stratton, Bromley, Bretton Woods, and

even Wachusett Mountain to the south-
east.

After his parents died, Webster reno-
vated his old bedroom for Rowan, building
a closet and bookshelves and a desk with
drawers. Rowan still sleeps on the old oak
bed Webster once had, but gone is the
Bruins blanket, replaced now with a patch-
work quilt Rowan's grandmother made,
the quilt and half the top sheet now on the
floor. Webster, an inexpert bed maker himself, has never been able to teach Rowan
the proper way to do hers. Webster sometimes finds the blanket drawn up to the pillows with what looks like one strong swipe.

In the corner of the room are Rowan's
guitar and clarinet. Webster hasn't heard
her play either in months. Webster knows
that if he opens Rowan's desk drawers, he
will find various tubes of lip gloss, several
dozen Bic pens with the tops chewed, a
photo of Sheila and Rowan shortly after
the baby's birth (the photo viewed so often
that it no longer holds any power over
Webster or Rowan—or does it?), costume
jewelry Rowan received as presents years
ago and can't bear to throw away, and various coins. Periodically Webster has Rowan

collect all the loose change in the house,
put it into wrappers, and take it to the bank,
Rowan getting half the score. One recent
Christmas, Webster gave Rowan a machine that sorted and wrapped the coins.
Before Christmas dinner, Rowan presented
her father with $260 in neat tubes.

But Webster will no longer look through
Rowan's drawers, the result of an agree-
ment on Webster's part not to pry. In the
fall, right after Rowan's seventeenth birthday, Webster found a card of birth control
pills in the desk and called her on it. It was
a mistake that led to the worst fight father and daughter had ever had. Webster
winces just to think of it, his own anger (at
what, really? His daughter's sexuality? Her
preparedness? Her common sense?) just
as immediate and sharp as Rowan's, with
all sorts of pent-up frustrations leaking out
on both sides: a mysterious dent on the
front bumper of the Toyota neither would
claim; a C– on a Spanish test that Rowan
defended by proving that she knew the
material—she brandished the corrected
paper annotated with sympathetic com-
ments from her teacher—but couldn't finish the test on time; and a curfew that

Rowan thought punishing and laughable. The invasion of privacy, Rowan insisted, was unforgivable. In the end, Rowan took care of the dent in the car, though Webster paid. Webster relented on the curfew. Both agreed that a Spanish tutor might be a good idea. Webster promised never again to pry.

He rolls, and his radio digs into his waist. He takes it off.

Before he died, his father sold the store for a modest sum that after taxes and debts went to Webster. He was thirty-two then with a ten-year-old daughter and no wife. The bulk of the money went to day and night child care over the years, and he set aside most of the rest for Rowan's education.

Now Webster makes $57,000 a year. He's reached the top. He'll never make more than that, apart from yearly incremental raises. Not even yearly lately. The next four years will be rough, but not impossible.

Or maybe they will be impossible now. He thinks of the present Rowan gave him at breakfast. That forecast might as well have been a picture of his daughter in the space of any given day: a sun, a sun with cloud, rain, and another sun.

His radio sounds the tones. "Webster," he says.

"I need you to come in early. Actually right now," Koenig says.

"Be right there."

"No. You're closer."

Koenig gives Webster the address.

"What is it?"

"Forty-eight-year-old male. Difficulty breathing."

The patient, confused and sweating, is sitting on a Persian rug and leaning against a wall. Webster has enough time to register the cathedral ceiling, the oversized flat-screen television, and the wall of glass with the view of the Green Mountains beyond. Koenig finds the man's radial pulse and applies the blood pressure cuff. The redheaded wife stands, puts her hands to her head, and spins with anxiety. Two girls with similar hair, about five and eight, have been banished to the kitchen, but Webster can see small toes hugging the doorsill.

"Where does it hurt?" Webster asks the man.

The patient puts his hand on his chest and runs it down his left arm.

"BP seventy-eight over thirty-six," Koenig reports. "Can't get a pulse. Respirations thirty-two and shallow."

Webster applies the electrodes from the monitor. Right arm, left arm. Right leg, left leg. "Get a line in," he says to Koenig. "He needs a fluid challenge to get that pressure up."

"We were just having coffee," the wife says in a high-pitched voice, as if she can't believe it. She's jumping up and down, and Webster wants to tell her to knock it off, she's scaring the children. In the kitchen, the kids are crying.

"On a scale of one to ten," Webster asks the man, "how bad is the pain?"

The man loses consciousness and lists to one side. Webster and Koenig line up the backboard and the two lift him onto it while checking his carotid pulse.

"What's his name?" Webster yells.

The wife hesitates long enough that Webster has to turn his head.

"Mr. Dennis!" the kids shout from the doorsill.

Mr. Dennis?

"Dennis!" Webster shouts.

No response.

"Dennis, stay with us!" He checks the monitor. "V-fib," he says to Koenig. "Any pulse?"

"Can't find one," Koenig reports.

"Remove the oxygen."

Webster checks to see that the pads are in the proper position. He yells, "Is everybody clear?" He scans to make sure no one is touching the patient. He shocks the man.

The wife begins to keen—an eerie sound that rises to the ceiling.

Webster completes a round of CPR, then sets the machine at 100 joules again. He administers another shock. He gives the patient epinephrine and then raises the level to 150 joules. It takes four tries before Koenig reports a pulse. Koenig secures the airway by intubating the patient.

"Let's load him," Webster says.

"Where are you taking him?" the wife asks as they head toward the door.

"Mercy," Webster answers. "We're doing everything we can for your husband." He glances at the children, who are white-faced now.

"He's not my husband," the woman says in a small voice.

Webster nods. Of course. The way the children yelled *Mr. Dennis* while the woman hesitated. The way she hasn't touched or talked to the patient in all the time they've been at the house.

**Never make assumptions.**

"Ma'am, I want you to wait for someone to get here for the kids and then drive yourself to Mercy. Then get someone to drive my car to Rescue. Leave the keys under the seat. You need to calm down a little. We're doing everything we can for him."

But boyfriend Dennis is not OK. Again, he falls into V-fib, and this time, in the ambulance, Webster can't shock him out of it. They wail down the ridge, sparsely populated with expensive vacation homes, the owners thrilled at the prospect of six times more square footage than they have back in Manhattan.

Webster and Koenig approach the ER with lights and sirens turned off. Jogging alongside the stretcher, Webster gives his report, being precise about the order of the procedures, the amount of medication, and the number of shocks. "No pulse since nine forty-seven," he says.

As good as dead.

He wonders if the girlfriend will come to the hospital and if the man was married. If the woman's spinning meant more than just distress, meant, *This can't happen here.*

After leaving Mercy, just outside the town limits, Koenig and Webster head to Rescue, passing a sign that announces that Hartstone is tobacco-free. Webster and Koenig are silent because no matter how hard they've worked, a death is a failure. As they drive south with the Taconic range to the west and the Green Mountains to the east, Webster thinks about the girlfriend. Koenig put her address in the report, and maybe that will be fine with her, but Webster doubts it. Had the woman been unconcerned about anyone finding the boyfriend at her house, she'd have been more forthcoming with information. She'd have gone to her children and would have spoken to Dennis. Webster wonders who the next of kin really is. The true wife might be back in Manhattan or she might have her own six thousand on an adjacent ridge. Webster is a cynic. Too many of his calls unearth infidelities. Other calls are often marital disputes gone spectacularly wrong. He thinks he's seen pretty much everything one spouse can do to another.

Koenig parks the rig in its spot: facing out, ready to go again. Webster heads for the building while Koenig finishes cleaning out the rig. No blood, Webster notes in passing, which is a blessing.

"What happened to Pinto?" Webster asks when Koening enters the squad room. Koenig walks to the coffee machine and presses the lever six times to get half a cup. Webster checks his watch again. Three hours since his daughter made him breakfast.

"He called in sick," Koenig says, setting his cup on the Formica counter that runs the length of the room.

"Again?"

"Burnout," Koenig says. Koenig isn't a probie, but he has less seniority than Webster.

"After only two years?" Webster asks.

"He's always been a stressed-out dude."

Burnout. Webster knows all about it. Emotional anxiety coupled with physical damage to backs and knees from having to lift patients causes many rookies and veterans to leave the field before their time. Some go back to school to study to be nurses. A few of the younger ones try for the police academy. Others merely drift away or, in the case of his first partner, Burrows, die in their living rooms. Burrows in his last year a burnout and, at the end, a cardiac. Webster, out of service, heard about Burrows's death an hour later, which sent him into a frenzy. If only he had been on duty. He was certain he could have saved his old partner, whom he'd come to love like a cranky uncle.

Only once has Webster had to deal with personal burnout. After Sheila left, Webster was unable to answer a single call. He lay on the couch as he watched his mother take care of his two-year-old daughter. It wasn't entirely burnout that was causing his paralysis, but it was the job that took the brunt of his anger: the bloody messes, the fat bodies, the houses that smelled of urine and cat food, and the sudden deaths

of teenagers, suicides the worst. He'd seen
guys lose it at the scene, screaming at
the rookie and terrifying the patient. He'd
watched them sob in public or throw equipment back at Rescue. Worse, he'd known
them to start down the short path to alco-
holism. Unwilling to resign, the burnouts always found a way to force themselves off
the job.

After Webster spent a week on the
couch, his mother stood over him and told
him he had no choice but to be the man
he used to be. Webster was his daughter's
sole provider. Even now, he can see the
way his mother looked at him: a sheet of
parental anger over eyes filled with sym-
pathy. Her fists were knots on her hips.
She and Webster's father would help when
they could, she said, but Rowan was Webster's responsibility.

After that day, Webster has never let
himself get close to burnout. He can't afford to.

"The weather's going to be good tonight for the rehearsal dinner," Webster
says to Koenig to change the subject. His
tall partner, who both runs and smokes,
looks younger than his forty-seven years,

with his close-cropped blond hair and his light brown eyes. Once a math teacher at a private school, Koenig had his own personal burnout. He decided he needed a job that wouldn't bore him to death. Webster was surprised to learn that being an EMT paid better than being a math teacher. So much for four years of college. Koenig, relieved never to have to enter a classroom again, loves his job, and it shows. Webster has never had a better partner and doubts he ever will. Often the two switch roles to keep up Koenig's skills. Webster doesn't want to lose his partner, but he hopes for Koenig's sake that he gets the lead position on the number two ambulance when it comes in.

"You like the guy?" Webster asks. The wedding isn't exactly shotgun, but it came on fast because Jim (Joe, Jack?) has to ship out next week for Afghanistan.

"I'm worried for the guy, but I'm worried more about Annabelle." Annabelle, who at twenty-one shares Koenig's height and love of running. "I might get to like him more when he gets back," he adds. "He's rabid right wing, which is normal for a guy committed to the military. I never go near politics with him. But Annabelle worked for Obama. I don't know what the hell they talk about."

"How'd they meet?"

"Blind date."

"Sometimes, they end up the best," Webster says.

Unlike meeting your wife at the scene of an accident she caused because she was drunk, which ought to have told Webster all he needed to know if only he'd been paying attention.

"I just hope he doesn't come home with a head or spine," Koenig says. "I know Annabelle. She'll stick with him forever. But, Jesus, one week of a marriage, and then you're taking care of a guy you hardly know, wiping his ass and trying to teach him to talk again. No kids? Main breadwinner? What kind of a life is that?"

"Hey," Webster says, "you're getting ahead of yourself. Let the girl get married. Enjoy the wedding, Koenig. It's your only job tomorrow."

"That and writing the checks."

"Right. Oh, jeez, I almost forgot." Webster fetches an envelope from his back pocket and opens it on the table. "I have to renew my license."

"You have a birthday coming up?"

"Today."

"Hey, happy birthday. What? Forty?"

"Yup."

"Just a baby," Koenig says.

"Watch it."

Webster reads the letter. "I have to get a new pic this time. Do they really think the color of my eyes is going to change?"

"No, but your weight might. You might go gray."

"My parents went gray in their forties," Webster says.

"I'll be bald at fifty."

"Your mother's father?"

"I loved the guy. He had an ugly head, though."

Webster checks the computer that is always open on the center table. "Weather's going to be great tomorrow," he tells his partner. "Sixty-eight and sunny."

"May the gods smile on Annabelle."

"Hope the gods smile on the soldier, too."

"Jackson."

"I knew that." Webster puts down the letter and sips his lukewarm coffee.

"You OK?" Koenig asks.

"Yeah, why?"

"You look preoccupied."

"No, you know, the usual. Worried about Rowan."

"Until six months ago," Koenig points out, "you hardly ever worried about Rowan."

Webster says nothing.

"What's different?" Koenig asks.

"Seventeen?"

"Maybe she's got a romance going."

"She does have a romance," Webster says. "Guy named Tommy. Good kid, as far as I can tell."

Koenig is silent. He crushes his empty cup and lobs it toward the trash bin. "Rowan's a straight-up kid," he says as he unlaces his boots. "These new Timberlands hurt like hell."

"How long have you had them?"

"Three weeks."

"Wearing them the whole time?"

Koenig nods.

"Get rid of them, then. You have to be sharp on your pins."

"Shame."

"Find someone on the squad who has your foot size," Webster says as the tones sound a call. He takes it.

"Seizure," he reports to Koenig. "Twenty-two-year-old female. Known epileptic."

"Super," Koenig says, lacing his boots as fast as he can.

Webster cleans the kitchen, moving the silver cube from the center of the table to the sill. There's a different fortune in the box: *Go slowly and be careful.* He thinks that Rowan, the previous night, must have given the box another shake, and he wonders what advice she was looking for. After he finishes with the kitchen, he gives the bathroom a punishing scrubbing. The windows are winter-filthy, but he knows that Rowan will tackle them, still tickled by the novelty of the Windex sprayer that sheets them clean. The day is fine, as promised, and Webster from time to time thinks about Koenig and Annabelle and the soldier. Mostly, however, he thinks about Rowan.

It wasn't so long ago that Rowan used to give him a hug and a kiss when she walked in the door. Then she'd ask him how his day went while she sliced apples for them to eat with a sugar and cinnamon mix. He'd want to know about her day, and she'd tell him—when she planned on hiking with Gina; how she was glad she no longer had to take history; and could he loan her fifty dollars until she got paid so that she and Gina could go shopping in Manchester for good deals on winter jackets? When had that been? October? November? Had the change in Rowan happened gradually or all at once? He can't remember. It seems to him that one day she gave him a hug and a kiss, and the next day she didn't. That all of a sudden he no longer knew where she was or who she was with. That by Christmas a petulant tone had crept into her voice, there one minute, gone the next. And that by March, she was questioning his authority and letting him know when he irritated her with his questions and his always *wanting to know.* He supposed the change had to happen, that it would help when Rowan had to leave in the fall. All that made theoretical sense. What didn't make sense was the day-to-day reality of not knowing his daughter anymore.

Webster hears the specific whine of Rowan's Corolla before it hits the driveway. He's still vacuuming when Rowan comes in, so it isn't until he turns off the machine that he hears voices in the back hallway, those of Rowan and Gina, a blond genius who might also one day be a beauty once she rids herself of the small landmasses of pimples that cross her facial continent. Webster strolls into the kitchen, hands in pockets. "Gina," he says, "how are you doing?"

"Hey, Mr. Webster."

"Hey, Dad," Rowan says, opening the fridge, the first move she makes whenever she enters the house. "Want some OJ?" she asks her friend.

"Sure."

"How was work?" Webster asks. "You two have the same shift today?"

Gina's sweatshirt is dotted with what looks to be meat blood.

"It was OK, not great," Gina says, as Rowan fills two tall glasses with orange juice. "I was mostly at the back door, opening cartons. Least I got some sun."

"I had this lady at the register went nuts on me," Rowan announces, sitting at the table, glass in hand. "All of a sudden she starts screaming that I'm trying to cheat her. I haven't even totaled her order yet, much less taken her money. And she's screaming—I mean *screaming*—that I'm ripping her off." Rowan downs the juice in one go, looks for a napkin. Webster tears off a piece of paper towel and hands it to her. "The assistant manager comes over, takes the tape out, and compares it to every item in her bags. Then the lady says she's entitled to two boxes of strawberries for the price of one, and that I charged her for both—she's pointing her finger at me now—and Mr. T explains that was last week's offer. And before he gets a chance to tell her he'll extend the offer, she throws her purse at him, and all this crap falls out. Coins, keys, dollar bills, used tissues, breath mints . . . a jar of makeup breaks and gets all over my sneakers and Mr. T's shoes, and then the lady starts sobbing. Mr. T tries to put everything back into her purse except for the used tissues and the makeup. He gives her pocketbook back, bags her groceries, and wheels them out to her car for her, and of course she hasn't paid for anything."

Gina laughs. "I love the makeup."

"You wouldn't if it was all over *your* sneakers," Rowan points out. "I had to clean that up and pick up the tissues and the millions of pieces of glass."

"So," Webster asks, "what are you two up to tonight?"

"Gina's over because her computer broke again," Rowan says, "and she needs to get some notes and a take-home quiz off mine."

They both know this to be a white lie. Gina's mother doesn't have the money for a computer, and Gina is expected to use the one in the library, which always has a long line. At least two or three times a week, the girl comes to the house to use Rowan's laptop. Gina had to complete all her applications on it, and some of those applications had four essays. Despite the hardship, Gina has excellent grades, which proves something, though Webster isn't sure exactly what. He likes it that Rowan spends time with her.

"There's homemade pea soup in the freezer," he says.

Sometimes Webster worries about what Gina is getting to eat at home. The girl lives with her mother, Eileen, and a housebound grandmother. Eileen works part-time as a receptionist at Blake Ford because she can't leave the grandmother alone all day. Eileen is probably pulling in twenty-five, thirty at best, Webster guesses. Gina will be able to go to Columbia only because she has a full ride.

On Saturdays, Webster doesn't make dinner. Gina and Rowan are eating the first of two meals they'll have that afternoon and evening, the other away from home and not a real meal—more like cows grazing. On Saturday nights, Webster consumes leftovers and watches TV until he can't keep his eyes open. Rowan used to wake him up when she came in, but she's stopped doing that.

"Well, I'll let you be," Webster says, eyeing Rowan, who returns his gaze and shrugs.

"You'll do the windows today," Webster announces on Sunday morning. "It's going to rain tomorrow, so it has to be today."

Rowan, sleep hanging off her face like a net, nods.

"Nana used to love the days when Gramps would wash the windows in the spring. 'I've got new eyes,' she'd say."

Rowan, in her flannel pants and T-shirt, says she has to go to Liz Foster's at four. "We're finishing up a physics project."

"Fine. Don't be too late. I'm guessing you have a lot of homework."

"A ton of reading."

"What book?"

**"Gravity's Rainbow."**

"What's that?" Webster asks.

"A really stupid seven-hundred-sixty-page book."

Webster turns from the stove with a pan of fried eggs and bacon. "They're asking you at the end of your senior year to read a seven-hundred-sixty-page book? Mrs. Washington assigned it?"

"She says it's the best novel in the English language."

"Your class make fun of her this year?" Webster asks as he slips the eggs and bacon onto Rowan's plate.

"No. Maybe. A little."

"You reap what you sow."

Rowan shrugs.

"Bad luck for you," Webster says. He puts a plate of toast between them.

"No kidding."

"You and Gina have fun last night?" he asks.

"Pretty much." There's a trim of tiny pimples at her widow's peak, a rose growing near a nostril. Rowan's morning smell—the sweet scent of her hair, the particular fragrance of her skin—is so familiar to Webster that he thinks he'd know the girl anywhere: in the woods, in a crowded department store. He remembers a trip to Boston he and Rowan made during spring vacation when she was nine. After touring the Freedom Trail, he took her to the Aquarium and promptly lost her when he became engrossed in an exhibit on penguins and she wandered away. Panicked, he snagged a security guard, which alerted other security guards. Rowan was startled to find herself the center of attention at an exhibit of dolphins. "I knew where *he* was," she said, bewildered.

"Rowan, eat. You need your strength."

Rowan rolls her eyes. Webster wonders how many times he's said that to her. Sometimes he gets into a groove, and he can't get out. "It's just that Friday, at breakfast, you went from zero to sixty in nothing flat. Everything OK?"

"Everything's *fine,* Dad."

"Well, good," he says, though he knows now that it isn't.

Rowan scratches her left arm, a sign that she's anxious.

*"You OK?"* Rowan mimics as she points to her father's untouched breakfast.

Webster stabs a cold egg. "You don't have to take that tone with me."

Rowan sops up her eggs with a slice of toast.

Webster puts his fork down and glances at the dirty windows. He can't eat the eggs. Wrong breakfast. He'd have done better with something sweet. "Rowan, I'm getting tired of your moodiness."

"Dad, just fuck off, OK?"

The word, like a scratch of fingernails against a blackboard, creates a physical reaction along his spine. Webster can see that Rowan is waiting for him to reprimand her, punish her. When he doesn't, she pushes her chair back. "Where's the hose?" she asks.

From the garage, Webster watches as Rowan washes the outside windows. She stands on a stepladder and starts with the back attic window of her bedroom. She points the hose with the attached Windex and sets the switch to "soap," letting the foamy water shimmy down the panes. Rowan waits a few seconds, turns the sprayer to "water," and washes the soap away, leaving a clean window with droplets that will shortly dry. Just the way he's taught her. He's had to assure her that the fluid won't damage the bushes and the grass, and though he wonders how that can possibly be true, neither the bushes nor the grass has been hurt. He wishes Windex would invent a product to wash the insides of the windows as easily as the exterior ones. Old houses are great, but a bitch to keep clean.

She climbs down the ladder and washes the next level of windows, two at a time. Soap two, then rinse two. She's wearing her rubber boots, her pajama pants, and a slicker that once was yellow. Her boots are already wet from the sprayer and the dew in the shaded grass. He likes the flowers of late May, early June. The crab apple, the lilacs, the trillium. One day the color isn't there; the next day it is.

He thinks his not mentioning the *fuck* rattled Rowan more than if he'd laid into her.

Rowan reaches the front of the house and tackles the other attic window. She untangles the hose and takes it with her up the stepladder. She aims it, soaping up the mullions. She slips past the frame of the window and points the nozzle at the vinyl siding.

What the hell? Is she trying to give the house a wash, too?

Rowan makes wild loops and crazy brushstrokes. An angry sound escapes her. She turns her weapon on the bushes with their new leaves, at the lilacs with their potent scent, at a pine tree that she covers with what looks like wet toilet paper.

Rowan shoots as far down the driveway as she can. Then she raises the hose and lets it rain straight over her.

Webster takes off at a run. Rowan lets the hose fall and begins to climb down the ladder. When she stumbles, Webster catches her, keeping her upright. He pulls her head, soapy hair and all, into his shirt.

Webster and Koenig are backup, second rig on the scene. A six-vehicle pileup on the road coming off the mountain. The fog moved in fast, visibility nil. The fog halos the whites and blues on the cruisers. Webster spots five of them and another rig. He and Koenig report to incident command, and Webster is told to head for the bus. He sees a tractor-trailer on its side, a yellow school bus mounting it like a dog. A crumpled red Mercury, a navy Jeep that looks to have skidded into a tree, a silver Touareg that has accordioned a foreign car, a Hyundai maybe. Webster grabs what he can from the back of the rig and heads for the school bus. He and Koenig are part of a larger team now.

Children are always top priority. He notes the noise as he jogs: the cruisers, ambulances, fire engines, tow trucks, and the screams of the injured or frightened.

Two cops have pried open the front door of the bus. Webster hoists himself up and in. The driver is unconscious but is being rapidly extricated by a medic and a cop. Webster heads down the aisle, bracing himself against the seat backs. Kids are calling out, but Webster is more worried about the ones who aren't. No seat belts on the local school buses, and some of the bodies have been thrown as far as their backpacks, most toward the rear of the bus, which can't now be opened because of the Mercury. Cops have broken the emergency exits, crawled up and in, and are handing out children. Some of the kids look like grown men. A rural K-through-twelve. The place will be swarming with parents in fifteen minutes.

Knees bent, searching each bench, Webster finds a blond girl in a purple tank top wedged beneath a seat on his right, her ass so deep in, it's almost on the floor of the next bench back. Lying on her side, her knees and shoulders are caught by the steel bars that support the seats.

Webster gets down on his hands and knees and lets the shouting and the screaming float away, concentrating on the single case. He fears spinal injury, maybe paralysis. No blood. No movement. He speaks to the girl in a loud voice, trying to rouse her. He checks her airway and listens for breathing. He feels her carotid and finds a weak pulse. She's alive but in bad shape. He fastens a c-collar around her neck. He checks her pupils. Equal and reactive to light. Probably not a spinal injury.

When he looks up, he sees a boy, maybe thirteen, in a brown zip-up, sitting three benches down with his head in his hands. "Hey, son," Webster calls. The boy looks up. Dazed, but not in shock, Webster hopes.

"What's your name?"

"Edward."

"You OK to move?"

"They told me to stay here."

"Give me a hand. I've got a girl who's stuck."

The boy pulls himself upward to get to Webster, who points to the bench he wants the boy to sit in. The kid falls backward, straddling the girl's butt with his feet.

"You got any injuries?" Webster asks.

The boy shakes his head.

"OK, listen. On my count, I need you to gently push her behind forward so I can get her out and check her. You feel any pain yourself, you stop at once. Am I clear?"

The boy nods. "What's wrong with her?"

"I don't know yet. You know her name?"

The boy pulls himself up and over the bench to look down at her face. "Jill," he says.

"Jill!" Webster yells. No response. He calls again. No response.

Webster opens the belt of the girl's jeans, making sure the leather is in symmetrical loops so he can pull her forward. "My count and gentle now. One. Two. Three." With the boy's help, Webster, arms extended through the bars of the seat ahead of Jill, drags her straight toward him. She's slight, maybe 105.

"OK, now come around and help me get her onto her back and straighten her out. When I say so, you're going to *gently* draw her legs into the aisle. I'm going to get behind her and lift her shoulders forward."

It's one of the many decisions a medic has to make. Moving the blond could harm her already hurt body, but not to move her, to wait until an emergency crew can unbolt the bench, could cost her vital minutes.

The boy crawls into position. Then Webster has the girl supine, her feet into the aisle and then some. The boy straightens them.

Webster does the acronyms and looks for lacerations. He performs a neuromotor scan and checks her pupils again. Equal and reactive. Her knee jerks and she shifts her leg.

"Keep calling her name," Webster instructs Edward.

An older boy in the back is screaming, an EMT's yellow coat blocking Webster's view. Webster is losing focus and has to exert his will to concentrate on the task at hand.

One, maybe two, dislocated shoulders. A contusion the size of a baseball at the back of her head. Blood pressure 110 over 72. Pulse rapid and thready. He presses lightly against her clavicle and can feel the break. She should have woken screaming at the touch.

"You stay here," he says to the boy. "I'm going for the stretcher and the oxygen. Don't move, no matter what. And *do not* let anyone step on her."

Webster exits the vehicle the way he entered, most of the other medics using the side door that the cops have now freed. Webster runs for the stretcher and sees a unit pulling in from New York. He puts out a hand.

"Come with me," he tells the medic. "Bring your backboard, your stretcher, and your portable $O_2$. I've got a patient."

Webster and the medic climb back into the bus. They turn the girl's body into the aisle and slide her onto the backboard. They strap her on, and Webster applies a head restraint. They inch her toward the front door. Webster exits first, shouldering the weight, but the medic has the trickier maneuver—getting out of the bus without losing his grip on the backboard. They put Jill on a stretcher and walk her back to the waiting ambulance, Webster leading, the EMT and Edward following. The other EMT from New York has the back door open. "We've got it," he tells Webster.

"Unresponsive, breathing shallow, pulse rapid and thready, BP hundred ten over seventy-two, one, possibly two dislocated shoulders, broken clavicle, suspect head injury, name's Jill."

Webster turns to the kid standing to one side. The boy is quivering like a heart in V-fib.

"Take this kid with you," Webster says to the EMT. "His name is Edward. Give him a phone to call his parents or do it for him. Get him to tell you the girl's last name and call it into Dispatch."

Webster helps the kid, who has lost all his strength, up into the passenger seat. "You did good, Edward," Webster says, buckling him in.

Webster shuts the door and steps back. He checks his watch, a digital. He's been at the scene nineteen minutes.

As far as he can see up the hill, there are emergency vehicles, lights strobing in the thick fog. Critical injuries, some fatalities. The smart medics have made U-turns on the shoulders before stopping so that later they'll be able to exit the scene. The other emergency vehicles will serve as mini–trauma centers with EMTs and medics dispensing urgent care.

Webster, being among the first to arrive, is almost the last to leave, negotiating the shoulder on his way to Mercy, with Koenig and two hurt but not critical patients in the back. Mother and son, from the Touareg, she with face and chest bruises from the air bag, the boy, nine, with a broken wrist sustained when he tumbled, long after the accident, from the passenger seat of the car onto the road, and otherwise unhurt.

Four dead at the scene, three of them children, the fourth the driver of the Hyundai. An unhurt woman from an adjacent vehicle hysterical, sobbing that she couldn't stop in time, until finally a cop put her into a cruiser and took her home just to shut her up. Local news channels from two states criminally blocking the exit routes. Small children on shortboards, red and blue sweaters peeking through the thermal blankets. Webster has called in to Dispatch to find out where Jill was taken, but no one has an answer yet. Webster thinks of

Rowan, of how the girl in the purple tank top might so easily have been her.

It isn't the first mass-casualty incident Webster has had, but a school bus ups the ante, flooding the scene with anxious parents, some of whom had the good sense to dig in and help. The driver of the Jeep looked bad ten different ways when the stretcher carrying him raced past the bus. Webster treated broken bones, mild concussions, lacerations, two serious wounds. He kept his eyes averted from the parents who had to learn that their children hadn't made it. Webster can't bear the deaths of children; the images haunt him at night. It's a parental grief he can imagine so well that he's occasionally brought himself to tears.

On the way back from Mercy, Koenig, in the driver's seat, says, "Fucking nightmare. They ought to outlaw semis on 42."

"Where would they go?" Webster, one hand on the wheel, sitting back now. "It's the only route up the western side of the state."

"Put the stuff on smaller trucks. That semi had no business on that road going that fast."

"How fast?"

"The estimate from the statie was sixty."

"Never buy a Hyundai."

"The Touareg on the other hand . . . ," Koenig suggests.

"Like you could afford one."

"The cops just drove it away."

"I hate these kinds of calls," Webster says.

"No shit."

"How was the wedding?"

Koenig shakes his head. "Almost a disaster."

"What happened?"

"Annabelle's smarter than I gave her credit for. She cried in the car, and I had to wait a good twenty minutes for her to stop. She was scared. She didn't want to marry Jackson before he shipped out, but she didn't think it was morally right to let him go off without being married. And she couldn't bear the thought of leaving him at the altar, or whatever you call it when you have a wedding at an inn."

"Jesus."

"She'd been agonizing over this for weeks."

"So what did you tell her?" Webster asks.

"That I felt bad for her. I knew that Ruth, sitting right up front as mother of the bride, would have a fit if Annabelle backed out at that late stage. But I told Annabelle that all I had to do was put the car in gear, and we would drive away, and I would go back and explain it to Jackson and Ruth and the guests. I put the car in gear and went about ten feet before she begged me to stop. I finally said she either had to get out of the car or let me drive on. She fixed herself up as best she could, and then I took her into the inn. It felt like I was leading her to the slaughter."

"Hey, I'm sorry," Webster says as he makes the turn in to Rescue.

"She seemed happy enough at the reception, so maybe it was mostly nerves. That's what I'm hoping, anyway. She's going to have a lot of time over the next year to wonder if she did the right thing."

"She'd be better off not to think about it at all," Webster says. "She can't undo it while he's in Afghanistan."

Webster drags himself from the cruiser and through his own back door. Twelve thirty a.m., the end of one of the longest and worst days on the job he's had in ages. A shift and a half. Rowan is sitting at the kitchen table with leftovers waiting to be put in the microwave.

"You're still up?" Webster asks, surprised. "You cooked?"

"Just stew. You look tired."

"Rough day."

"I heard about the pileup. What was it like?"

Webster has always answered Rowan's questions about emergent care and its aftermath. Lately, he's been hiding nothing, even the gruesome deaths. "A horror show. Four dead, three of them kids. I worked on a girl who was stuck under a bench on a bus. Head injury, I think, though I hope not. She can't have been more than fifteen."

"How did the adult die?"

"Crushed, in her Hyundai."

Rowan is silent at this news. Does she try to picture it?

Webster peels off his jacket. He wants to take everything off right then and there and carry it to the washing machine. All deaths still make him feel slimy.

"It's great what you do," Rowan says, looking up at her father.

She's waited up all night to tell him that.

"Thank you," he says. "That makes it all worthwhile."

"Good," she says, standing.

"You'd better get to bed. You have to get up for school in six hours."

"I took a nap."

Webster watches his tired child climb the stairs.

Reparations. For the *fuck?* For shooting the leaves and flowers?

In the afternoon, after his nap, Webster is working in his newly dug garden. He hears the squeak of the back door and glances up. For a second, not even a second, he thinks it's Sheila. Not as she might be now, but as she was then: the long brown hair, the slightly defiant posture, the gray sweater and jeans, the sunglasses back on her head, even the dress boots. But it isn't Sheila—it's his daughter looking about two years older than she did the last time he saw her.

He meets her in the driveway.

"Where are you going?" he asks. He

wipes his hands on his old jeans. He has on a short-sleeved maroon T-shirt that reads HARTSTONE MARAUDERS.

"Out," she says.

"Rowan?"

"I'm meeting Tommy at the mall. We're going shopping for his mother's birthday and then we're going to the talent show at the high school. There might be a party after that."

"What party?"

"I'm not sure."

"You know I don't like that."

"I'll call you when I get there."

Both know a cell phone call is only slightly better than meaningless. If she wanted to, she could easily lie about her whereabouts. Would she lie to him?

"You have gas in your car?" he asks her.

"Enough."

She lifts her head and tosses her hair, a gesture he hardly ever sees her make. Webster doesn't want Rowan to go, but there's nothing he can do.

He aches to put his arms around her. Three months ago, he would have done it. He worries about car trouble, about her getting lost, about predators. But he can feel the shield she's put up against him.

"So," she says.

He wants to say, *Don't drink.*

He watches his daughter slide into the Corolla. He knows he's making her nervous. He ought to move away, go back into the garden, but he feels as though he has to see her out of the driveway. It's an old habit, impossible to break. He's watched her leave in the backseat of a girlfriend's mother's van, and driving away after she got her license. The old impulses just don't go away.

She backs the car around, slides her sunglasses forward, adjusts her hair, and heads down the driveway. He watches until she makes the turn onto 42.

He likes the feel of the earth, the smell of it, the mounded rows of seedlings. He's already harvested lettuces, and the peas should pop soon. He has a lot of weeding to do tomorrow, the tomatoes to put in. The day before, he worked on the fence, securing it against deer, though he's heard from others that a vegetable garden in Vermont is a crapshoot. Koenig's wife, Ruth, said that last year the deer ate all the pink and blue flowers she'd put in. They left the rest alone. Webster has planted marigolds all around the inside border of the fence. It's supposed to work with small pests. Already he has bigger pests, the tunnels in the lawn suggesting moles. Squishy places where the foot sinks in. He supposes it's just a matter of time before the critters reach the garden.

He pictures Rowan on the road. Does she drive with only one hand? Does she text while she drives?

By the time she heads for college, he'll have had her for eighteen years. Maybe that's all he'll get. He has to be ready to settle for that. Sheila had only two.

He squats, digs the spade deep into the black dirt, and rests the heel of his hand against the wooden end. He wants to lie down. He wants to let the worry sink into the dirt.

When he gets home after his shift, Webster can smell the alcohol as soon as he enters the kitchen. He takes the stairs two at a time and yanks himself into Rowan's room by the doorjamb. She's not there. He can't tell if she's slept in her bed or not. After nearly falling down the stairs to get to the living room, he finds Rowan on the couch wrapped in a summer quilt.

"Rowan!" he yells, standing over her. The reek of alcohol is strong and so is something else. He glances at the carpet and sees a dried stain of vomit.

Jesus Christ.

He shakes her and gets a moan.

Shit, he thinks. Is his daughter having a blackout?

He shakes her again and says her name. She opens her eyes and focuses. He sees the moment of panic. Conscious and alert.

"What the hell?" he says to her.

Rowan moans. "I don't feel good," she says.

"How much did you have to drink?"

There's a slight movement under the blankets. Rowan's hand going to her stomach. "I don't know."

"Did Tommy do this to you?" Webster demands, his blood pressure soaring.

"No," Rowan says. "He was getting pissed at me."

"Did he drive you home?"

"Oh, God, Dad, why are you doing this?"

"I'll do a hell of a lot more if you don't answer my questions!"

"Tommy got me into his car," Rowan says. "He was sober. I don't remember anything after that."

"Jesus Christ, Rowan. Why?"

"Why what?"

"What the hell happened to you?"

She coughs, and he thinks she's going to throw up again. Was she in such bad shape earlier that she couldn't even make it to a toilet or grab a pan from the kitchen?

"I don't know," she says weakly. "I guess it runs in the family."

Webster roughly pulls her to a sitting position. Her head bobbles. Her skin is green. Just looking at her nauseates him. "You listen to me," he says to his daughter. "This I will not tolerate. There's nothing alcoholic about you, so don't goddamn use that as an excuse. You did this to yourself. I don't know what game you're playing here, but you'd better knock it off." When Webster lets her go, she slumps back onto the couch. She turns her head away.

When Rowan was twelve, Webster told her that her mother had been an alcoholic and that was why she had to go away and get help. He never dreamed that his daughter would see this as her legacy. He's pretty much told Rowan everything that's fit for an adolescent girl's ears about Sheila and him, but he's withheld one important fact. He hasn't told her that it was he who sent her mother away. He should have done it years ago.

Webster rakes his scalp with his fingernails. Shit. There's nothing he can say to his daughter now. For all he knows, she might not even remember this conversation.

She isn't so sick that she needs to go to the emergency room. He'll just have to wait until she's slept it off. She's already on her side, so that's OK. He'll wake her up every half hour for another two hours. He hopes she'll have a pounding headache.

He falls into a chair across from her. Sleep will be impossible now. As his eyes adjust more and more to the gloom, he can see that there are two stains on the carpet. He heaves himself out of the chair and finds a bucket and a rag from the kitchen. He should have Rowan clean it up in the morning, but he doesn't know if he can tolerate the smell. The more he scrubs and rinses, the more infuriated he becomes. If his blood pressure keeps rising, he'll have a heart attack. He thinks of getting out his cuff. He can't remember the last time he was so angry with his daughter. Maybe never.

She can't remember the drive home. And Tommy? He'll ream that kid out the first chance he gets. Tommy her boyfriend? Jesus Christ. Who would sit by and watch his girlfriend get shitfaced unless he had ulterior motives? Webster shakes his head. He can't go there.

When Webster is done with the cleaning, he washes his hands, makes himself a cup of coffee, and sits again in the chair opposite the couch. Being angry with someone he loves brings on a sick feeling inside his chest. Too close to the bone. Memories he doesn't want rise up to meet him. Sheila drunk with the baby in her arms. Sheila at Rowan's birthday party. The image of Sheila weaving on Route 222. He will not, *will not,* let that become Rowan.

When he wakes, there are streaks of light around the shades. Something else, too, a knocking at the door. What time is it? He checks his watch. Almost eight a.m.

When he peers through the glass of the kitchen door, he opens it fast and closes it again behind him. He's so rough with his movements that Gina takes two quick steps backward. Tommy stands to one side.

"I'd like to know what you have to say for yourselves," Webster barks at the pair. For an instant, Webster remembers the Tommy he once liked. Six three, maybe six four. A dark hairline going straight across a high forehead, full lips, a nice smile. The first time he met the boy, Tommy came to the door to pick Rowan up, his car not much better than hers. Rowan, employing manners she'd never needed before, came to get Webster to introduce them. She warned Webster ahead of time, and because he was surprised and pleased for Rowan that she had a date, he didn't ask a lot of questions. "Be home by midnight?"

Rowan didn't answer, but Tommy did. "Will do."

Webster liked the kid straight up. Shy, but giving it his all. Honest face. Dark eyes that didn't slide away when they met Webster's. Good handshake. Not trying to prove anything. And the way he looked at Rowan. She'd said something funny—what was it?—and the kid laughed and gazed at her in a way that told Webster everything he needed to know. That's all you could hope for, really.

But now? Webster feels betrayed.

"It wasn't Tommy's fault," Gina says.

"Then you explain to me," Webster says, pointing back and forth to each, "how a girl can get so drunk, with friends who care for her just sitting by and watching. Was it funny? Did you get a kick out of it?"

Tommy puts his hands up. "Mr. Webster, I should have been there, but I wasn't. We went to the party together, but we both knew I would have to leave at some point to go home to see my grandmother, who just came from Indiana. When I got back to the party, I found Rowan stumbling around."

"How long were you gone?" Webster asks.

"An hour maybe?"

"She got that drunk in an hour? And where were you?" he asks, looking at Gina.

"I wasn't there," she says. "I never went

to the party. But I heard that when Tommy left, she went for the vodka in a big way. I'm so sorry. I wish I'd been there. I would have stopped her."

"Some class of friends you hang out with," Webster says.

"How is she?" Gina asks.

Webster opens the door and cocks his head in the direction of the living room. Gina slips around Webster and heads for Rowan.

"She's right where you left her," he says to Tommy as the kid enters the kitchen. "You're the one who brought her home?"

Tommy nods. "I was the designated driver all night."

"Why didn't you call me?"

"I don't know," the boy says, flustered. "I knew you were on duty."

"You think I wouldn't come home to take care of my daughter?" Webster asks. "And why did you leave her here alone?"

"I had to go home," Tommy, stricken, says. "My parents insisted I be home early."

"You realize she could have died," Webster points out. "She vomited twice. Thank God she had enough sense to puke over

the side of the couch. Never leave someone in that position."

Tommy lowers his head. He looks as
though he might be sick, too.

"It's not your fault," Webster says, relent-
ing and putting a hand on the boy's shoulder. "It's entirely Rowan's fault. I should be
thankful you got her out of there."

When they reach the living room, Gina is
already kneeling on the floor in front of the
couch, murmuring to Rowan, who seems
awake enough to listen.

Tommy stands awkwardly behind the
couch. Entitled to be there, but not.

Webster paces.

"Where's Tommy?" he hears his daughter ask.

He watches as Tommy puts a hand on
Rowan's shoulder. She reaches up from
the covers to hold it. It's a simple gesture,
but it means something. The boy held his
ground against Webster's roaring. Back-
bone there. Restraint as well. Webster
might have provoked another boy to be
defensive. He takes another deep breath.
He has to calm down.

The late morning light is garish. Rowan

shades her eyes and begins to cry. Webster leaves the three of them and crawls upstairs to his bed, trailing unwanted memories behind him.

While he sleeps, he dreams of Sheila.

A cop meets them in front of the warehouse. "Jumper down," he says.

"Really?" Webster asks. "I couldn't believe it when the call came in. Has anyone ever had a jumper down?"

"Not in my memory," the cop says. "Quechee Gorge maybe." He motions toward the back of the building.

Koenig has the backboard, the trauma bag, his jump kit. Webster carries the rest. They set out on a run. A clot of cops stands around a limp patient. They move out of the way when they see Webster and Koenig coming.

"He's conscious. He's talking," one of the cops says.

A security light illuminates the scene: surreal, metallic, framed in black. The patient has fallen onto his back. His left knee is bent backward in an unnatural way. A bone is sticking through his skin. A new cop to the scene says, "Oh Jesus," and turns away.

Webster glances up. Two stories. *Maybe* you could kill yourself falling two stories.

"The guy in front, security, actually heard the thud," the first cop adds. "Ran around back here to see what was going on."

Webster squats next to the patient and applies the c-collar. "We'll have to splint that," he says to Koenig, pointing to the fracture.

"ETOH," Koenig says, sniffing. He wraps a blood pressure cuff around the man's arm.

"Sir, can you tell me your name?" Webster asks.

Why isn't the guy screaming? Even though it's late May, he has a multicolored cap on his head, as if knit by a grandmother, blood pooling under it. Webster applies a pressure bandage. The man has on a denim jacket and jeans, one boot. The guy should be yelling his head off with pain.

"Randall," the man says.

"OK, Randall, can you tell me where you're hurt?"

"My back. Knocked the wind outta me, I guess."

"Your head hurt?"

"Not too bad."

Webster stabilizes the head. Head wounds bleed profusely. It's not as bad as it looks. He checks the pulse in the guy's ankles.

"How old are you, Randall?"

"Thirty-four."

Koenig glances at Webster. The guy looks to be in his late fifties, if a day. Hard living.

"Randall, were you pushed or did you jump?'

"I guess I jumped."

"Can you feel either your right or your left leg?" Webster asks.

The man tries to look up. The exertion seems to tire him, and he lies back.

"BP one hundred twelve over sixty-eight,"

Koenig reports. "Pulse thready and weak. Respirations twenty-four. Breath sounds equal and bilateral."

"You got the warming blanket with you?"

Koenig takes the shiny blanket out of the trauma box and covers the man up to his chest.

"Lumbar fracture?" Webster asks Koenig.

"Think so."

Webster can overhear the cops talking behind him. "Who would try to kill himself by jumping off a two-story building?" one of them asks, and another starts laughing.

"Call it in," Webster says to Koenig. "Tell them we got a jumper, possible L-1, compound tib-fib fracture, knee dislocation, bleeding profusely from the back of the head. ETOH. Conscious and talking."

"I want full-body immobilization," Webster says. "Bring the rig around," he tells one of the many cops who have gathered just to see the novel scene. Webster tosses him the keys. "Make it quick," Webster says.

By the time Webster and Koenig slide Randall onto the stretcher, the cop has the rig waiting, the back door open. "I can feel the guy shivering right through the stretcher," Webster says. "He's in shock."

Webster climbs in back with the patient and starts a line, the first of two. He can hear Koenig calling it in. Webster warms the IV liquid and jacks up the thermostat.

The guy is shivering so much, he can barely make himself understood. Webster wants to keep the guy talking and awake.

"So why did you do it?" Webster asks.

"Girlfriend."

"Randall, stay with me. Look at me. You with me?"

Randall nods once.

"What about the girlfriend?" Webster asks.

"She died."

It's an answer Webster wasn't expecting. "I'm sorry for your loss," he says in a loud voice. "How did she die?" he asks while taking the man's vitals.

"She killed herself," the man says.

"Really," Webster says.

"She jumped."

Oh God.

Webster feels it coming on and tries to suppress it. The more he tries to suppress it, the worse it gets. A deep, cosmic laughter rumbles up through his chest.

He turns away from the patient just in

time. Facing the back corner of the rig, Webster opens his mouth wide, suppressing the sound as best he can. Tears run down his cheeks, and he wipes them with his sleeves. The laughter stops. Webster catches his breath. Thinking it's over, he starts to turn, and then has to whip back around. He puts an arm over his mouth. He can't stop himself. He bites on his sleeve. He puts his forehead against the padding. The guy behind him says something unintelligible, which sets Webster off again. He pounds his fist into his palm to make himself stop. He keeps it up until he's good to turn around again. Koenig pulls into the bay, Webster opens the doors, and he can see an ER nurse running toward him. Tears still in his eyes, he gives his report as quickly as he can. He motions with his head for Koenig to go in with the stretcher.

When Koenig comes out, Webster is in the passenger seat.

"What the hell happened to you?" Koenig asks. "I couldn't believe my eyes."

"Oh God," Webster says. "I asked the guy why he tried to kill himself, and he said his girlfriend died. So I asked him how she

died, and he tells me she jumped. And . . ."
A high-pitched sound escapes him. Koenig
shakes his head and starts laughing. Webster pushes the heel of his hand hard
against his knee. Koenig snorts.

After a time, they stop.

"That was awful," Webster says.

"That was pretty bad. You might be losing it."

"I *am* losing it." He remembers Rowan
with the hose.

"We don't ever have to talk about this
again."

"No, we don't."

Koenig puts the rig in gear and heads
back to Rescue.

Chelsea seems to Webster to be a maze of industrial, abandoned, and triple-decker residential buildings. He makes his way to a water tower at the top of a hill and drives by what appears to be a hospital straight out of the First World War. When he passes the fire station, he searches for an attached building for Rescue, but can't see one from the street. He drives past a church called Saint Rose and a number of flat-roofed buildings on a busy road.

In spite of his MapQuest directions, Webster can't find the address. He's sure he's circled and recircled the same teal and brick school. Because he needs gas anyway, he pulls into a Mobil station and asks the guy there if he has a local map for sale. There are no Chelsea street maps in the stack, but the man asks him what he's looking for and Webster gives him an address. The man, with the name Peña embroidered on his pocket, draws out the directions for Webster. Webster tries to thank the guy with a five, but he won't take it. Webster buys a coffee and a doughnut.

Webster follows the new directions, paying attention at every turn, and finds himself driving up a residential hill. He spots the sign he wants and then the correct house number. He parks across the street.

The house is a triple-decker with asphalt shingles: pink on top, gray on the bottom. The building runs right up to the sidewalk with only a chain-link fence holding it back. He takes a long sip of the coffee and then a bite of the doughnut. The sun is high. From where Webster is parked, he can see that whoever lives in that house has a terrific view of the Boston skyline and of a large body of water. Boston Harbor? The Mystic River? On his side of the street, in front of a pale green vinyl-sided house are a pair of Virgin Marys cemented onto concrete pedestals that form a front gate. Adjacent to that house is a dwelling with a Santa in a fake well. It's the last week of May. The porch is covered with linoleum tile.

Finding Sheila was easier than Webster imagined. According to the Internet, there were twenty-two Sheila Websters in Massachusetts, but only six Sheila Arsenaults, one of them in Chelsea. He couldn't be sure that one was his ex-wife; maybe there was a large clan of Arsenaults in the city. And for all he knew, Sheila could have settled in New York or California. It would be nearly an eight-hour drive round trip, and Webster wondered if it was worth going just to find out he had the wrong Sheila. He thought of calling to make sure, but he didn't want his first contact with her to be over the telephone. They had to see each other face-to-face.

He thought of calling McGill over at the police station and requesting a search through their records, but then they might discover an outstanding warrant for Sheila Arsenault that could cause her all sorts of

problems. What was the statute of limita-
tions on vehicular assault, anyway? Webster wanted only to see Sheila. Ever since
Rowan came home drunk, he's felt that
she might be able to help him with his
daughter. The plan isn't well thought out—
he's come on an impulse, the urge to see
Sheila strong. What does he think she can
do? See Rowan? Talk to her? He can't really imagine either.

Long after the coffee in the cup is cold
and he's finished the plain doughnut, he
steps out of the car and walks over to the
porch. There are three residences in
the building, each with its own buzzer. The
third buzzer has the name *Arsenault* beside it. He rings the bell.

He hears footsteps coming fast down
an interior stairway. He braces himself. For
all he knows, the cop from Chelsea might
open the door.

"I wondered when you were going to
come in."

It's Sheila, and it isn't. He feels the same
as he did at his twentieth high school reun-
ion, seeing hidden faces within faces, features morphing as he watched. Only this

time, the sensation is so interior that he feels he is observing himself change in a mirror.

"Sheila," he says.

The hair is long and dark brown and gray near the temples. She must be forty-two now. She has on jeans and a plaid shirt, both paint-splattered. No shoes. There are crow's-feet around her eyes, but the mouth is precisely as he remembers it. She's slim but not athletic-looking.

"What are you doing here?" she asks.

Webster puts his hands in his pockets. "I came to talk to you about Rowan."

There is no thought of shaking her hand or embracing her.

"You came from Vermont?" she asks.

"I did."

She says nothing.

"Can I come in?" he asks.

She stands aside so that he can step over the threshold. He takes in the dark interior, the steep staircase, the stained glass in a side window.

She gestures with her hand toward the stairs. "Third floor," she says. "All the way to the top."

"You saw my car," he says when he reaches the landing.

"Well, it's a different cruiser. How many have you had?"

"Since the first, three."

Since she drove away in the first.

"I thought it was an undercover stake-out. Then I saw the license plate."

The scent of turpentine is strong. Webster follows Sheila into a large room with several windows on three sides. The sun makes rectangles against the white walls. There's a long wooden table that has on it paintbrushes in glasses, old rags, bottles of turpentine and linseed oil, a palette, dozens of squeezed tubes of color, and various rags. On the floor, all along the perimeter, are canvases of different sizes, each facing the wall.

"You're a painter?" he asks.

She spreads her hands.

He knows nothing about the woman in front of him. They spent nearly three years together and fifteen apart. Though everything about her is somewhat familiar—her stance, the sound of her voice, her body, her gestures—she's a stranger to him.

"I came to talk about Rowan," he repeats.

"Is she all right?"

"She is, and she isn't."

"Is she sick?"

"No," he says.

Sheila stands at the other side of the room, her arms crossed over her chest.

"Could I get a glass of water?" he asks.

She gives him a dull look, but walks past him. He follows her to the kitchen, cluttered but not unappealing. The table and the chairs have come from an older generation. The walls retain a printed wallpaper, definitely a relic from years ago. Utensils are lined up on hooks near the stove. Along another wall are bookcases, one shelf filled with cookbooks.

"You live here alone?" he asks.

She nods, turns on the tap, and lets the water run. She pours him a glass of water and sets it on the table. He reaches for it.

"You still living with your parents?" she asks.

"They died years ago," Webster says.

"I'm sorry," she says, and she looks as though she means it.

"I still live there," Webster says. "I inherited the place."

"My sister sold me this house for a buck. I grew up here."

Webster is amazed at their civility. Shouldn't they be screaming at each other? Weeping? Throwing things?

From where he stands, Webster can see planes coming in to Logan. That he would enjoy. Watching the five o'clock rush hour from that balcony out back. A beer in hand.

"What are you doing here?" Sheila asks again.

"I thought it might help. To talk to you about Rowan. She came home drunk a few nights ago. She's not herself. She seems to be spiraling off the rails."

Sheila is silent.

"Rowan's changing. And not for the better."

Sheila bites the inside of her cheek.

"She's beautiful, Sheila. She looks just like you. She's been a real good kid—up until now."

Every cell in Sheila's body has changed since he last saw her.

"Are you sober?" he asks.

"I am. Ten years."

He'd taken a chance. He might have found a drunken Sheila.

"I assume we're officially divorced," she says.

"We are."

"On what grounds?"

"Abandonment. It was all I had. My lawyer tried to find you, but you weren't in the system anywhere."

"What year was this?" she asks.

"Ninety-eight?" he replies, not quite sure.

"I was in Mexico."

"I don't think he tried very hard," Webster says.

She twists her hair in the back and lets it fall onto one shoulder. It's a gesture he remembers, and it startles him. It's Rowan's gesture now.

"So you're not married?" he asks.

"No. Are you?"

He shakes his head. He points to a gold ring on the middle finger of her left hand.

"It belonged to someone I once loved," she says.

**Once loved.**

A threadlike pain moves from one side of Webster's chest to the other.

"I'm sorry," Sheila says, "but I can't do what you ask. I know you came all this way for a good reason. But you don't know me anymore. You don't know me at all."

The silence in the kitchen lasts so long that Webster finds his breathing shallow. "She's seventeen," he says.

Sheila shakes her head.

"She thinks she's an alcoholic. Or maybe I think she thinks she's an alcoholic."

"Is she?"

"She's acting out, and it's dangerous."

Sheila winces. He notices that her hands are trembling.

"This is a shock. Your coming here." She pauses. "I was her mother," Sheila says, "and then I wasn't. You of all people should know that. I severed the mother-daughter tie the minute I got in the car drunk with Rowan in the back."

Webster thinks of reminding Sheila that it was he who sent her away, but he doesn't want to argue about who is to blame. He sees no good outcome to that conversation.

"Will you at least think about it?" he asks.

"Meeting her?"

"I suppose so, yes."

"You came all this way for nothing."

"But you'll think about it."

Sheila was silent.

"May I see a painting?" Webster asks in desperation.

Sheila seems confused by the abrupt request. When she leaves the kitchen, Webster follows her. In the front room, she turns a painting around. It's of an old wooden table, an aged plaster wall behind it, a shiny blue and white bowl on top of the table with a red chili pepper in the foreground. It's beautifully executed. He recognizes the blue and white bowl. It used to be his mother's, but she gave it to Sheila.

One by one, Sheila turns all the paintings around. He watches as she bends, handles each item with care, and then leans it against the wall.

Each is a domestic scene, painstakingly rendered. Another picture shows three bowls against the backdrop of the horrible flower-print curtains they had in their apartment. Another is of a cut lemon, so realistically painted that one can almost taste the juice. The background is the wallpaper in Sheila's kitchen. Another is of a chair against a table, a trio of apples, and a book.

"They're called sharp-focus still lifes," Sheila says.

"Where did you learn to paint?"

"In Mexico."

"You paint from memory."

"I do."

"They're really very good," Webster says.

"Thank you."

There is a long silence between them. What does he hope? That she'll change her mind right here?

"Well," he says. "I'd better go."

Reluctantly, he walks to the door. He examines Sheila for another few seconds. He wonders if this will be the last time he'll ever see her. Her hands are tight fists. Her entire body is rigid.

He won't beg. He won't try to negotiate. In a way, he gets it.

"I shouldn't have come," Webster says.

Sheila opens her mouth and then closes it.

He jogs down the steps and shuts the front door behind him.

He drives furiously out of the city, having no idea where he's going until he comes to a sign that reads, ENTERING QUINCY, which he knows is south of Boston and not where he wants to be. He pulls the cruiser onto a side road. He's lucky he didn't get a ticket.

He rolls down the window and breathes in metallic air.

He takes out his cell phone and punches in his daughter's number. She picks up on the second ring. "Hello?" she whispers.

"Rowan, it's Dad," he says.

"I know."

"I just wanted to see how you're doing."

"Dad?"

"Yup?"

"It's twenty past one."

"OK," he says.

"I'm in *history* class. If I don't hang up, Mr. Cahill is going to kill me."

"Oh, sorry. I wasn't thinking."

"You OK?" Rowan asks, still in a whisper.

"I'm fine. Talk to you later."

Webster leans his head back and shuts his eyes. He decides he'll stop at the first decent restaurant he finds and eat a proper meal. Then he'll find a map and drive like a normal person back to Hartstone.

*Caddyshack* is in the DVD player for the hundredth time. The probies watch it over and over during their first three months. They need the mindless laughter to calm their nerves.

The radio sounds out the tones at 3:10 a.m. Powell, a probie who has the haircut of a marine and the skinny frame of a geek, pops up from the couch like a jack-in-the-box.

"Attention, Hartstone. We need a crew at 35 High Street. Fifty-one-year-old female, difficulty breathing and severe chest pain."

Webster responds: "602 and 704 in the building. Any other info?"

"Patient made the call. Appears to be alone."

"You drive," he tells Powell as they run to the rig.

It's Webster's first shift with the kid, and he needs to monitor him as well as take care of the patient. Webster glances at the speedometer. "You want to push it as high as you can without danger of causing an accident. Almost all rig accidents take place in intersections."

The probie is memorizing acronyms. Webster can see it on his face.

"Remember how to get to each call, not only because you might be called back to the same place, but because it's the best way to learn the geography. Though you should be studying the maps, too. You studying the maps?"

"Yes, sir."

"Name's Webster. We don't do sir."

"Understood."

"Where did you train?"

"Saint John's Hospital. This was the only job I could find."

"You move here?"

"Yes."

"Family?"

"No."

Webster shakes his head. The guy's probably renting a single room in someone's home. Bathroom down the hall. A probie's salary is grim. "You ever had a code ninety-nine before?"

"Just in training."

The house is at the end of a driveway badly in need of a regrade. Powell has to slow down for a massive bump.

The probie takes the backboard and his jump kit. Webster has the med box and a flashlight. They walk straight in and find a middle-aged woman sitting forward on a kitchen chair, a large cooking pot by her feet. Webster can smell the vomit.

"You take the vitals, I'll do the history," he tells the newbie.

Webster has a pen and pad in hand. "Ma'am, can you tell me your name?"

"Susan."

"Susan, we're here to help you. How old are you?"

"Fifty-one."

"Can you tell me where your pain is?"

Webster watches the rookie take the

pulse as the woman vomits into the pot again.

"Susan, on a scale of one to ten, can you tell me how bad the pain is?"

"Eight."

"Can you show me where your pain is?"

The woman pats her chest. "Heavy," she says.

Elephant on the chest.

Webster puts an IV line in. He can see that the newbie is having trouble with the blood pressure cuff. "Probie, what's your problem?"

"No problem."

"What's the BP?" he asks.

The newbie hesitates. "One-eighteen over eighty," he says.

"Other vitals?"

"Pulse, a hundred twenty-four. Respirations, thirty-six," he snaps out.

The patient seems confused by Webster's presence. More confused than when Webster entered the house. "Probie, we need another light. The switch over there," he says as he points.

Powell turns on the overhead while Webster checks the woman's airway and listens to the lungs. He slaps on the non-rebreather mask. Webster examines the cardiac monitor. "Let me see that cuff," he tells the probie. "Watch for vomit."

Webster takes the blood pressure. "Eighty-six over fifty-eight," he says aloud.

Webster hands the cuff back just as the cardiac monitor signals V-fib. Webster catches Susan, and he and the probie lay her on the wood floor.

"I'm going to shock her," Webster says.

Webster checks to see that the pads are securely in place. The probie has done something right. He removes the oxygen. "Is everybody clear?" he calls out.

Before he can administer the shock, he sees, from the corner of his eye, Powell reaching for the IV bag.

*"Don't touch that!"* Webster shouts.

The probie freezes, his hand six inches over the bag.

"Sit back," Webster says. He waits a second. Powell looks like he wants to swallow his arm. "Is everybody clear?" Webster repeats. He administers the shock.

"Keep the compressions going," he tells the probie. And then, after a minute, he adds, "I'm going to shock her again. Is everybody clear?"

This time, the probie scuttles backward so fast, Webster thinks he'll fall over.

Webster turns up the joules and shocks Susan again.

"Let's get her onto the stretcher and into the rig. Keep up the CPR."

They slide Susan into the rig. Webster goes with her, taking over the CPR. Still V-fib on the monitor. Webster wants to bring her in alive. He removes the oxygen and administers another shock, this time a hundred fifty joules. He gives her one milligram of epi, shocks her at two hundred joules, and then delivers one hundred milligrams of lidocaine.

He radios the hospital. "Hartstone Rescue to Mercy. "

"Go, Hartstone."

"We are en route to your facility with a fifty-one-year-old female. Patient was conscious initially, but arrested shortly after our arrival. The monitor is showing V-fib. Patient shocked and defibrillated a total of four times. We've administered a total of two migs of epi and two hundred migs of lidocaine. Patient is intubated."

"What's the down time on this patient?"

"Four minutes."

"Continuous CPR?"

"Yes."

"Per MD number twenty-three, administer one amp sodium bicarbonate. ETA?"

"Five minutes?"

"We'll be waiting for you."

"OK, Susan," Webster says to his patient, who looks as dead as a person can be. "You and me, we're going to do this together." Webster removes the oxygen. "I'm clear, you're not." Webster shocks the woman again. He replaces the bag valve mask and administers the sodium bicarbonate.

"You married? Your husband at work? Kids? You a smoker?" Webster stops the CPR, removes the oxygen, turns up the joules, and goes through the procedure again. "Hey, Susan, seriously, you gotta do your part." He starts the CPR again.

"OK, Susan, we got nothing to lose. Hold on to your eyeballs." Webster repeats the routine and turns the joules up to two hundred fifty. "I'm clear, and you're dead if this damn machine can't do the job."

The woman's body rises right off the

stretcher. Webster's eyes are locked onto the monitor. He watches as Susan converts to a normal sinus rhythm.

"Beautiful, beautiful!" Webster says with awe. He loves the normal sinus rhythm. Loves it. "Way to go, Susan!" Webster says, pretending to high-five the woman.

"ETA," he shouts to Powell.

"Two minutes."

"Step on it."

When they reach the ER, a med tech and a nurse run out to the bay and take over. After the ER has transferred the patient from the rig stretcher to the hospital's, the probie rolls it back to the rig. Webster heads for the medic room and completes his report: what they saw and what they did. He tears off the ER copy, takes it back to the cubicle, and lays it across Susan's legs.

"Good work," says the attending. "I was sure you were bringing in a DOA."

Webster shrugs and nods.

Back in the bay, Webster sees that the rig's back doors are closed, indicating that it has been cleaned and disinfected. Powell is in the driver's seat already. Webster climbs in and faces the kid.

"You lied about the BP," he says to the newbie.

Powell has red circles on his cheeks. His ears are enormous. "I couldn't get it."

Webster doesn't need to raise his voice. "Never lie. Never. Just tell me you can't get it. A wrong BP can lead to wrong treatment. And wrong treatment can lead to a disaster. Do you understand me?"

The probie nods his head.

"And what the hell was that with the IV bag?" Webster asks. "You could have shocked yourself to Montreal."

"I didn't think," the rookie says.

"You didn't think. From now on, probie, *think*. Think so much your brain hurts. Every move, every procedure. I can't have a situation where I've got two patients on the floor."

"No, sir."

Webster rolls his eyes. "Everyone you come in contact with for the next week, I want you to take his BP. I see you without the cuff, you're suspended. I want you taking BPs twenty, thirty times a day. We clear?"

"Yes, sir."

"The name is Webster. You can't say

your partner's name, you're going to have a real problem. Let's go."

The ambulance rolls out into the night. On the horizon is the first lining of dawn.

Webster leans his head back and closes his eyes. He hasn't had a save in three months. He smiles. Nothing better than waking up the dead.

Webster sits in the cruiser, uniform on, the field not twenty feet from him. The kids are used to his car. Even the uniform won't bother anyone. He checks his watch. He has maybe a half hour before he has to report to Rescue. During the season, he tries to get to as many games as he can.

Today, he feels the need to see something normal taking place—something so far removed from what he does for a living and his visit to Sheila that he might as well be in Kansas. At some point, he'll have to tell Rowan about his trip to Chelsea. What the hell will he say? I found your mother, but she wants nothing to do with you?

He locks the cruiser and walks, with his hands in his pockets, to the end of the bleachers. The girls have games on Saturdays and Wednesdays, mostly Wednesdays, which allows Rowan to keep her job. He can't tell what inning it is because there's no scoreboard. He could ask, but he doesn't need to socialize. He knows most of the parents in the bleachers—by sight, if not by name. He's been sitting with them for years at one game or another. Rowan, in her maroon uniform, plays first base, her reach and her stride long, her arm accurate. She likes the spot because it provides her with action.

The runner is off the bag two long steps. Rowan, glove extended, is watching the pitcher for any sign of a pickoff. Webster hopes for a double play. He's made it to about half the softball games this season. Just watching his daughter on the field brings back memories of sitting for hours during Little League games when Rowan was six, seven years old. Rowan with her cap too big for her, her T-shirt hanging down to her knees, running as if she had a load in her pants. At some point, her posture changed and with it her center of gravity, but those early years were the great ones.

The batter gives the ball a good wallop. Rowan leaps into the air to catch it. The runner takes off to second and keeps going when she sees that Rowan has missed it and that the ball has rolled out onto the field. Another player, whom Webster doesn't know, shoots it back to Rowan for the cut-off. Rowan throws it to the catcher in time to prevent a homer. The runner waits on third.

Rowan couldn't have caught that ball off the bat anyway, Webster decides. Too high.

When the team runs off the field at the third out, Rowan, ponytail flapping through the hole at the back of her baseball cap, gives a quick wave in his direction. Though it isn't cool to wave to your dad during a game, Rowan usually does. A teammate throws Rowan a bottle of water, and she drinks it straight down.

Webster asks a guy standing near him what the score is.

"Seven–five, Hartstone's losing."

Rowan ditches the empty water bottle and walks to the batting circle, searching for her favorite bat. The first batter flies out, so Rowan makes her way to the plate. Webster can tell by Rowan's stance and her practice swings that she wants to hit it over the fence.

Rowan swings and misses. Strike one. Webster loves the chatter from the dugout. Hey, batta, batta, batta. Rowan sets up for the second pitch.

It's as solid a hit as he's seen from his daughter all season. Keeping his eye on the center fielder, Webster watches Rowan take off, running as if the World Series were at stake. Part of her speed is due to the fact that Webster is watching—the Parental Effect—but part is pure Rowan. As Rowan rounds second, he feels the old familiar hope soaring. The center fielder leaps, doesn't even get her glove on the ball. While she is scrambling behind her, Rowan keeps up the pace, beating the shortstop's cutoff throw to the catcher. Home run.

All right, Rowan.

Webster watches her team high-five her. Rowan grabs a towel to wipe off her face.

Webster checks his watch. He has ten minutes left. Maybe he'll get to see another inning.

He's aware of a person moving toward him from the direction of the bleachers. He turns to see a woman he thinks he knows but can't immediately place.

"Mr. Webster?" she asks.

He turns. "Yes, hello."

"Hi, I'm your daughter's English teacher, Elizabeth Washington."

"Of course," Webster says, wanting to smack his forehead. "How are you?"

"I'm fine," she says. "My daughter just joined the team this year. She's a sopho- more. Julie Washington?"

"Is she playing today?"

"No, she's on the bench for now."

"The coach will give her playing time," Webster assures her.

"I was wondering," Mrs. Washington says, "if Rowan has been OK at home."

The hair prickles on the back of Web- ster's neck. The woman has on a gray blazer and sneakers. He puts her in her late forties. Her eyes look pinched, or maybe that's just the sun in her face.

Webster doesn't want to tell Elizabeth Washington about Rowan's drunken epi- sode. On the other hand, he doesn't want to seem an oblivious parent, because he isn't. "She baffles me sometimes," Webster says. "Sweet one day, moody the next. I don't always know why."

Elizabeth Washington nods. "That's just normal teenage behavior, and maybe this is partly that, too. She's letting her grades slip. All second-semester seniors do it to some extent, but she's in danger of failing English. Calculus, too. I checked. She's not doing the homework, not paying attention. Not doing the reading."

Webster rocks back on his feet. Elizabeth shades her eyes.

"I'm . . . I guess I'm shocked," Webster says. "Rowan's always been such a good student that I long ago stopped checking her homework. I talk about it with her sometimes, but I always thought she had everything under control."

He tries to remember her last report card. B+ in English, he's pretty sure. C+ in math, and he questioned her about that. He can't remember what Rowan's response was. She didn't seem worried, even though her grades weren't as good as they'd been in the past.

"She could make up some of the work," Elizabeth says, "but it's only two weeks to graduation. I'm concerned. If she fails English and calculus, UVM may not take her in the fall. We have to send the final transcripts along to the college."

"Will she graduate?"

"She'll graduate. She's had enough credits since early fall. But it isn't just the grades. I guess I'm trying to find out if anything's amiss at home."

"Hard to read her right now," Webster says. "You assigned a big book recently. Something about gravity?"

Elizabeth smiles. *"Gravity's Rainbow.* Yes. A lot of the students found the book challenging—mainly its length. But as far as I can tell, Rowan never read a word."

Webster lets out a sigh.

"I'm sorry," the teacher says. "I should have said something earlier. There's really little that can be done at this point. But I've been curious. And I thought I'd ask."

Webster opens his hands and shakes his head. He knows the woman's motives are pure, that she has Rowan's best interests at heart, but he feels as though he's being called on the carpet, too. To not know what's going on with Rowan at school makes him feel like an idiot. "I'm completely surprised," he says. "Thanks for telling me. Obviously there is something wrong. You can bet I'll talk to her about it." He checks his watch. "I'm late for my shift," he says.

Elizabeth touches his arm. "I didn't in any way mean to suggest you've been a bad parent. Personally, I think you've done a tremendous job with Rowan. She's one of the few students I'm really fond of. But lately, she seems to be undergoing a personality change."

Webster shakes her hand, simply because he can't think of any other way to say good-bye. He has two minutes to make it to Rescue. He wishes he could pull Rowan aside and ask her about the bad grades, but unless there's an emergency, it's understood that a parent doesn't pull a player away from a game.

But failing English and calc? Isn't that a valid emergency?

He glances in Rowan's direction, but though he can see her face, she doesn't look his way. Her lips are pressed together hard.

Webster strokes his rough chin while gazing at a pile of bills he's been neglecting for weeks. Usually, he practices triage, dividing them into three piles: those that have to be paid immediately, those he could pay at the end of the month, and those he could let go for a few more weeks. Today there will be no triage: all the bills are late. He ponders the tuition bill that will soon come due. He'll have to take on more shifts at Rescue or mortgage the house. At least UVM's tuition for in-state students is reasonable.

Since Elizabeth Washington took him

aside the day before, Webster completed
his tour and was waiting for Rowan when
she woke up this morning. In the kitchen,
he confronted her with what he knew.

"So?" Rowan asked, trying and failing to
brush it aside.

"*So?*" Webster asked. "*So?* You might
not get to go to college."

"So?" Rowan repeated.

"That's it," Webster, fuming, said. "Give
me the keys."

"Seriously?" Rowan asked. She had her
backpack over her shoulder. She hadn't
planned on having breakfast.

"You bet," he said, holding his ground,
though he could already feel that platform
shift beneath him.

"How will I get to school?" Rowan asked.

"Walk. Lots of kids have to walk."

She tossed the keys onto the table.
They slid in Webster's direction. "No one
walks, Dad," she said in a tone that suggested she felt sorry for his ignorance.

He watched her leave the house. He
did not stand to see her make her way
down the driveway.

At the table with the bills, he checks his
watch. One thirty.

Tomorrow night is Rowan's senior dance. He wonders if she'll be speaking to him by then. The talk this morning didn't go as he imagined it would. Why does he continue to expect reasonable conversations with a seventeen-year-old whose moodiness is taking over her entire personality? Because he used to have sane conversations with his daughter.

He takes a sip of cold coffee. He could heat up the coffee in the microwave, but he decides to make another pot. He has at least an hour with the paperwork ahead of him anyway.

He wipes a spill of water with the tail of his cotton shirt. He'll stick it in the laundry basket when he goes upstairs. He has on the beat-up slippers Rowan gave him two Christmases ago. They have fur inside and are too warm for this time of year. He'll have to find his boat shoes.

He hears a sound. The front doorbell? Only FedEx and UPS ever use the front door.

A package for Rowan, he guesses. He pads down the hallway. So few packages are for him. Because she shops online and is, for the most part, frugal, Webster doesn't mind the odd delivery or two. He likes the look on Rowan's face when she catches sight of a package on the kitchen table.

Webster opens the door.

A package he never expected.

"You have some nerve," he says.

"So do you."

"I thought I'd never see you again."

"One good surprise deserves another," Sheila says.

Webster feels his body gearing up for an emergency.

"I came to talk about Rowan."

Webster takes a step backward, which she reads as an invitation.

He closes the door behind her. She glances around at the small foyer, the dining room to the left, the kitchen straight ahead.

"You haven't changed too much."

He can't tell if that's a compliment or not.

Sheila has on a short black jacket over a pair of slim gray jeans. She's wearing leather sandals. She has an unusual necklace made of large beads. She's worn her hair up in a kind of a smashed ponytail. He watches her take in the house.

He hasn't shaved. The cotton shirt is well past its sell-by date. He probably smells. He hasn't brushed his teeth.

Why the abrupt change of mind? he wonders.

"Come into the kitchen," he says.

Webster goes ahead and sweeps up an armful of papers from the kitchen table and lets them fall onto the dining room table. "Bills," he says when he returns.

Webster wishes there were acronyms for what's about to happen.

"Would you like some coffee? I have a pot on."

"Sure," she said. "Thanks. I'll leave before she gets home. There's no need for her to know I was here."

"Rowan and I don't keep secrets."

A lie. Especially lately. He wonders how long it's been since he and Sheila had a conversation about their child's welfare. Did they ever?

He notices that her hands are trembling. "I've thought about Rowan every day since I left her," Sheila says.

She raises her chin and purses her mouth. Her mouth is still lovely, he'll give her that. Her long neck is mostly unwrinkled. He refuses to look at her body.

"If you've thought of Rowan every day, why haven't you called her? You say you've been sober for ten years."

"It's complicated," she says.

"Try me."

"I was afraid," Sheila says. Webster sets a cup in front of her. "The sobriety still feels new. I was afraid that if I opened that door on . . . you, Rowan, Vermont . . . I'd start drinking again. It wasn't something I positively knew. It was something I felt."

"Past tense."

"It's why I'm here."

Webster waits.

The grandfather clock in the hallway chimes the hour. Sheila smiles. "You kept that running," she says. "It's nice."

"You hardly notice it when you live with it all the time." He takes a sip of his own coffee. "Rowan's a great kid. But she's right at the edge. The edge of what, I don't know. She's testing, testing all the time. And, as I mentioned at your place, she seems to think she has a genetic disposition to alcohol. I told you that I found her here one night in a state of near blackout."

Sheila winces. "Webster, I'll do whatever I can to help, but I've missed a lot."

It's a bald statement, as true as anything she's said. He tries to imagine himself in her shoes, but his mind won't let him.

"Rowan's spinning just beyond my reach," Webster says. "She's let her grades go. She was about to go to college at the University of Vermont, but because she's currently failing English and calculus, she might not be able to enter in the fall."

"College," Sheila says with a wistful tone.

"She worked hard for it, too," he says. "And now she's almost blown it."

Sheila glances around the room. "I'm really surprised you didn't marry," she says. "You always seemed like the marrying kind."

"No time," he says. "When I didn't have work, I had Rowan. I had to be mother and father to her both." He pauses and stares at his ex-wife, wondering how she is taking this. An unwanted thought enters his mind.

"It's amazing," he says, "given where you

came from, that you were in Vermont that night at all. And then you married me." Webster pauses. "It's almost as though you decided, spur of the moment, to try on a life, like trying on a new dress. Then you realized that the waistband was too tight, that the sleeves weren't long enough. And so you chucked it. Me and Rowan and Vermont. Tossed it onto a heap on the floor."

"It was a dress I loved," Sheila says. "It didn't fit, but it was a dress I loved."

"As in adored? Couldn't live without?"

"I adored Rowan. You know I did."

"Tell me one thing," Webster says. "That night, on the land, the first time we made love, you weren't on the pill, were you?"

"I don't remember."

"Sure you do."

"It wasn't what you think," she says. "I didn't con you into marrying me. I felt that I could be careless with you because you made me feel safe."

Webster doesn't trust himself to speak.

Sheila leans forward. "Webster, I would like to see her."

"I'll have to ask Rowan," he says. "At the moment, she doesn't even know I've found you, never mind that you're sitting in her house."

Sheila smoothes her temples.

Webster looks out the kitchen window. "When I went to Chelsea, you were so cold, such a stranger, I decided I didn't want her to meet you."

"But I want to meet her," Sheila says. "I *am* her mother."

"I think you have to earn the title of mother," he says.

"You took that away from me."

"No, you took it away from yourself."

She picks up her purse. "This is ridiculous," she says.

Webster realizes he doesn't want her to leave. "What happened to you after you drove away that day? I've always been curious."

She gives him a hard stare. "I ditched the car and made my way to my sister's in Manhattan. I was drinking all the time then. She had a young child, too. I could hardly stand it. I made her life hell. At a bar, I met a man who lived in Piermont, just north of the city. I was nuts about him. I went up there to live with him, but I was still

drinking." She pauses. "One night, we had
a spectacular fight, and I went out into the
streets, drunk, swearing my ass off. I was
arrested on a drunk-and-disorderly and
put in jail overnight. Paul said he'd bail me
out on one condition: that I go into rehab.
That day. And so I did. In upstate New
York. When he came to pick me up after
my stint was done, he drove me to Mexico,
where we lived for eight years. His idea
was that if I was far away from familiar sur-
roundings, I wouldn't be as tempted to drink.
And . . . it worked."

"What happened to him?" Webster asks.

She tears the elastic off her ponytail
with an angry gesture. Her hair falls down
her back. "He died of pancreatic cancer."

Webster closes his eyes. "I'm sorry," he
says. "That must have been awful."

He gets up and walks around the room,
jiggling the change in his pockets. The love
of her life, and he died. He feels sorry for
her. On the other hand, she was the love of
*his* life. So where does that leave him?

The same place he's been for fifteen
years.

"I'll think about it," Webster says. "About
whether you should meet Rowan or not.

I'll speak to her. I'll give her that choice. I might not do that right away, though."

"Thank you," Sheila says.

"What changed your mind?" he asks.

"After you left, I leaned against the wall and slid right to the floor. I've made a life, Webster. A good life, but it's fragile. When you came—and I wondered if someday you would come—I was shaken. I reacted badly. But later, I thought about how you said Rowan was in trouble. I don't believe I can help at all, but I feel I should do something. That's all I can tell you."

He nods. That will have to be enough for now.

He will ask Rowan if she wants to do this. He suspects that she'll be wary at first, but then maybe curious enough to agree.

"I guess I'd better go," Sheila says. "Can I use the bathroom? As you know, it's a long ride."

"You remember where it is?"

"You never made a powder room?"

"I'll do it when I can't get up the stairs."

It's a good three minutes before Webster realizes his mistake. He bolts up two flights of stairs and finds Sheila sitting on Rowan's bed, weeping. She holds a stuffed animal that might once have been a dog.

"What the fuck? Sheila?"

Sheila looks up. "I gave her this," she says. "I had no idea she—you—had kept it. To think it's been here all these years." She hugs it to her chest, as if the toy were a child. "Webster, I've missed so much. Every bit of this room is a part of Rowan I know nothing about. All those years." She moans. "The desk, look. And the clarinet. And that mural? My God, Webster. There's so much in here, and I never saw any of it."

He didn't want her to experience this—or did he? He walks to Rowan's desk and rummages around in the top drawer. He finds what he wants and holds the picture out for Sheila to see. It's the photo taken right after Rowan's birth, the snap of Sheila holding Rowan. "She's had this with her all this time," he says.

Sheila takes the small wrinkled scrap, studies it, and holds it to her chest. She bends her head.

Webster turns away. Sheila's loss is horrific. As he listens to his ex-wife sob behind him, he wonders, were the situation reversed and he the alcoholic, would he be doing the same? He's pretty sure he would. He stands in the threshold, facing away from her, giving her some privacy.

He wants to go to her. He's used to caring for a person who's sobbing. It happens to him at least once a week. But he can't go to this particular person.

When he turns, she's standing. Her face is ruined. She glances around the room one more time, as if trying to memorize it.

"You good to drive?" Webster asks. He shakes his head. "I meant . . ."

"I know what you meant," Sheila says. "Yes, I'm good to drive." She pauses. "I know I'm different, Webster. But you're not. I recognize you."

"Is that good or bad?" he asks.

"It's good," she says.

He watches her walk to her car, which she parked on the street. Hers is a problem he can't fix. He wanted to help Rowan when he went to Chelsea, but what he really did was cause a fault line in his ex-wife to crack wide open.

Webster climbs up to Rowan's room to make sure Sheila hasn't left something behind, that the stuffed dog is back in its regular place. He stops as soon as he crosses the threshold. Sheila's perfume, which he didn't notice downstairs, is heavy in the room.

Shit.

He starts for the Lysol spray, but then thinks Rowan will want to know why he used it in her room. He decides to open the window. When he tries to raise it, however, he discovers that it's stuck. He checks that the latch is undone, and still the window won't budge. He tries the other window at the other end of the room. That one won't budge either.

What the hell?

He should have fixed these for Rowan months ago. He goes back to the first window. Should he wax the sash? If he gets it open and cracks only one window downstairs, he can always say he was trying to draw the heat out of the house. He gives it one more hard shove, loosening the frame, and something falls from a piece of molding above the window. A white notebook, measuring maybe three inches by two.

He stands with the thing in his hands. That Rowan has hidden it tells Webster to put it back, though he doesn't know which side of the molding it came from. Left or right?

He's royally screwed.

He opens to a random page.

**I don't want to be the star of my own afternoon special. I dislike drama in others. How it suddenly manufactures itself.**

Another page:

**How can a person be allowed to do that? Just leave her baby for fifteen years?**

And another page:

**Though he's often clueless, he's a good dad. I try not to forget that, even when he's at his most exasperating. He means well. He tries. He's mine. He loves me. And he's a hundred times better as a parent than most of my friends' parents.**

There are entries about Tommy and Gina and school that Webster skips. Another entry catches his eye.

**When Allison told me just before Christmas, I was shocked and couldn't fake it. My mother was pregnant with me when they got married! I realized**

**then that I didn't even know what their wedding date was. Why didn't I ever ask Dad? Because I was afraid it would make him sad? Allison knew because her mother, who worked for Gramps, knew. I still can't get used to the fact that I'm a mistake.**

Webster winces. He never told his daughter this simple fact?

And yet another entry:

**Don't you actually have to raise a child to be called a mother? I don't think I'd trade my life for anything. But there were days when I could have used a mother's advice about female stuff. A lot of nights when I had to be alone and didn't want to be. But no one can trade a life. It's a hypothetical. My mother wasn't here. It's like trying to imagine a sister or a brother. I can think about it for a couple of minutes, but then it doesn't go anywhere because it's . . .**

"What are you doing?"

Webster shuts the notebook with a snap.

Rowan, in maroon sweats, stands at the threshold.

"I was opening the window," Webster says, "and this fell, and I picked it up . . ."

"You're reading it," she says.

"It just . . ."

"You had no right to do that," Rowan says.

"It just fell open . . . ," he says, knowing how lame that sounds.

"YOU HAD NO FUCKING RIGHT!" his daughter yells. She puts her hands up against the jambs, as if holding herself back from charging. "That was mine! That was personal!"

"I know it was, I know it is," Webster protests, dropping the diary onto the bed.

"Get out!" Rowan screams. "Get out of this room, and don't ever, ever, ever come back. Ever. DO YOU HEAR ME?"

He has never seen this level of rage in his daughter. Rowan moves inside the room to allow her father to leave. As soon as he's gone, she slams the door so hard the attic shakes.

Webster knows that Rowan spent some part of the afternoon at the hairdresser with Gina. He won't make it easy for her to ignore him tonight. In his shirt and jeans, he waits for her to come down the stairs. Every time he thinks about the notebook, he cringes.

He can hear the clicking of high heels on the floor above him. He gapes when Rowan descends the stairs and walks into the kitchen. She's chosen a black dress, high waisted, that looks disturbingly like the one Sheila wore to their wedding. Rowan has pearls at her throat, a gift from her grandmother. His daughter walks to a mirror in the back hallway. She turns from side to side as a model might. His daughter is a woman, he tells himself. He's had this thought before, but each time he realizes it, it strikes him anew. He tries not to think about it at all, but Rowan reminds him again and again. When he sees the way she is with Tommy, his head fills with static, like a TV on a channel with no signal. It's none of his business, Webster tells himself over and over, but of course it is. How can it not be?

"Those are some heels," he says, the first time he's spoken to her since he left her room.

Rowan doesn't respond.

"I want to get your picture."

If she refuses him this, he'll know the rift is even deeper than he fears.

"Where?" she asks, her tone sullen.

"Where we always do them."

Rowan walks to the bare patch of kitchen wall, against which he has taken many pictures of his daughter: dressed as a bunch of grapes at Halloween; holding her softball trophy aloft, her eyes popping with pride; in her Girl Scout uniform, trying and failing to look serious.

Did she choose the black dress because he told her Sheila wore a similar dress to their wedding? Has he never shown Rowan the wedding pictures? He doesn't even know where they are—packed up in one of the many boxes in the cellar, he imagines. Was Rowan's an unconscious choice or a conscious one?

Rowan shakes her hands at her sides, trying to loosen herself up. He's seen her do that before games. He aims the digital in her direction, studies the screen, finds an angle he likes. She isn't smiling. He presses the silver button.

She doesn't ask to see the picture.

She wrestles with the small purse she is taking with her, performing her own triage. Lipstick in, hairbrush out, ditto hair spray, keys in, mirror in, cell phone in, hand cream out.

It's a beautiful summer night. He remembers similar weather for his own prom, now called the senior dance. He rented a tux. Do boys do that nowadays? He also remembers his date, Alicia, who had on a poufy dress with big shoulders. At the time, he wondered if she would put out, but she didn't. He's pretty sure they both had a decent time.

Webster glances at the clock over the sink. He can hear Tommy's car in the driveway.

Rowan opens her purse and studies the contents once again.

Of all times to look heartbreakingly lovely.

She snatches up a wrap from a chair. She opens the back door and closes it without a word. Webster walks into the dining room and watches through the window. Tommy is out of the car and on his way toward the house. He and Webster would have shaken hands. Perhaps a look of understanding might have passed between them.

Rowan's mincing walk in her stilettos might have made Webster laugh. Tommy opens the car door for Rowan, a nice touch. He walks around the back of his car, straightening his sport coat. No tux. When the engine starts, Webster turns away.

No kiss good-bye. No hug. No chance to tell his daughter she looks beautiful.

\* \* \*

Webster waits fifteen minutes and then climbs into his cruiser. He has an hour before he has to be at Rescue.

Webster drives away from town and up a long ridge. The moon will be .95 tonight, full tomorrow. He opens all the windows and lets the warm air blow through the car. If he had the radio on, and if he were twenty years younger, he'd sing. He hasn't been to the top of the ridge in nearly two decades. He's had calls halfway up, but he's never gone back to the place he once considered his life's dream.

He parks the cruiser at the edge of the road and slips out. The mountains are purple, green, and rust-colored, depending on the light and the high clouds. He wades into the tall grasses. He's amazed that whoever owns the land hasn't sold it to a developer or built on it himself. The previous owner passed away.

What were his dreams all those years ago? What did he hope for?

A house with a window.

Now his hopes are so much more complicated.

The grasses move. Part of what used to

be the owner's house has caved in, creating an oyster shell of a roof.

Would he have had a sheep or two? Dogs? A vegetable garden worthy of the name? A house he'd built, over time, having done much of the work himself?

Webster gazes in the direction of the high school, but he can't see it. Below him somewhere is the town he's lived in all his life. Will he die here, too? Will Rowan live nearby or will she move away with a family, the husband needing to live closer to a city? Webster can't imagine the future. For the first time since he was a boy, he feels alone.

Somewhere nearby is the place where Sheila and he conceived Rowan.

The what-ifs are dizzying.

Webster doesn't want to end the year on a sour note. He doesn't want his time with his daughter to come to such an ugly close. He's heard of teens who walked out the door without so much as a wave and went their own way, never to be heard from again.

He checks his watch. He has twelve minutes to get to Rescue. He can do it in five.

He decides that when Rowan leaves Hartstone, he will too. Maybe move closer to a city, see what that's all about. Maybe leave Vermont altogether. He wonders if he could hack being a medic in Manhattan, say, or in the Bronx. Shit, they'd toss him out the door. Emergency medicine is geography-specific. He remembers the "jumper down" call, how odd that was in Vermont. On the other hand, he guesses the medics in the Bronx have never seen a leg mangled by a tractor and baler.

There's something in the landscape, and he can't catch it. He wants it. Inside him, there's a powerful longing to hold on—a feeling both new to him and old.

He cuffs the high grasses.

What are you doing here?" Koenig asks.

"Switched my schedule so I'd have graduation free," Webster answers, pumping for his coffee. "What are you doing here?"

"They pulled in extra crew. Fireworks on Turnip Hill and the . . ." Koenig stops, catching himself.

"Senior dance," Webster finishes for him. "Yeah, I know."

"Rowan there?"

"She is," Webster says. "But she's with a good, responsible kid. More responsible than she is, truth be told."

"So you're not going to pace all over like you did last year the night of the junior prom?" Koenig makes a whirligig motion with his finger above his head.

"No," Webster says, taking a hot sip. What he really wants is an iced tea. "I'm worn out from worrying. Seriously, Koenig, how did you survive Annabelle's teenage years? What a ride."

"And Rowan's a *good* kid," Koenig reminds him.

Webster waves his hand back and forth. "We're not doing so well right now," he confesses.

"What's up?" Koenig asks.

"She caught me reading her diary," Webster says.

"You didn't."

"I did."

"You've stepped in it now."

"Don't I know it," Webster says. "She's not speaking to me."

"How the hell did you let that happen?" Koenig asks, shaking his head.

"Long story. It fell off a ledge, and I picked it up, and . . ."

"Yeah, yeah, yeah."

"Who you riding with tonight?" Webster

asks. Koenig now has the lead position on the number one ambulance. Webster has the new rig.

"Dunstan. Transfer from Bennington. Wife moved up here for a teaching job. Teaching jobs are harder to get these days than medic jobs."

"Really? I didn't know that. Seems like we've all had budget cuts."

"Yeah, but the town can't cut too far back on Rescue. The high school budget has been slashed to pieces over the last few years. Finally, they voted to reinstate the reading program. They needed a teacher."

"Don't know Dunstan. I'm riding with the probie."

"The guy with the ears?"

Webster nods. Koenig moves in closer and lowers his voice. "The guy's obsessed with blood pressures. He cuffs everyone he comes across. He even tried to do me."

Webster glances over at the probie, who's sitting in a corner with a manual. He smiles. Maybe it's time to let the kid off the hook.

"Probie," Webster says, walking toward him.

The probie stands, and Webster thinks he's going to salute. "Webster," he says.

"How you doing on those BPs?"

"Pretty good."

"OK," Webster says, rolling his sleeve. "Take mine."

The probie sets up the cuff. He seems confident. "One forty-two over eighty-six," he says when he's finished.

"You sure?" Webster can't believe the number. "Take it again."

The probie, nervous now, repeats the procedure. Webster notes how shiny the guy's shoes are.

"Same," says the probie.

"Precisely the same?"

"One forty-six over eighty-six."

"Koenig, come over here," Webster calls.

Koenig stands and walks to where Webster is. "Boss?"

"Take my blood pressure."

The probie gives Koenig the cuff. Again, the ritual is repeated. "One forty-two over eighty-eight," says Koenig. "Little high, don't you think?"

Webster groans. "Thanks," he says to Koenig.

"You're off the hook," Webster says to

the probie. "I'd better make an appointment to see my doctor."

Webster, shaken, sits in an armchair. He should get back on the treadmill at the workout center in the next room. Cut out the pies and the pasta. He's always had low blood pressure and because of that hasn't given it much thought. Age, stress, or lifestyle? he wonders.

He's asleep in the armchair when the tones come and he misses the beginning of the call. He sits upright and looks for the probie, who's already by the door.

"What is it?" he asks the guy standing next to him. Maybe it's the new transfer, Dunstan.

"Two females, seventeen and eighteen, at Gray Quarry. One's not breathing, suspected drowning. The other's not conscious, but breathing."

Webster springs out of his chair. His eyes find Koenig's.

"I'll be right behind you," his old partner says.

"I'm driving," Webster yells to the probie as he crosses the room. He runs to the rig.

Webster pulls out, siren wailing. The probie, alert, is pale.

Webster takes the rig right up to seventy and blows through the two intersections in Hartstone. "Do as I say, not as I do," he yells at the probie. A hundred yards behind him, he can see the lights of Koenig's rig, following.

Webster refuses to form a picture. Instead, he recites acronyms in his head. As good as a prayer in this case.

Webster speeds down 42, cars scurrying onto the shoulders. He knows precisely where the marble quarry is. When he was a kid, he used to swim there. He remembers, early in his career, when he was only a probie, saving a boy who nearly drowned in the dark water.

Two girls in the water at night. They wouldn't have been able to see a thing.

The rig bounces over the ruts of the road leading into the quarry. Ahead of him, Webster can see light from a wood fire.

He's out of the rig before the probie even has the door open. A boy who's been kneeling beside one of the girls stands up.

It's Tommy.

Webster's stomach falls to his shoes.

Webster straddles his daughter. Her eyes and mouth are covered in blood. He can see that someone—maybe Tommy—has tried to wipe it away.

"She went up on a dare," Tommy says. "I begged her not to. She wasn't breathing when I got her back on the ledge," Tommy says, "but I checked her airway and did CPR until she coughed. She vomited, too."

Webster bends his head in close to Rowan's mouth and counts. Ten respirations a minute. His daughter reeks of alcohol and vomit.

"Ten respirations," he shouts to the probie. "ETOH. Get the radial pulse and BP. I need the c-collar."

The probie hands it to him. Webster applies the collar. He whips out his flashlight and checks Rowan's pupils. Equal and responsive. He yells, "Rowan!" He checks her ears. No cerebral spinal fluid from the ears. He feels a pair of hands on his shoulders.

"I'm treating," Koenig says.

"It's Rowan," Webster says, refusing to move.

"I know it's Rowan, Webster. Stand up!"

Webster stands and moves to one side.

He watches as Koenig kneels beside Rowan. The medic yells for the backboard. For the first time, Webster sees that Rowan is in her bra and underpants.

"For God's sakes, Koenig, cover her."

Koenig lays a warming blanket over her. Tommy is crying, his own briefs soaking wet. Webster twists his head to see a pair of medics from yet another rig performing CPR on another girl. Unresponsive. Her skin already going gray, even in the artificial light. A cop next to the medics is asking questions and taking names. Above them, under the full moon, the branches sway. The light plays with the dark water.

"Get this kid a blanket," Webster yells, pointing at Tommy. "What happened?" he asks the boy.

"Rowan and Kerry were daring each other to climb onto the tree limb there, and another guy was egging them on." Webster notices that Tommy doesn't say the name. "Rowan had been drinking, and I was begging her not to go. I was actually holding her back. She shook me off and started climbing. I took off my clothes just in case. And then she fell, and she must have hit her head beneath the water, because I could see right away that something wasn't right. I went in after her."

"Who went in after the other girl?"

"The guy who was egging them on."

"You brought Rowan to the edge. You did the CPR."

Tommy nods.

"Where'd you learn to do that?"

"Boy Scouts. Years ago."

"The protocol has changed, but you probably saved her life," Webster says.

Koenig is doing the sternal rub and getting nothing.

Rowan. Wake up, honey.

"Probie, call it in," Koenig yells. "We're going to need an airlift."

"Seventeen-year-old unresponsive female needs airlift to Burlington," the probie says into his radio. "Head trauma resulting from fall onto rocky ledge. Suspected fractured dislocated right shoulder. Pupils equal and reactive. ETOH. Respirations ten. BP one ten over sixty-four. Not responsive to pain. And we'll need an ETA and rendezvous point for the airlift."

The probie helps Koenig perform the logroll in order to put Rowan onto the backboard. Koenig attaches the orange head blocks at either side of her forehead and chin with Velcro. In the shiny blanket, she looks like a mummy from a strange world.

"We're taking her to the track at the high school," the probie says to Koenig. "The flight medics will prepare her for an airlift."

Webster turns and vomits. He knows what an airlift means.

A cop takes his arm. "You OK?"

"I'm fine," Webster says, standing and wiping his mouth with his sleeve. "I'm riding with her," he says to Koenig.

"I'm treating," Koenig reminds him.

"Do another sternal."

"She's not responding."

"Do it anyway."

Koenig gives it everything he has.

"Was that a moan?" Webster asks.

"I didn't hear a moan."

Webster holds Rowan's hand as the rig speeds to the high school, the building his daughter so recently left. He massages her fingers, then just holds her hand, as if it were a lifeline: she giving the life to him, because without her . . .

Webster feels Rowan's hand stiffen just as she begins to seize. Webster has seen seizures dozens of times, but the adrenaline shoots through to his fingertips. Koenig is already at work. Two milligrams of Ativan IV to quell the seizure. Webster's heart rate increases with Rowan's shaking. A seizure is never a good sign.

Webster watches as the seizure subsides. The last thing a medic wants to do is to give an alcohol-depressed patient Ativan, but it has to be done. Webster and Koenig don't say a word. Webster fingers the hair away from his daughter's face.

He thinks about the procedures that await Rowan before the airlift. The Seven Ps. Prepare: get all the equipment ready, none of which Webster wants to think about. Preoxygenate for five minutes. Premedicate: 1.5 milligrams per kilogram of weight of lidocaine two minutes before intubation. Paralyze: the medics will paralyze Rowan for the duration of the trip to Burlington so that she won't seize on them. The idea of his daughter being medically paralyzed makes Webster want to scream.

Pass the tube. Proof of placement. Postplacement care.

The fire department sent all of its engines to set up a landing zone. Webster squeezes Rowan's hand. It's good to talk to an unconscious patient. According to some, Rowan might be able to hear what's happening around her even if she can't respond.

"So, Rowan, honey," Webster says. "Here's what's going to happen. We're at the high school track so a helicopter can land. The helicopter is going to take you to a very good hospital in Burlington. In fact, it's the university hospital. Ironic, huh? You're going to college. I'll be with you every step of the way. Even though you got a good hit on the noggin, this is just routine. You remember I've told you about airlifts before? Nothing to it. Just like answering a call, but on a different vehicle. I'm going to keep holding your hand. You're tough, Rowan. We both know that. Pretty soon, after they get you to the hospital, it will be time to wake up. This is important, Rowan, so listen up. You'll have to concentrate when you get there. It might feel hard to do, but you have to do it. And don't worry if you don't remember everything I just said, because I'll be there with you, holding your hand and making sure they do everything right. You're in good hands, OK? The best."

Webster watches the helicopter circle and then land. The pilot won't want Webster on the bird. He moves behind Rowan when he sees the airlift crew running toward the rig with their own stretcher. The nurse and the medic will hear Koenig's report, switch Rowan to their equipment, and then return to the helicopter.

"Weight?" the flight nurse asks.

"About one twenty-five," Webster says.

"That medic is the girl's father," Koenig explains.

"The patient's father is a medic?"

"He's been keeping her calm," says Koenig. "Talking to her."

Webster jumps out of the rig as soon as the chopper crew has Rowan on their stretcher. He walks with them, holding Rowan's hand. He talks to the helicopter medic ahead of him.

"I promised her I'd go with her," Webster says.

The medic doesn't reply.

"I'm one eighty. She's one twenty-five. That's three hundred five. Under the limit."

The medic is still unresponsive. Webster wants to yell at him, but he knows that to do that is the fastest way to get himself kicked off the chopper.

The fire engines have booted up their lights, making a fierce perimeter that's hard to look at. Webster can feel his shoes on the cinders, then on the grass, the wind from the propeller blowing his hair. The scene feels dreamlike and terrifying. He has to break his handhold when they reach the bird.

The pilot radios back to the medic, wanting to know weight and how long it's going to take to go through the Seven Ps. "Ten to fifteen on the Ps," the medic says. "The girl is one twenty-five. The dad's a medic. Can we extend a courtesy ride?"

"Weight?"

"One eighty," says the medic.

"You're looking at him," the pilot says. "Weight?"

"One eighty," the medic repeats without hesitation.

"Give him the protocol."

"I know what to do," Webster says before he needs to be told. He climbs into the chopper and sits up front with the pilot.

He won't be able to hold Rowan's hand, but he'll be there. Maybe she'll sense his presence, even through all the medication. He's heard of unconscious patients who claim to have heard conversations.

The fifteen minutes prep seems like an agony of time to Webster. He wills the chopper to take off. He wants Rowan in the ER as soon as possible.

When he feels the odd angle of the lift, Webster goes into silent medic mode, as if he were a rookie, observing. Head turned, he concentrates on the medic's hands, the lines, the monitor, the nurse—watching it all unfold as it should. He tries not to look at Rowan's face, which is far too calm.

He has little sense of time during the ride. He notes the lights of Burlington and can feel the helicopter descending to the roof of the hospital. Another team will meet the chopper, and once again Rowan will be transferred.

Webster remembers his mother's admonition: *You can't regret anything that leads to your children.* Webster wants to add a corollary: *You will regret something you did that caused your child harm.* If only Webster had forbidden Rowan to go to the dance. If he hadn't read her diary, she might have lingered at the house, waited for Tommy to knock on the door, and somehow those few minutes might have altered the universe in such a way as to cause her not to drink so much, not to be so willing to take a dare. If he'd tried to get in touch with Sheila sooner. If he hadn't sent his wife away, depriving Rowan of a normal family life.

Webster feels the jolt as the chopper lands. The ER doc and nurse have the door open at once and are already wheeling Rowan into the hospital, the chopper medic giving his report as he jogs. Webster hops out and runs to catch up. He won't have a problem with the ER personnel. Any parent would be allowed access to his child.

The ER doctor assesses Rowan. He orders blood tests, an X-ray on the shoulder, a CAT scan of the brain. If that doesn't show what he wants, he'll order up an MRI. Webster hopes that Rowan will wake up on her own before the MRI.

"You the dad?" the ER doctor asks.

"Yes. How is she?"

"Right now, critical. I've ordered tests, but we don't know what we'll find. As you know, prognosis is guarded with head injuries. We need to know how much swelling of the brain there's been. You ought to get yourself a cup of coffee and some food. After the tests, they'll wheel her up to the ICU, and you can be with her then." The doctor wraps a solid hand around Webster's upper arm, and the gesture frightens him. Does the doctor know more than he's telling?

Webster finds his way to the cafeteria and stands in line. All hospital food is the same: fattening and unhealthful. He wonders how much he actually weighs. He might not get back on the scale until he's been running for a couple of weeks. He passes through the entire line and finds nothing he can stomach except a tangerine and the cup of coffee. He searches for an empty table. He doesn't want to talk, and the uniform might elicit talk.

He wonders what happened to Rowan's dress. Where Tommy is and how he's doing. Maybe later, he'll call the kid and report and ask him to drive the cruiser up to

Burlington. No, Tommy can't do that; Webster has the keys in his pocket. It doesn't matter. None of it is important.

The only relevant fact is the nature of the swelling inside his daughter's head.

Webster holds Rowan's hand. The low beeps from the IV, the steady signal from the monitor, and the crackling from the blood pressure cuff—all of it make a symphony both horrific and comforting. Proof that she's still alive, waiting, as he is, for a moment of recognition. He pictures the long fall in the night, the unseen rock protruding, the black water. A boy, standing in his underwear, calling out and begging. Amid the low laughter, the thunk, the odd trajectory, the shallow splash of feet, the audible warning to hurry . . . hurry . . .

He imagines the glow of the firelight, the

dumbstruck faces, some alert at once while others gape. The boy diving into the inky quarry, calling out again and crying. The resistance as the boy drags the girl to the edge, the weight like heavy cloth moving through the water.

In the ICU, the lights are harsh and unforgiving. Already the purple-blue below her eyes, the gauze wrapped around her head. Webster prays as he hasn't in years. "Please," he says aloud.

He brings Rowan's slender hand to his forehead and whispers.

After a while, he stands up and goes outside into a corridor, where he is allowed to make a call. He rummages in his wallet for a piece of paper Sheila gave him as she left his house. He waits through the rings and is relieved when the phone is answered.

"You'd better come," he says.

The longer the patient is in a coma, the less likely that patient is to recover. This is a fact Webster knows, and he wonders, as he sits in a chair beside the bed, what kind of healing is happening inside her skull, and why it's taking so long.

When Sheila comes, she has on a pair of black cotton pants and a white dress shirt and looks as helpless as he feels. She carries a small duffel.

"They said the next forty-eight hours will tell," Webster reports as they stand in the hallway.

Will tell what? Webster wants to know. He didn't ask, afraid of the answer. "They said an MRI might be necessary."

Sheila leans against a wall.

"Today they're going to attempt surgery on her shoulder. I asked the neurosurgeon whether or not they'd have to drill into Rowan's head to relieve the pressure, and he said they didn't expect to have to do that just yet."

"Yet."

"Yet."

"You look utterly exhausted," Sheila says.

"I am, but I don't dare leave her."

When he sits with his daughter, he talks to her, no longer believing that she can hear him. He does it the way an agnostic might say a prayer, hedging his bets. He has told her everything he can remember from her childhood, which isn't much, his memories limited to the photos he's taken of her, and most of them celebrating special occasions. According to the pictures, all of Rowan's life has been a special occasion. He hasn't talked to her about the last photo he took, of Rowan against the wall in her black dress and stilettos, no smile on her face. He doubts he will ever be able to look at that picture. Should it come to it, he'll have Koenig print out the pictures on the disk, give him everything but that one.

But it won't "come to it." It simply won't.

"Let me sit with her," Sheila suggests.

Webster is surprised by the offer. "It might upset her too much if she wakes up and you're there."

"We should be so lucky," Sheila says.

Webster leads Sheila into the room. He watches as his ex-wife gets her first glimpse of their daughter at age seventeen. A thin body under the sheet, attached by lines to different monitors, a head bandaged. The color drains from Sheila's face.

"I know. It's terrible," Webster says.

"She's beautiful," Sheila says.

"Sometimes I talk to her. I hold her hand."

Sheila sits. For long time, she is still. Then she makes a tentative gesture toward Rowan's hand.

"It's all right," Webster says. "The injury is on the other side."

"My hands are cold."

"She'll warm you up."

Sheila reaches for Rowan's slender hand. It's a calm moment, though Webster feels electricity in the room. He remembers his vigil at Rowan's side fifteen years earlier, the one Sheila couldn't participate in.

"It'll be a miracle if I sleep," Webster says. "I'll probably be back in an hour. There's an inn attached to the hospital they tried to get me to go to after I got here. You have my cell phone number. Call me if there's any change at all."

"Of course," she says.

"Are you afraid?" he asks.

"Yes," she says.

When Webster returns, he tells Sheila that he's booked her a room at the inn. He gives her the key.

"Did you sleep?" she asks.

"I might have dozed."

"Well, that's all right then."

"Did anything happen here?"

"I held her hand," Sheila says.

"Oh, God," Webster says. "This is all wrong."

"I talked to her."

"What did she say?"

"She said she was fine."

Webster smiles at the mild joke.

Tommy and Gina come bearing flowers, which they don't allow in the ICU. The sight of Rowan makes Gina cry and causes Tommy to look away. Koenig and his wife, Ruth, make the trip, bringing a meal that Webster can't eat. Even the probie comes straight off his shift, silently standing near the door, awkward in the situation. Webster thanks him before he leaves.

Webster bends to kiss Rowan on the cheek. He wants to feel her breath.

"Your mother is here," he tells his sleeping daughter. "She came all the way from Boston. Actually, Chelsea, where she lives. She came to watch over you. I think you

might like her. She's an excellent painter.
I've seen the paintings. You'd like them,
too. It seems pretty obvious to me that
she's been thinking about you all this time.
She cried when she saw Puppy. No, forget
that."

Webster thinks.

"I forgot to tell you that she has a sense
of humor. I thought she'd lost it, but it's
there. Maybe it will come back full force,
I don't know. She sat here with you while
I dozed in a room at the inn attached to
the hospital. She held your hand. I don't
know if you could feel that or not. She
said she talked to you and that you told
her you were fine. I hope you were telling
the truth . . ."

Webster is running out of things to say
to Rowan. Is she slipping farther and farther away from him with each passing
hour? This is what he fears the most. That
everything is already lost, and he doesn't
know it.

He panics when he wakes and sees the
clock. Rowan is now in hour forty-nine. He's
aware of other people in the room.

He stands, alert. "What's happening?" he asks.

"We're taking her for another CAT scan," one of the nurses answers.

"She's already had the MRI. Why?" Webster asks.

"The doctor will be in shortly to talk to you. This is routine," the nurse adds. "Nothing to be alarmed about."

"Routine?" Webster asks, incredulous. "What's routine about a child being in a coma for forty-nine hours?"

"This shouldn't take long," the nurse says.

Webster walks to the window and stares at the lit parking lot. It's still dark, three thirty in the morning. Two solid days since Rowan and the other girl, Kerry, fell into the quarry. He thinks about the other father, living with his own awful news. Webster should have given the parents a call. He doesn't even know the girl's last name. Not a friend of Rowan's that he knew about. He could call Tommy, but he doesn't want to call only to tell the boy that there's been no change.

Two days is nothing, he tells himself. He knows of cases in which the patient was out for a week or more and then recovered. Not a hundred percent recovery, but a comeback just the same. No, it's not the same. Rowan has to come back as herself with all her faculties. He is still praying for that. Maybe there will come a day when he'll be able to accept less. He can't imagine it.

"Mr. Webster."

Webster turns to see the neurologist in the doorway, a guy named Lockhart. He has a sport coat on, a tie loosened. A thick head of dark hair. He looks twenty-two. "We've taken your daughter down for a CAT scan," the doctor says. "It's been forty-eight hours, and I think it's time for another look. I don't have to tell you that the longer it takes for her to regain consciousness, the more difficult the outcome may be."

No, you didn't need to remind me of that.

"I'm hopeful that we'll be able to see something that will give us a clue as to how to proceed. If we need to drill into her skull to relieve the pressure, we will. But it's not something we want to do."

Webster is silent. Appalled.

"I've personally witnessed a lot of miracles, Mr. Webster. I don't want to get your hopes up, but I've seen patients come fully alert after a week, two weeks . . ."

"What's taking so long?" Webster can't help but ask.

"The brain remains a mystery. If we had a drug to wake her up without risk, we'd give it to her."

Webster thanks the man and makes his way down to the cafeteria. The room, without Rowan in it, is a place of horror.

Later that morning, Sheila arrives to spell him. Webster stands and meets her in the doorway. She asks Webster if there has been any change. He tells her what Lockhart told him. Sheila shuts her eyes and shakes her head.

"Don't do that to me," he says.

"Don't do what?"

"Shut your eyes and shake your head. I can be afraid, but you can't. I need you to stay strong. Just keep telling me she's fine."

"All right."

Webster stands outside while Sheila enters the room and takes the chair. This time, she reaches for Rowan's hand at once. Webster can see that she is talking to their daughter.

Webster sleeps for five hours and then returns to the room. Sheila says she'll get something to eat. When he's alone with his daughter, he sits and looks at the same impassive face he's been looking at for more than two days. He tries to remember what it felt like to be her Little League coach.

"OK, Rowan. You can do it. It's game time. Nothing to be afraid of out there. You've gotta step up to the plate. Get into your stance. Take your time. Do not swing at the first pitch. But the next fat pitch you see coming your way, you give it everything you've got. I've seen you hit it over the fence, so I know that you can do this. The game's on the line. It's the bottom of the ninth, your team is down a run, one out. You've got a runner on first. All you need is a good solid hit. A good hit gets the runner home. Then you still have two outs to go. I see you winning this game. But it's up to you. No double plays, right? This game is not going to end with you barely off the plate. I'm your coach, and you need to listen to me."

Webster pauses.

"Anything?" he asks Rowan.

He waits.

"You got anything to say to me? Questions you need to ask? 'Cause you're up at bat right now, and you need to do this."

Webster waits.

"Honey?" he asks. "Sweetie?"

Nothing.

Webster sits with his face close to hers. He's used Listerine. Maybe that will snap her out of it.

"OK, listen. I'm going to wait here. The game will wait, too. But whenever you're ready, you just give the signal, and we'll be ready. I'm going to hold your hand. I'm not going to leave you. You give me the high sign."

The second CAT scan shows no improvement.

Sixty hours pass.

Sheila and Webster spell each other in six-hour shifts. Once, when he passes by the room, Sheila is sitting close to Rowan's face, speaking in a soft voice. Another time,

Sheila is sitting near the foot of the bed, her head bent to the covers.

On Webster's watch, Tommy comes with his father. "We brought you a car," Tommy says.

Webster stands and shakes hands with Tommy's father, who is shorter than his son. Barrel-chested, going bald. "We're all waiting with you," the father says. "We're all praying with you. Here are the keys. It's a navy VW and has a pink daisy in the vase on the dashboard."

Webster looks from father to son. Tommy has eyes only for Rowan.

"My wife's," Tommy's father says. "Sorry about the flower."

"Thank you," Webster says. "Tommy, you want to sit there with Rowan a minute? I'm beat. I need some fresh air. I'll be back in ten."

Tommy's father and Webster take the elevator to the lobby. "Why don't you walk me to the car, so I'll know where it is," Webster suggests.

"My son blames himself," the father says as they set out. "He believes that if he tried harder, it wouldn't have happened."

"That's not how I see it. Your son did everything he could to stop her, but Rowan was drunk and wouldn't listen to him. You should be proud of your boy. He saved her life with the CPR. I'm proud of him. I'm grateful."

"He's useless now," the father says.

"I'm not surprised."

"This must be hell for you."

"On a scale of one to ten, it's a god-damn ten," Webster says as they approach the parking lot. "But not as hard as the other girl's parents have it."

Tommy's father shoves his hands in his pockets. The sun sparks off the windshields.

"The funeral is tomorrow. Tommy doesn't know whether to go or not."

"I'd go if I were in town," Webster says. "To pay my respects."

"I'll tell him that," Tommy's father says. "There's the car."

Webster shades his eyes and sees the navy bump. "Got it," he says. "Thank you again. I can't say how long I'll be here."

"Not to worry," the father says, shaking his hand. "My wife wanted to do this for you and Rowan."

"I'll send Tommy down."

* * *

When Webster makes it back to the ICU, he can see through the glass that Tommy is crying. Good for you, Webster thinks. He waits a minute and then spots a nurse coming his way.

"Do me a favor," he says to the nurse. "Just go in and pretend to be checking Rowan. That kid there is her boyfriend, and he's crying, and I want him to be able to collect himself before I go in."

The nurse smiles. "Done," she says.

Webster stands out of sight and gives it another minute. When he walks in, Tommy is at the foot of the bed and his nose and eyelids are red.

"Your dad's waiting in the parking lot. Please thank your mom for me."

"I will," Tommy says.

"She's going to be OK," Webster promises the boy.

Webster can see that Tommy doesn't believe him.

After five and a half more hours of sitting, the nurses arrive and ask Webster to leave the room while they give Rowan a sponge bath. Sheila finds him in the cafeteria.

"It's stopped raining?" he asks her.

"It's hot and sticky."

She examines the tray before him. "Your usual? Coffee and a pastry?"

"I don't seem to be able to eat anything else."

"I'll be right back," she says.

Webster picks up his cup, sets it down again. When this is over, he might swear off coffee. Sheila returns with a tray. She removes a bowl of soup and hands it across to Webster. "Minestrone," she says. She does the same with a small plate. "Ham sandwich." She gives him utensils and a napkin.

"Thank you," Webster says.

"You look terrible," she says.

"You look nice."

A memory is triggered. Webster tries to grab it. Keezer's when she was a waitress, and he was just getting off the graveyard shift. Eighteen years ago.

Surprising himself, Webster reaches for Sheila's wrist. "I don't think I can take this much longer," he says. "This is hell, just hell."

"You have to take it," Sheila says. "You don't have any choice."

He releases her. He's left pink marks on the inside of her arm. "It must be hell for you, too," he says.

"It is. But I'm glad to be here. I don't think it helps Rowan one bit for me to sit with her, but it helps me."

Webster nods. He understands.

Just after midnight on Wednesday, with his head resting at the edge of the bed, Webster thinks he feels Rowan's fingers move inside his own. He sits up with a start, not sure if he is dreaming or not. "Rowan?" he asks.

He waits ten minutes before she does it again. He has to be sure it's not a reflex.

"Rowan, this is Dad. Your hand is in mine. If you can hear me, squeeze my hand or wiggle your fingers."

He feels the movement of her fingers right away.

"Oh, God. Oh, Rowan."

Webster stands, opens the door, and shouts for a nurse.

The nurse, when she comes, bends over Rowan, prepared to examine her pupils, but his daughter, bless her heart, opens her eyes on her own, startling the nurse.

Webster has never seen anything more beautiful.

Rowan seems dazed, unable to focus. She can't speak. But Webster is OK. He knows she will.

Ow," Rowan says, her first word. "My head."

Webster clutches her hand. He may never let go.

"I'm not surprised," he says. "You've had a nasty crack."

"I did?"

"You don't remember it?" Webster asks.

"No," she says, trying to think, but he can see that the effort is too difficult.

Dr. Lockhart booms from the doorway, "I hear we've got good news!" He walks to the other side of the bed. "Well, I guess so. Welcome back, Rowan Webster."

Webster can see that Rowan is confused. Who is this man?

"I'm Dr. Lockhart," the neurologist explains. "I've been treating you. You had a
serious head injury."

Webster observes Lockhart as he inspects Rowan's pupils. He asks her to move
her arms and legs, wiggle her toes, press
down on his hands, and squeeze his fingers. Then he asks Rowan questions. What
year is it? Who's the president? What month
is it? What's her address? Rowan is OK
with the year, a little slow with the president,
completely confused about the month, but
she knows her address.

"I'll give you a B," the doctor tells Rowan.
"I'll come back and ask you again in two
hours, and I guarantee you'll get a better
grade."

"I'm at Mercy?" Rowan asks her father
when the doctor has gone.

"No, we're in Burlington."

Rowan glances around the room. "Why
are we in Burlington?"

"You were airlifted here. What's the last
thing you remember?"

She studies him for a minute. He hopes

he's not the last thing she remembers. "I was at a dance," she says.

"You remember anything after that?"

"It was hot in the gym," she says. "And someone said we ought to go swimming." She pauses. "And I remember being afraid, but I don't know why."

It would be surprising if Rowan remembered every minute leading up to the crack on the head. Trauma erases time.

"I'll tell you what happened," he says to her. "You tried to climb a tree over Gray Quarry. You fell and hit your head on a hidden ledge in the water. This was at two thirty in the morning on Saturday. Tommy went in after you, but when he got you on shore, you weren't breathing. He did CPR on you. You coughed up water and started breathing on your own, but you wouldn't wake up. Let's see. The incident happened very early on Saturday. It's early in the morning of Wednesday right now. You've been out for four days."

Rowan tries to comprehend this. "Where did I go?" she asks.

"That's what I'd like to know!" Webster says, laughing.

"So that's why you look like a wreck."

"You have no idea," he says. "The worst four days of *my* life, that's for sure."

"The nurse said I went up in a helicopter."

"You certainly did."

"And I missed it? I never even knew I was there? I've never been in a helicopter."

"You didn't miss anything," Webster says. "It was a horrible ride. Someday, when you're better, I'll tell you all about it. And you and I will take a helicopter ride just for fun."

"Did you know I would wake up?"

"No."

"I'm sorry, Dad," Rowan says.

Webster smiles. "Rowan, you don't have to be sorry about anything in the world. You woke up. That gives you a totally free pass."

"Forever?" she asks.

He squints. "I didn't say forever."

A team of nurses asks him to move outside the room. He's happy to do whatever they require. They explain that they want to try to get Rowan to sit up and then to stand. They'd like to be able to take the

Foley catheter out, and they might try to clean her up, depending. They suggest he get something to eat.

"She'll be right here when I get back?" Webster asks, making sure.

"She'll be right here."

"Because I don't like leaving her."

"I *promise* you she'll be right here," the nurse says, "but she might be sleeping."

"All right," Webster says reluctantly, reaching in his pocket for his phone.

By the time he descends to the cafeteria, he's unexpectedly ravenous. He wants sugar. He selects two pieces of apple pie and a doughnut, accompanied by a cup of coffee. The pie tastes so good, he moans with pleasure. When he finishes, he calls Sheila, Tommy, Gina, and Koenig, in that order. Tommy is speechless, Gina starts to cry, and Koenig whoops. Sheila is the most relieved. She says, *I'm so happy,* and he can feel the release in her voice, the lifting of the terrible worry.

"I'll come right now," she says.

"I think you'd better wait. She doesn't know you're here. She doesn't even know I've been in touch with you. Let me talk to her first, and then I'll call you."

"Will she make her graduation?"

"If I have to carry her."

When Webster returns to his daughter's room, she's asleep. He sits next to her, as he has been doing, but doesn't wake her, even though he wants to, just to make sure.

The room looks better for her having woken from the coma. The curtains aren't as dreary, the television not as dull. Webster knows it's simply his state of mind. He gazes at his daughter.

The doctors had to shave the top of her head in order to suture a deep laceration, and, as a consequence, she has a four-by-two-inch bald spot with a little fuzz starting. When she was in a coma, her hair was flattened to her skull, and she seemed to be all widow's peak. But someone in the last hour has taken the time to comb her hair so that her bangs cover most of her forehead. Rowan will think the bald patch a problem for graduation.

Though now she might not care.

A nurse stands in the doorway. Webster turns.

"She was still woozy when she sat up,

so we didn't try to get her to stand. We took the catheter out, and she was able to use the bedpan. She'll be moved to a semi-private room and be there at least two or three days, maybe longer. She has to be able to walk unassisted. There may be issues with balance."

"She graduates from high school on Sunday."

The nurse chews a lip. "That's going to be pretty tight." She pauses. "How are you doing?"

"A hundred percent better."

"You need to get some sleep," the nurse says. "I can't order you to do it, but you know I'm right."

"I hate to leave her."

"This is the ICU. She's being monitored every second." The nurse smiles. "She's out of the woods, Mr. Webster. I think you can start to relax now."

He stands immobile in the shower for twenty minutes, letting the hot water remove the kinks. Then he scrubs and washes his hair and slides between the covers. It's nearly dawn when he shuts his eyes.

It's noon the same day when wakes up.

He comes alert and has to remind himself that his daughter has come out of the coma. He lies back against the pillow, his arms crossed behind his head, and savors that sweet sensation. A bright sun tries to enter the room at the edges of the curtains. He wonders if today will be too soon to mention Sheila to Rowan. It's a gamble on his part—the notion that Rowan might better absorb the idea of Sheila visiting in a hospital setting than at home, which is full of memories—but he thinks he should try it.

He dresses and half jogs back to the hospital. He finds Rowan in her new room, awake, sitting up and eating lunch. He stands, wide-eyed, in the doorway. A simple sight and yet so astonishing.

"Hey," he says.

"Who are you?" Rowan asks.

Webster's heart thuds against his chest.

"Are you my doctor?"

"Rowan, this is Dad. You don't remember me?"

"My father works with the Hartstone Rescue Squad."

His heart kicks again.

"Rowan. Sweetheart."

"Oh, I had you good! You should see your face."

"You . . ." He grabs her foot under the sheet and shakes it.

She laughs. "I'm having a turkey sandwich. And custard. I never knew how much I loved custard."

"You're a rascal," he says, still finding it hard to believe his eyes. "You look wonderful."

"Dad, I look like a freak! I've got a ten-inch bald spot on top of my head and a cast on my shoulder."

"The bald spot is four by two inches."

"It feels huge. I wish I could wear a hat."

"Let's see what the nurses say about that. I'll go buy you one."

"A Red Sox hat," she says.

"How about a UVM hat?" he asks.

"We're close to UVM right now, aren't we?" she asks, as if just registering that fact.

"We're *at* UVM," he says.

"But don't get me a baseball cap. Get me one of those, oh, you don't know, it's like a golf cap, except bigger, and I can get my ears under it. I should really pick it out."

"I'll see what I can do," he says.

"If only Gina were here. She'd know what I meant. Do you know what happened to my cell phone?"

He hasn't seen her cell phone or the purse she took to the dance. Maybe Tommy has them. "I'll see if I can find out," he says.

Webster sits on her bed. Who gets reprieves like this?

"Want half my sandwich?" she asks.

He tells her no, even though he's hungry. "Gina came," he says. "Tommy came with his dad. Tommy saved your life. Did I mention that?"

Rowan looks concerned. "I wish I could remember something."

"Maybe you will, maybe you won't," he says, deciding to take Rowan up on her offer. He picks up the other half of her sandwich. Turkey, white bread, no dressing. Tastes delicious. "It's probably better off if you don't."

"I was drinking, wasn't I?" she asks, wiping her mouth with a napkin. She has to do everything now with her right hand.

"Yes, you were."

"Are you mad?"

"Mad? Yes." He meets her eyes. "But

mostly all I've felt is fear. You're a very lucky girl."

Webster won't tell her about Kerry, the girl who didn't make it. Not yet.

"But I'll be rip-roaring furious if you ever get drunk again," he warns.

"I'm sorry."

"Do you know why you did it?"

"I just did it," she says, moving the tray out of her way.

"You were angry when you left the house."

"Maybe I was still angry," she says. "It's hard to know."

"A lot of people came here to visit you," Webster tells her. "Tommy's dad lent me a family car. The cruiser is back at Rescue, and I had the keys in my pocket. They're a good family."

"I knew you'd like them," Rowan says. "Dad, I'm so sorry. I can't imagine how horrible this was for you. And I've been such a bitch."

"You certainly have," he says. "If you feel up to it, I'm going to ask you to do some makeup work. If you fail math and English, you won't be able to go to UVM."

"I'm *at* UVM, remember?"

"Do you remember the last time you saw me?"

"The night of the dance. I was furious with you."

"Do you remember why?"

"You read my diary."

"So you're not angry now?"

"Now? I'd have to be crazy to be angry now. Though I'm a little pissed off about my hair."

"I didn't read much, if that's any consolation."

She shrugs and sits up straighter. "It doesn't seem like such a big deal. But I don't want to think about it. It's embarrassing."

"Nothing's embarrassing now," he tells her.

"I'm still hungry. How long did I go without eating?"

"Four days."

"Cool. I wonder if I lost weight," she says. She presses the sheets down at the sides of her hips and stomach.

"The last thing you need to worry about is your weight." Webster finds her foot again under the sheet and holds on to it. "Look, there's something I want to tell you."

Rowan waits.

"Your mother has been here nearly the whole time you've been unconscious."

"My what?"

"I found her just last week. When I told her about the accident, she came right away. She kept me from losing my mind."

His daughter's eyes open wide. He waits for the fact to sink in.

"Where did you find her?" she asks.

"She's been living in Chelsea," he says, moving closer to her on the bed.

"Where is that?"

"It's a city near Boston. I think once when you were younger, we talked about where she came from, and I showed you on a map."

Rowan leans back and inches the covers closer to her chin. "How did you find her?"

"On the Internet. It was easier than I thought. I drove to Chelsea and talked to her."

"And you didn't tell me?"

"You weren't in a mood to hear about it," he says. "I had to think about how to tell you. And then, next thing I know, I'm in a helicopter with you strapped to a backboard."

"What's she like?"

"She's an artist, Rowan, a painter. She's very good. She's had a complicated and difficult life. But the reason I'm telling you this now is that she wants to meet you."

"She wants to meet?" Rowan pulls the covers right to her mouth. She looks stricken.

Webster hopes that a nurse doesn't choose this moment to come to the door. "If you would like to meet her," Webster says, "it can be arranged."

"Meet her *here*? Like this?"

"Would you rather wait until you get home?"

Rowan lowers her eyes, thinking. "Will I make it home for graduation?"

"Absolutely. But probably not much sooner than that."

"Can I think about it?"

"Of course," he says.

Rowan scrutinizes him. "Are you and she . . . ?"

"Are we what?"

"You know . . . like, reuniting?"

"No," he says, shaking his head and smiling. "No, Rowan, we're not. We've talked, but it's mostly been about you."

"What's she like?"

"The same and different. Not as feisty. Older. All of which means nothing to you, since you don't remember her when she was younger."

"No, but I can imagine. Or try to."

"There's something I should tell you before you and she meet."

"What is it?" Rowan asks.

"Your mother didn't just go away. I sent her away."

Rowan looks blank, as if she doesn't understand.

"I sent her away," he repeats.

"She didn't just drive away?" Rowan asks, baffled.

"Well, yes, she did, but it was because I made her."

Rowan glances out the window. All she can see from her bed is the sky.

"You remember I told you that she left because she was sick, she was an alcoholic, and needed professional help?"

"Yes."

"Well, she did. But after the accident with you in the car, I couldn't trust her with you, and I couldn't be with you every second of the day. So I sent her away."

Webster watches Rowan.

"If I hadn't sent her away," he says, "she'd have gone to jail."

"Then you saved her life," Rowan says.

He shakes his head. "No, Rowan. I saved your life."

"And your own?"

"I don't know about that."

Rowan nods. "But didn't she say she would go to rehab?"

"We couldn't afford rehab. It wasn't an option. Not as many places to go then as there are now."

Even though he's a medic and knows what nerves produce—the heart pounding, the dry mouth, the sweaty palms—he's powerless to prevent the symptoms. He has them all.

"You couldn't afford it?" Rowan asks.

Webster remembers his father's offer to finance rehabilitation. Only Webster's pride had kept him from accepting that help. "It wasn't an option that minute. That day. If she stayed in town another two hours," Webster says, "the police would have had to arrest her."

Rowan's face is pale. "Would she really have gone to jail?"

"I believe so, yes," Webster says. "It was

her second DUI, her second accident. In this case, she'd injured a man. They were going to put her away for a while."

Rowan raises her knees under the sheets. "Wouldn't they have made her go to rehab?"

"Well, I suppose jail is rehab in a way. Though not always. Jail is a bad place to be. Almost no one comes out the better for it. And she was in no shape to survive that."

For a moment, Rowan is silent.

"But she'd have been out years ago," Rowan says finally, "and maybe she'd have gone into rehab, and we could have been a family again."

The words sting. A family again. He's had this thought himself a thousand times. By sending Sheila away, he had destroyed the family. "The truth is," Webster says, "I think your mother and I would have been divorced within the year. I couldn't trust her anymore. I'm sorry to have to tell you this. I'd hoped I'd never have to. The drinking was a clue to who she was. Or maybe it made her who she was. She was reckless, she wanted adventure. She hid things."

"If she wanted adventure, what was she doing with you?"

Webster smiles. "When I met your mother," he says, "she was outrunning an abusive boyfriend from Boston. They were both drunks. She was looking for a place to rest. I must have seemed like a good place to lie low. She actually said that once: lie low."

"She was pregnant when you married her."

"Yes," Webster says.

"Allison Newman told me just before Christmas. Her mother used to work in Gramps's store."

Webster tries to remember the women who worked for his father. He can recall only three of them, but he knew their first names only.

"Would you have married her if she hadn't been pregnant?"

Webster sits forward. "I can't honestly say, Rowan. I loved her. There was a time when I loved her so much, it hurt." He pauses. "But if the relationship had run its normal course," he adds, "and I'd seen the lying and the drinking, I might have ended it. We weren't even living together when she got pregnant."

"So," Rowan says, "I'm what? A mistake?"

Webster turns to his daughter. "Rowan, look at me," he says. "Do you feel like a mistake?"

It takes her a while to answer. "Sometimes I do."

Webster briefly closes his eyes. Why didn't he talk to Rowan about this when she was younger? But how does a dad know when his daughter is ready for a conversation like this?

"Rowan, listen. A baby, when it comes, is never a mistake. Never. A baby is the exact opposite of a mistake."

Rowan turns her face away.

"You were deeply loved from the moment you were born," Webster adds. "Certainly by me, that goes without saying. But by your mother, too."

"If she loved me so much, why did she leave me? And why did she drink so much? Why did she risk my life?"

"I think you're going to need to ask her those questions."

He pauses.

"Somewhere inside, the drunk has to want to get better. Otherwise, nothing works. Your mother wasn't there yet."

He stops again.

"I couldn't have her driving around drunk with you in the backseat. End of story. And I'm guessing that wasn't the first time she'd had you out in the car after she'd been drinking. You and she were incredibly lucky that day. On Route 222, an unexpected curve, a slow reaction time? She's lucky she didn't go head on with a tree."

"Is she sober now?"

"Yes, she is."

"What did Nana and Gramps think of her?"

"They didn't like her at first. Or they didn't like the fact that I was marrying her. But after the wedding, they were fine. And after you were born, they were over the moon."

Rowan taps the empty can on the patio table. "Were they happy when you sent her away?"

"No, they weren't. I had to explain it to them. I mean, they knew, they could see it, but I talked to them anyway. I could hardly avoid it. You and I were living with them at the time."

"What was I like when I was born?"

Webster smiles. "Wrinkly. Red-faced. You had a pointed head."

"I did?"

"All babies have pointed heads. The ones that are birthed naturally. And, boy, were you in a hurry. You were practically born in the car."

"I was?"

"I was all set to deliver you."

"What did . . . my mother . . . think?"

"She wasn't thinking anything, Rowan. She was in pain."

"Is the pain really terrible?"

Webster tosses his cup into a wastebasket. "I think that's another question for your mother."

"I might have had brothers and sisters."

Webster leans forward. "Rowan, honey, listen to me. You didn't. OK? That's your given. You didn't have a mother most of your life. That's another given. You've been dealt that hand, and that's what you play with. You can wish you had a different given, but it won't do you any good. People start feeling sorry for themselves, that's pretty much the end of them."

"What makes you know so much?"

Webster shrugs. "I don't know so much. I know a lot about a few things. I know about raising a child from birth to seventeen."

Rowan narrows her eyes. "You don't know everything."

There's been enough conversation for one day, Webster decides.

"You have months, years, to digest this. The most important thing you have to do now is rest."

"The most important thing I have to do is grow my hair," she says.

Webster waits until the next day before re-introducing the subject of Sheila. Webster has alerted Sheila that the visit is likely to happen in the morning. Tommy and Gina are scheduled to come later in the day. Webster has to make this happen in the morning, if at all.

"So how are you doing today?" Webster asks when he walks in the door.

"Good," she says. "They're going to begin physical therapy for the shoulder, and they have to make sure I can walk a fair distance without losing my balance. I can't risk falling on the shoulder."

Webster sits on the bed. He smiles. "You didn't notice they washed my hair."

"I did notice. You look great."

"I tried to figure out how to handle the bald spot." On a hook on the back of her door is the hat Webster bought her. He went to the campus store and asked a young woman if she knew what Rowan meant. The woman sent him to a boutique not far away that sold the right kind of cap.

"Rowan, do you remember I asked if you'd be willing to meet your mother?"

"Yeah."

"And have you thought about it?"

"I'd like to do it," she says. "I'd like for you to be here, and I'd like to work out a prearranged signal with you for when I want her to leave. You can go get a nurse and have her interrupt us, or something."

"And what will the signal be?"

Rowan ponders possible codes. "I think I'll just say, 'I need a nurse.'"

Webster laughs. "That's pretty straightforward." He stands. "I'm not allowed to make phone calls in here. I have to go out into the hallway. Be right back."

"OK," Rowan says. "Maybe you should get me my hat."

Webster tosses it to her.

Ten minutes later, when Webster sees Sheila in the corridor, he says to his daughter, "She's here, Rowan. Do you want me to bring her in?"

"I'm scared," Rowan says.

"So am I."

Webster walks out into the corridor and signals to Sheila.

"Are you sure this is a good idea?" Sheila asks.

"Not positive, but I think it is. She may not be able to handle more than a minute or two."

Sheila has on a short white jacket with a long black T-shirt and a pair of jeans. She has her hair down and behind her ears. He has no idea how this will go. It is a risk, maybe a terrible one. If Rowan can't handle the meeting, the consequences for both of them could be serious and long-lasting.

Webster steps to one side to allow Sheila into the room. "Rowan, this is Sheila Arsenault."

Sheila takes a step forward. "How are you?" she asks Rowan.

His daughter cannot speak. It's as though her vocal cords have been paralyzed. She seems to want to say something, but can't.

With Rowan alert, Webster sees the uncanny resemblance between the two women.

Sheila takes a step closer to the bed. She tilts her head and looks right at Rowan. "Is it OK if I sit down?" she asks. From Rowan's point of view, Sheila must look intimidating. Webster notices that his daughter is still clutching the hat.

"Sure," Rowan says, finally finding her voice. With her good arm, she hitches herself a little higher against the pillows.

"You had a nasty accident."

No one has said the word *mother* or *daughter* yet. Sheila might be a friend of Webster's who's just stopped by. He wonders if either Rowan or Sheila is registering the similarities between them.

"You look well," Sheila says.

Webster is expecting the summons from Rowan any minute now, and even he is beginning to think this meeting may have been a bad idea. Rowan, in the bed, resembles a cornered animal.

"The doctors say she'll be able to go home in a couple of days," Webster explains.

"Just in time for your graduation," Sheila says.

Rowan seems surprised that Sheila knows about the graduation. "I hear you're a painter," Rowan offers.

"I am," Sheila says, setting her purse on the floor beside the bed. While Sheila sits, Webster stands at the foot of the bed so that he can see his daughter's face. To be ready for any signal. How small his personal universe is.

"My dad says they're very good." Rowan hitches herself up farther. She's still holding the hat, but not clutching it. She's revealed her bald spot but appears not to know it.

"Your dad is very generous," Sheila says. "I recognize you, but you're so different. You're beautiful."

Rowan's blush is instantaneous. Webster holds his breath for a two-beat. This could go in any direction now.

"How tall are you?" Sheila asks Rowan.

"Five nine. And you?"

"Five ten, or I used to be. Who knows now? They say you start to shrink."

"You looked very tall when you were standing."

Sheila smiles.

"Our hair is the same color," Rowan says.

Sheila nods. "That's one of the first things I noticed. Yours was much lighter when you were a baby."

And there it is. Connection made. A history together, even if Rowan knows little about it.

"This is completely weird," Rowan says. "I have, like, a million questions."

"I have two million," Sheila says.

No mention yet of abandonment or guilt. Anger or remorse. That will come, Webster knows. But maybe not today. Each of them smart enough to avoid it. Now, instead of a stranger, it's as though a long-lost aunt has come to visit.

Sheila takes off her white jacket, either hot or maybe just sweating from nerves. Rowan sits straight up in the bed and bends forward, showing Sheila the bald spot. "What am I supposed to do with this?"

Rowan asks. "I have to be at graduation in three days."

Sheila takes the question seriously. "Won't that cap you have to wear—the mortarboard—cover it?"

"But then you have to toss them in the air at the end," Rowan says.

Sheila tilts her head again. "May I?" she asks, reaching for Rowan's hair.

Rowan nods yes.

Sheila fingers Rowan's hair and inspects the bald spot again. "You could cut your hair," she suggests. "Do one of those short, spiky things. Your hair is thick enough. Then just wear the bald spot as part of the new cut. There's no way you can really hide it. I was thinking you could do some sort of comb-over, but that would be worse in the end."

Rowan runs her fingers through the ends of her hair. "I've always had long hair," she says.

"Have you?" her mother asks.

"Since twelve, anyway."

"Maybe it's time for a change."

"Do you know how to cut hair?" Rowan asks Sheila.

"I don't," Sheila says. "But I can find someone who does."

"They'll come here?"

"I'll arrange it that way, if the nurses will let me."

Webster, baffled, can only watch. He knows this is surface, that there will be pitfalls ahead, perhaps an entire crater. Odd how females bond over crises in appearance. With guys, it would be sports.

Sheila, having checked that the haircut would be all right with the nurses, arranges for a hairdresser to come to Rowan's room that afternoon. Webster steps outside the door when the hairdresser arrives, and he's pretty sure that Rowan doesn't even notice his absence. He watches for a moment. The nurses have put Rowan in a wheelchair and covered her with sheets. Sheila sits on the bed and observes as the hairdresser fingers Rowan's hair. She asks if Rowan is sure she wants to do this and nods when Rowan bravely says yes. Sheila explains what she has in mind. Webster, watching the tableau, thinks: She might have been a good mother after all.

\* \* \*

After the physical therapy and the visit by Gina and Tommy (Webster and Sheila hear giggling from the room as they stand in the hallway), Rowan reports that the little physical therapy they gave her was brutal and that she has a lot of work to do on the shoulder. Because the nurses have encouraged Rowan to walk as much as possible, Webster strolls with Rowan along the corridors. Once he takes her outside to see the summer evening. Rowan sucks in the fresh air. From Webster's vantage point, the spiky hair doesn't hide the bald spot, but it makes it less noticeable. Webster asks Rowan what she thought of Sheila, but Rowan is less forthcoming than Webster hoped. He doesn't know if Rowan wants to keep her feelings about her mother to herself, or if she herself can't quite sort out this new development in her life.

"The nurse told me that the medics paralyzed me for the ride in the helicopter. Did you do that?"

"No," he says. "The airlift medics do that."

"The nurse said that she's known patients who recover from the original injury, but stay paralyzed."

Fucking nurse. "I've heard that, too," Webster says. "But I don't know of anyone that's happened to."

"But you knew this when they paralyzed me," she says.

"I did. I didn't like it, but it's standard procedure with a head injury prior to an airlift."

"So you must have been scared," Rowan says.

"I was terrified."

She hugs him with her good arm. "I'm sorry," she says.

When Webster arrives the next morning, he finds that Sheila has beaten him to it. She is sitting close to Rowan in the chair, and the two are talking. Rowan's eyes express wonderment and awe, and he can hear her giggle through the glass. Because he doesn't want to interrupt the pair, he meanders through the hallways, checking back every twenty minutes.

The second time he peers in, they are still talking.

The third time he nears the room, he can see that Rowan is laughing. Webster wonders if Sheila is telling her stories about what Rowan was like when she was a baby.

The fourth time he walks by, their heads are closer together, and each is serious. He walks into the room.

Both Sheila and Rowan look at him as if surprised to see him. Sheila sits back in her chair. Rowan says nothing.

"Did I interrupt something?" Webster asks.

Rowan shrugs.

"Anybody want anything from the vending machine?" Webster, in desperation, asks.

Rowan and Sheila shake their heads.

"OK. I'm going for coffee," he announces.

He gives them fifteen minutes. When he reenters the room, Rowan is crying.

Fuck.

Sheila turns to him and makes a downward motion with her hands, as if to say, *Don't get upset. Everything is not as it seems.*

Rowan reaches for a tissue and blows her nose. "If you hadn't sent her away, we'd have been a family all those years."

Sheila holds up a hand before Webster can respond. "Your father did the right thing

by sending me away," she says to Rowan.
"I might have killed you. It's sort of a miracle I didn't."

"So you're not angry that he sent you
away?"

"I have been at times," Sheila says. "But
there's no doubt in my mind that he did it
to save your life."

"I didn't save anyone's life," Webster
says, setting his coffee cup on the ledge
under the window. "It happened, and it
can't be taken back. We've all been dam-
aged by it." He pauses. Does he believe
that? Yes, he does.

"Rowan and I have a lot of catching up
to do," Sheila says. She stands.

"You're going?" Rowan asks with dismay.

"If my watch is right," Sheila says, "the
physical therapist is going to come grab
you in about five minutes. Besides, I have
to return to my house. I don't want to leave,
but I really have to."

Rowan throws off the covers and sits at
the edge of the bed. Her legs are thin and
white. Webster is always amazed by how
much muscle mass can be lost in so short
a time.

"When you go across that stage," Sheila

says, "you keep your chin up and forget about that bald spot. Besides, it's growing back in already."

"It is?" Rowan asks, fingering her head.

"I'll call you as soon as I get back. I have to run to check out of my room at the inn, or I'll be charged the extra day."

Rowan looks wildly at her father, as if to say, *Fix it.*

"Stay the extra day," Webster suggests to his ex-wife. "Unless you positively have to be back. Follow us to Hartstone. You can get a room at the Bear Hollow Inn."

Where they had their wedding lunch.

"Or if that's full, we'll find you another place. Wouldn't you like to see this sad, pathetic, bald creature graduate?"

"Yes," Sheila says. "Yes, I would." She turns to Rowan. "Are *you* asking me?"

"I am," Rowan says.

Sheila, having arrived at the house early from the Bear Hollow Inn, zips up the back of Rowan's dress, a chore that used to be Webster's, Rowan always pleading, "Don't look."

His girls. It's on the tip of his tongue. Webster remembers thinking it years ago one afternoon when he found Sheila and Rowan asleep together on the ground. But Sheila is no more his than the neighbor's lawn mower is. Still, there's something about the scene before him—a mother and a daughter helping each other with last-minute arrangements—that pleases him.

Rowan is nervous. Webster knows it's partly the hair, partly a slight unsteadiness on her feet, partly the idea of seeing her friends again.

It's been fifteen years since all three of them have been in this house together. But Rowan doesn't remember that.

Webster watches Sheila give Rowan her graduation present, a short necklace of powder blue stones and hammered silver balls. Even as Sheila hands the package to Rowan, the gesture seems tentative. As if she shouldn't be giving her daughter a present. The easy joy that Sheila took in Rowan just two days earlier appears to have left her.

"What do you think?" Rowan asks, standing before him in her light blue dress with a part of one sleeve cut to make room for the cast.

"You look fabulous," he says. "Very smart and chic."

Rowan wrinkles her face. "What do you know about smart and chic?"

Sheila adjusts her white jacket and fiddles with the waistband of her trousers. Webster catches a glimpse of a silky top under the jacket.

In the hospital, Webster told Rowan that his graduation present to her would be a four-night trip to New York City for her and Gina when Rowan is fully recovered. They could see museums, go to plays, eat out. "You won't drink," Webster warned. "You can't drink. You understand that."

"I do."

"My father used to say to me that I'd never been anywhere," Webster said. "He'd be glad that you're doing this."

"But, Dad, don't you want to go instead of Gina?"

He did. "I'd be a bore," he said. "I'd want to take long walks and visit other rescue squads. And I'd want to be in bed by ten. You'll have much more fun with Gina."

"She's going to *flip out* when she hears about this," Rowan said. "Thank you so much."

It has been arranged that Rowan will go to graduation first with Tommy because they have to put on their robes and line up for the procession. They will march out onto the field to the notes of "Pomp and Circumstance," just as Webster once did. He feels for the parents of the one student who won't be there. When Webster told

Rowan about Kerry, she cried for an hour. He worries that Rowan might not be able to handle the inevitable moment of silence. He worries about her standing in the hot sun. The doctor has warned both of them to be aware of the possibility of seizures. For the next two weeks, Rowan cannot be alone.

Webster and Sheila will go a bit early to graduation as well in order to snag a pair of seats near the front. Metal chairs will be set in rows before the stage. As soon as Webster sits down on his, one leg of the four will sink into the soft grass. Webster has his camera and has charged it for pictures afterward. He wants one of Rowan up against the bare patch of wall, but she might be embarrassed with her odd haircut and in Sheila's presence. And wouldn't Webster then be obliged to ask Sheila and Rowan to pose together, a request riddled with mines? He'll get Rowan after the ceremony, in her gown and in her dress.

"That's clever," Sheila says, noticing the silver box on the windowsill over the sink. "It really tells the weather?"

"It was my birthday present to Dad," Rowan says, lifting it from the sill. She explains its various features. She gives it a little shake and sets the cube on the table. "This side shows the future," she says. She tilts her head to read it. *"Go slowly and be careful,"* she reads. "Bummer. I already got that one. Whose future is it, anyway?"

"Yours," Webster says. "You shook it." He thinks it good advice for his daughter.

"But the box belongs to you," she counters. "I gave it to you."

"OK," he says, relieved that the liquid produced nothing worse. "I'll take it."

Rowan shakes the cube again. *"Treasure awaits if you can find it,"* she reads. She looks puzzled. "What does it mean?"

"I think it means exactly what it says," Webster replies. "Something wonderful is out there if you can recognize it."

"But what is it?"

"That's for you to discover," he says.

"You do it," Rowan says, holding the box out for Sheila. Sheila takes a step backward. "No thanks," she says. "Maybe some other day."

Surprises don't work for her either.

Sheila and Webster make their way across a field of green. They aren't as early as

Webster imagined they would be. The front rows are filled already. Sheila's heels sink into the sod, and once they have to stop so that Sheila can extricate a shoe.

Webster chooses a seat on the aisle. Always the need for the quick getaway, a habit from years on the job. Sheila sits beside him as he waves to Gina's mother, Eileen, who isn't hiding her curiosity about Sheila. Webster scans the large crowd. Grandparents and siblings next to parents his age and older. He'll know which clan belongs to which student when the seniors cross the stage. The family will shout and cheer and make catcalls to single out their child. Webster is glad he has Sheila with him. How much noise can a single father make?

His parents once sat here, as he is doing now. He remembers wanting only to get away with his friends and go to a series of parties that left him so wiped out by the end of the night that he fell asleep on a stranger's floor.

A woman he doesn't recognize approaches from the side. Beside her is a young man in black glasses. "Mr. Webster?" the woman asks.

"Yes?"

"This is the baby you helped bring into the world nineteen years ago. Aaron and I are here for Joshua, Aaron's younger brother."

"No kidding!" Webster says as he stands. He glances from mother to son. He's tickled and amazed. "Hello, Aaron."

The boy shakes his hand.

"I was so afraid that night," the woman says.

"You and me both. I was just a rookie."

"I've wanted to thank you for years, but our paths have seldom crossed, and when they did, you were always with someone else."

"Well, it was a great experience for me."

"The thing you said that made me not afraid? You said, 'This baby's going to come out hollering his head off. I can hear him already.' And that made me laugh, and I knew then that everything would be OK."

She gives Webster a quick pat on the arm. "I'll never forget it," she says.

Webster sits. He's treated a number of people in the crowd. He isn't a hero in town. In fact he's someone they hope never to see at their homes or in the middle of a highway. But he's part of the safety net that wraps itself around Hartstone, and for that they are grateful.

The sun beats on his head and the temperature rises. Maybe high seventies already? Webster watches as men shed their jackets, women their wraps. The field seems vast and fertile. Canned music begins from the speakers, and everyone stands. A line of students in maroon robes is poised at the entrance to the aisle of chairs. The teachers lead, some with academic gowns or sashes. Mrs. McDougal, the principal, has on a black velvet beret. Women in the audience have tissues out already. It's the music that sets them off.

The kids in line seem ebullient, ready for anything. Is high school so awful, they can't wait to be out? Or are they merely celebrating a milestone? Webster is aware of Sheila beside him and is glad she's tall enough to witness the spectacle coming down the aisle. Webster will have to wait until the end to see his daughter. He minds that by the time Rowan reaches him, many of the parents will already have turned away and sat down. Webster will stand until all the students are in place up front.

The lump is in his throat already—the music must have been composed for this effect. He glances at Sheila, who has a tight smile on her face. But she softens when she catches a glimpse of Rowan. Webster turns and watches his daughter approach the stage. She's unzipped her gown just enough to show off the blue and silver necklace—a gift to her mother. The mortarboard seems to be doing its job. Rowan's posture is for once erect. Her walk is steady, and she's a mixture of gravity and playfulness, winking at Webster as she passes.

The hooting and shouting dim as Mrs. McDougal takes the podium. She asks for a moment of silence for Kerry Coolidge, and Webster notices that many of the senior girls are crying. Parents, too. It's an awful moment, and Webster can't help but think that it might have been Rowan they were honoring with this brief silence. It's an unbearable thought. He wonders if Kerry's parents are in the crowd. Had it been his daughter who died, he would have stayed home. Or he'd be in Africa. Anywhere but on this field.

Mrs. McDougal swiftly returns to the ceremony by relating what a great year this has been for the seniors. She ticks off their collective accomplishments, the only interesting one being the fact that the debate team won the state championship. The football team didn't fare as well, nor did the hockey team. The principal tells the crowd that eighty-five percent of the senior class will go to four-year colleges. The crowd applauds. Webster thinks about the fifteen percent who won't. What will they do? Community college? The military? Farming? Mrs. McDougal adds that she's particularly proud of the community outreach by Rowan's class—how they've worked at shelters and volunteered their time to go into the elementary schools and work with special students.

And then Mrs. McDougal does something Webster didn't anticipate. She asks all the parents to stand. She commands the students to rise as well and give their parents a big hand for the love they've given and the sacrifices they've made to get the students to this point.

Webster has eyes only for Rowan, who

smiles and raises the fist of her good arm, her bad shoulder preventing clapping. He gives her a grin.

Webster glances down at Sheila, who looks as though she's been socked in the face. He tries to get her to stand with him, but she sits rigid, waiting for the applause to end.

"I'm sorry about that," Webster says when he sits down. "I had no idea they would do that, or I'd have prepared you."

Sheila gives a small shrug, as though it means nothing to her, but Webster can see the pain on her face. For fifteen years, she's had to make no sacrifices for her daughter. She simply wasn't there.

The heat rises as the speeches drone on. Sports awards are handed out, giving them greater weight than the academic awards, which were handed out at a separate ceremony the previous week. Webster doesn't mind this ritual. It's partly for the kids who have nothing else, some of whom have barely managed to graduate, who have nowhere to go next year. They get their shouts and cheers, their fifteen seconds of fame.

In the hospital, Webster and Sheila

managed to get Rowan to complete two take-home finals. His daughter finished them off with ease, which suggested to Webster that she'd deliberately sabotaged herself. Elizabeth Washington called the admissions committee at the university, explaining Rowan's recent and unusual circumstances. Rowan will go to college in the fall.

Webster sheds his jacket, and Sheila does so as well. The teachers, in their robes, fan themselves with programs. Webster yanks his tie. The weather will be a topic of conversation at graduation lunches: how off the forecasters were, how it feels more like August than June. Hairdos will be limp; shirtsleeves will be rolled.

When the principal reaches the Rs, Sheila nudges him and asks for the camera.

"That's OK, I can do it," Webster says of the moment when he will leave his chair and squat in the grassy aisle with the parents of the Ts and the Vs to snap a picture of sons or daughters receiving diplomas.

"I want you to be able to see it," Sheila says. "You can't see the real thing if you're trying to frame a photograph."

"You know how to use this model?" he asks, afraid that at the last minute Sheila won't know which button to push.

"I do," she says.

When the principal reaches the middle of the Ss (and there are always a lot of Ss), Sheila slides past him and makes her way toward the front, running bent over in her white silk top and black trousers. He notices that her feet are bare.

He glances up just in time to see Rowan on the stairs to the podium. He hears his daughter's name called. *Rowan Webster.* As she walks across the stage and shakes the hand of the vice principal, many students clap and shout. Webster, surprised, adds his own catcall and whistle. It's the injured-player syndrome, the audience applauding the fact that Rowan is there at all, that she can walk across the stage just like the others. Rowan smiles, flips off her mortarboard, bends, and points to the bare patch at the top of her head. The audience roars.

Before Rowan leaves the stage, she poses for the formal picture that every student will receive during the summer. In it, her face will be turned, and Webster and

Rowan will remember why. She's searching for her dad, who is waving with both hands.

*That's it,* Webster tells himself as he surveys the field with all the parents and their children. *That's all I need in life.*

Sheila slides into her seat. "I got some good ones," she says. She bends to put her shoes back on.

Webster, as if he's done it every day of his life, as if he did it just the day before, trails his fingers from the small of Sheila's back to the nape of her neck.

Sheila turns her head. "Go slowly and be careful," she says.

# Acknowledgments

My tremendous thanks go to Linda O'Leary, EMT-I with the Manchester Rescue Squad of Manchester, Vermont, for her hours of help with the EMT scenes. Any mistakes are my own.

Many thanks also to Genevieve Martland for her tour of Chelsea, Massachusetts. Again, errors in that chapter are mine only.

Thanks are not enough for Asya Muchnick, my lovely and gifted editor; for Jennifer Rudolph Walsh, my lovable, full-service agent; for Michael Pietsch, to whom I owe everything; for Terry Adams, my loyal and savvy paperback editor; and for John Osborn, love of my life.

Anita Shreve is the acclaimed author of fifteen previous novels, including *A Change in Altitude; The Pilot's Wife,* which was a selection of Oprah's Book Club; and *The Weight of Water,* which was a finalist for England's Orange Prize. She was awarded the John P. Marquand Prize in American Literature. She lives in Massachusetts.